GHOSTS

John Banville was born in Wexford, Ireland, in 1945. His first book, *Long Lankin*, was published in 1970. His other books are *Nightspawn*; *Birchwood*; *Doctor Copernicus*, which won the James Tait Black Memorial Prize in 1976; *Kepler*, which was awarded the Guardian Fiction Prize in 1981; *The Newton Letter*, which was filmed for Channel 4; *Mefisto* and *The Book of Evidence*, which was shortlisted for the 1989 Booker Prize and won the 1989 Guinness Peat Aviation Award. John Banville is literary editor of the *Irish Times* and lives in Dublin with his wife and two sons.

Also by John Banville

Long Lankin
Nightspawn
Birchwood*
Doctor Copernicus*
Kepler*
The Newton Letter*
Mefisto*
The Book of Evidence*

**available from Minerva*

GHOSTS

JOHN BANVILLE

Minerva

A Minerva Paperback
GHOSTS

First published in Great Britain 1993
by Martin Secker & Warburg Ltd
This Minerva edition published 1993
by Mandarin Paperbacks
an imprint of Reed Consumer Books Ltd
Michelin House, 81 Fulham Road, London SW3 6RB
and Auckland, Melbourne, Singapore and Toronto

A CIP catalogue record for this title
is available from the British Library
ISBN 0 7493 9979 1

Printed and bound in Great Britain
by Cox & Wyman Ltd, Reading, Berkshire

to Robin Robertson

There were ghosts that returned to earth to hear his phrases

Wallace Stevens

I

HERE THEY ARE. There are seven of them. Or better say, half a dozen or so, that gives more leeway. They are struggling up the dunes, stumbling in the sand, squabbling, complaining, wanting sympathy, wanting to be elsewhere. That, most of all: to be elsewhere. There is no elsewhere, for them. Only here, in this little round.

'List!'

'Listing.'

'Leaky as a – '

'So I said, I said.'

'Everything feels strange.'

'That captain, so-called.'

'I did, I said to him.'

'Cythera, my foot.'

'Some outing.'

'Listen!'

Behind them the boat leans, stuck fast on a sandbank, canted drunkenly to starboard, fat-bellied, barnacled, betrayed by a freak wave or a trick of the tide and the miscalculations of a tipsy skipper. They have had to wade through the shallows to get to shore. Thus things begin. It is a morning late in

May. The sun shines merrily. How the wind blows! A little world is coming into being.

Who speaks? I do. Little god.

Licht spied them from afar, with his keen sight. It was so long since he had seen their like that for a moment he hardly knew what they were. He flew to the turret room at the top of the house where the Professor increasingly spent his time, brooding by himself or idly scanning the horizon through the brass telescope mounted on his desk. Inside the door Licht stopped, irresolute suddenly. It is always thus with him, the headlong rush and then the halt. The Professor turned up his face slowly from the big book open in front of him and stared at Licht with such glassy remoteness that Licht grew frightened and almost forgot what he had come to say. Is this what death is like, he wondered, is this how people begin to die, swimming a little farther out each time until in the end the land is out of sight for good? At last the Professor returned to himself and blinked and frowned and pursed his lips, annoyed that Licht had found him there, lost like that. Licht stood panting, with that eager, hazy smile of his.

'What?' the Professor said sharply. 'What? Who are they?'

'I don't know,' Licht answered breathlessly. 'But I think they're coming here, whoever they are.'

Poor Licht. He is anything from twenty-five to fifty. His yellow-white curls and spindly little legs give him an antique look: he seems as if he should be got up in periwig and knee-breeches. His eyes are brown and his brow is broad, with two smooth dents at the temples, as if whoever moulded him had given his big head a last, loving squeeze there between finger and thumb. He is never still. Now his foot tap-tapped on the turret floor and the fist he had thrust into his trousers pocket flexed and flexed. He pointed to the spyglass.

'Did you see them?' he said. 'Sheep, I thought they were. Vertical sheep!'

He laughed, three soft, quick little gasps. The Professor turned away from him and hunched a forbidding black shoulder, his sea-captain's swivel chair groaning under him. Licht stepped to the window and looked down.

'They're coming here, all right,' he said softly. 'Oh, I'm sure they're coming here.'

He shook his head and frowned, trying to seem alarmed at the prospect of invasion, but had to bite his lip to keep from grinning.

Meanwhile my foundered creatures have not got far. They have not lost their sea-legs yet and the sand is soft going. There is an old boy in a boater, a pretty young woman, called Flora, of course, and a blonde woman in a black skirt and a black leather jacket with a camera slung over her shoulder. Also an assortment of children: three, to be precise. And a thin, lithe, sallow man with bad teeth and hair dyed black and a darkly watchful eye. His name is Felix. He seems to find something funny in all of this, smiling fiercely to himself and sucking on a broken eye-tooth. He urges the others on when they falter, Flora especially, inserting two long, bony fingers under her elbow. She will not look at him. She has a strange feeling, she says, it is as if she has been here before. He wrinkles his high, smooth forehead, gravely bending the full weight of his attention to her words. Perhaps, he says after a moment, perhaps she is remembering childhood outings to the seaside: the salt breeze, the sound of the waves, the cat-smell of the sand, that sun-befuddled, sparkling light that makes everything seem to fold softly into something else.

'What do you think?' he said. 'Might that be it?'

She shrugged, smiled, tossed her hair, making an end of

it. She thought how quaint yet dangerous it sounded when a person spoke so carefully, with such odd emphasis.

Softly.

The boys – there are two of them – watched all this, nudging each other and fatly grinning.

'So strange,' Flora was saying. 'Everything seems so . . .'

'Yes?' Felix prompted.

She was silent briefly and then shivered.

'Just . . . strange,' she said. 'I don't know.'

He nodded, his dark gaze lowered.

Felix and Flora.

The dunes ended and they came to a flat place of dark-green sward where the sandy grass crackled under their tread, and there were tiny, pink-tipped daisies, and celandines that blossom when the swallows come, though I can see no swallows yet, and here and there a tender violet trembling in the breeze. They paused in vague amaze and looked about, expecting something. The ground was pitted with rabbit-burrows, each one had a little pile of diggings at the door, and rabbits that seemed to move by clockwork stood up and looked at them, hopped a little way, stopped, and looked again.

'What is that?' said the blonde woman, whose name is Sophie. 'What is that noise?'

All listened, holding their breath, even the children, and each one heard it, a faint, deep, formless song that seemed to rise out of the earth itself.

'Like music,' said the man in the straw hat dreamily. 'Like . . . singing.'

Felix frowned and slowly turned his head this way and that, peering hard, his sharp nose twitching at the tip, bird-man, raptor, rapt.

'There should be a house,' he murmured. 'A house on a hill, and a little bridge, and a road leading up.'

Sophie regarded him with scorn, smilingly.

'You have been here before?' she said, and then, sweetly: 'Aeaea, is it?'

He glanced at her sideways and smiled his fierce, thin smile. They have hardly met and are old enemies already. He hummed, nodding to himself, and stepped away from her, like one stepping slowly in a dream, still peering, and picked up his black bag from the grass. 'Yes,' he said with steely gaiety, 'yes, Aeaea: and you will feel at home, no doubt.'

She lifted her camera like a gun and shot him. I can see from the way she handles it that she is a professional. In fact, she is mildly famous, her name appears in expensive magazines and on the spines of sumptuous volumes of glossy silver and black prints. Light is her medium, she moves through it as through some fine, shining fluid, bearing aloft out of the world's reach the precious phial of her self.

Still they lingered, looking about them, and all at once, unaccountably, the wind of something that was almost happiness wafted through them all, though in each one it took a different form, and all thought what they felt was singular and unique and so were unaware of this brief moment of concord. Then it was gone, the god of inspiration flew elsewhere, and everything was as it had been.

I must be in a mellow mood today.

The house. It is large and of another age. It stands on a green rise, built of wood and stone, tall, narrow, ungainly, each storey seeming to lean in a different direction. Long ago it was painted red but the years and the salt winds have turned it to a light shade of pink. The roof is steep with high chimneys and gay scalloping under the eaves. The delicate octagonal turret with the weathervane on top is a surprise, people see its slender panes flashing from afar and say, Ah! and smile. On the first floor there is a balcony that runs along all four sides, with french windows giving on to it, where no doubt before the day is done someone will stand, with her hand in her hair, gazing off in sunlight. Below the balcony the front porch is a deep, dim hollow, and the front door has two broad panels of ruby glass and a tarnished brass knocker in the shape of a lion's paw. Details, details: pile them on. The windows are blank. Three steps lead from the porch to a patch of gravel and a green slope that runs abruptly down to a stony, meandering stream. Gorse grows along the bank, and hawthorn, all in blossom now, the pale-pink and the white, a great year for the may. Behind the house there is a high ridge with trees, old oaks, I think, above which seagulls plunge and sway. (Oaks and seagulls! Picture it! Such is our island.) This wooded height lowers over the scene, dark and forbidding sometimes, sometimes almost haughty, almost, indeed, heroic.

The house is a summer house; at other seasons, especially in autumn, it wheezes and groans, its joints creaking. But when the weather turns warm, as now, in May, and the fond air invades even the remotest rooms, something stirs in the heart of the house, like something stirring out of a long slumber, unfolding waxen wings, and then suddenly everything tends upwards and all is ceilings and wide-open windows and curtains billowing in sea-light. I live here, in this lambent, salt-washed world, in these faded rooms, amidst this stillness. And it lives in me.

Sophie pointed her camera, deft and quick.

'Looks like a hotel,' she said.

'Or a guesthouse, anyway,' said Croke, doubtfully.

It is neither. It is the home of Professor Silas Kreutznaer and his faithful companion, Licht. Ha.

They had come to the little wooden bridge but there they hesitated, even Felix, unwilling to cross, they did not know why, and looked up uncertainly at the impassive house. Croke took off his boater, or do I mean panama, yes, Croke took off his panama and mopped his brow, saying something crossly under his breath. The hat, the striped blazer and cravat, the white duck trousers, all this had seemed fine at first, a brave flourish and just the thing for a day-trip, but now he felt ridiculous, ridiculous and old.

'We can't stand here all day,' he said, and glared accusingly at Felix, as if somehow everything were all his fault. 'Will I go and see?'

He looked about at the rest of them but all wanly avoided his eye, indifferent suddenly, unable to care.

'I'm hungry,' Hatch said. 'I want my breakfast.'

Pound the bespectacled fat boy muttered in agreement and cast a dark look at the adults.

'Where's that picnic that was promised us?' Croke said testily.

'Fell in the water, didn't it,' Hatch said and snickered.

'Pah! Some bloody outing this is.'

'Listen to them,' Felix said softly to Flora, assuming the soft mask of an indulgent smile. 'Rhubarb rhubarb.'

His smile turned fawning and he inclined his head to one side as if imploring something of her, but she pretended to be distracted and frowned and looked away. She felt so strange.

Sophie turned with an impatient sigh and took Croke's arm.

'Come,' she said. 'We will ask.'

And they set off across the bridge, Sophie striding and the old boy going carefully on tottery legs, trying to keep up with her, the soaked and sand-caked cuffs of his trousers brushing the planks. The stream gurgled.

Licht in the turret window watched them, the little crowd hanging back – were they afraid? – and the old man and the woman advancing over the bridge. How small they seemed, how distant and small. The couple on the bridge carried themselves stiffly, at a stately pace, as if they suspected that someone, somewhere, was laughing at their expense. He was embarrassed for them. They were like actors being forced to improvise. (One of them is an actor, is improvising.) He pressed his forehead to the glass and felt his heart racing. Since he had first spotted them making their meandering way up the hillside he had warned himself repeatedly not to expect anything of them, but it was no use, he was agog. Somehow these people looked like him, like the image he had of himself: lost, eager, ill at ease, and foolish. The glass was cool against his forehead, where a little vein was beating. Silence, deep woods, a sudden wind. He blinked: had he dropped off for a second? Lately he had been sleeping badly. That morning he had been awake at three o'clock, wandering through the house, stepping through vague deeps of shadowed stillness on the stairs, hardly daring to breathe in the midst of a silence where others slept. When he looked out he had seen a crack of light on the leaden horizon. Was it the day still going down or the morning coming up? He smiled sadly. This was what his life was like now, this faint glimmer between a past grown hazy and an unimaginable future.

The woman on the bridge stumbled. One moment she was upright, the next she had crumpled sideways like a puppet, all arms and knees, her hair flying and her camera swinging on its strap. Licht experienced a little thrill of fright. She would have fallen had not the old boy with surprising speed and vigour caught her in the crook of an arm that seemed for a second to grow immensely long. His hat fell off. A blackbird flew up out of a bush, giving out a harsh repeated warning note. The woman, balancing on one leg, took off her sodden shoe and looked at it: the heel was broken. She kicked off the other shoe and was preparing to walk on barefoot when Felix, as if he had suddenly bethought himself and some notion of authority, put down his bag and fairly bounded forward, shot nimbly past her and set off up the slope, buttoning the jacket of his tight, brown suit.

'Who is that,' the Professor said sharply. 'Mind, let me see.'

Licht turned, startled: he had forgotten he was not alone. The Professor had been struggling with the telescope, trying in vain to angle it so he could get a closer look at Felix coming up the path. Now he thrust the barrel of the instrument aside and lumbered to the window, humming unhappily under his breath. When Licht looked at him now, in the light of these advancing strangers, he noticed for the first time how slovenly he had become. His shapeless black jacket was rusty at the elbows and the pockets sagged, his bow-tie was clumsily knotted and had a greasy shine. He looked like a big old rain-stained statue of one of the Caesars, with that big balding head and broad pale face and filmy, pale, protruding eyes. Licht smiled to himself hopelessly: how could he leave, how could he ever leave?

Felix was mounting the slope swiftly, swinging out his legs in front of him and sawing the air with his arms.

'Look at him,' Croke said, chuckling. 'Look at him go.'

From the bridge it seemed as if he were swarming along on all fours. The nearer he approached to the house the more it seemed to shrink away from him. Licht was craning his neck. The Professor turned aside, patting his pockets, still humming tensely to himself.

Below, the lion's peremptory paw rapped once, twice, threefour times.

Here it is, here is the moment where worlds collide, and all I can detect is laughter, distant, soft, sceptical.

At that brisk and gaily syncopated knock the house seemed to go still and silent for a moment as if in alarmed anticipation of disturbances to come. Licht lingered dreamily at the turret window, watching the others down at the bridge. Then another knock sounded, louder than before, and he started and turned and pushed past the Professor and rattled down the stairs in a flurry of arms and knees. In the hall he paused, seeing Felix's silhouette on the ruby glass of the door, an intent and eerily motionless, canted form. When the door was opened Felix at once produced a brilliant smile and stepped sideways deftly into the hall, speaking already, his thin hand outstretched.

'. . . Shipwrecked!' he said, laughing. 'Yes, cast up on these shores. I can't tell you!' Licht in his agitation could hardly understand what he was saying. He fell back a pace, mouthing helplessly and nodding. Felix's sharp glance flickered all around the hall. 'What a charming place,' he said softly, and threw back his head and smiled foxily, showing a broken eye-tooth. He had a disjointed, improvised air, as if he had been put together in haste from disparate bits and pieces of other people. He seemed full of suppressed laughter, nursing a secret joke. With that fixed grin and those glossy, avid eyes he makes me think of a ventriloquist's dummy; in his case, though, it would be he who would do the talking, while his master's mouth flapped open and shut like a broken trap. 'Yes, charming, charming,' he said. 'Why, I feel almost at home already.'

Afterwards Licht was never absolutely sure all this had happened, or had happened in the way that he remembered it, at least. All he recalled for certain was the sense of being suddenly surrounded by something bright and overwhelming. It was not just Felix before whom he fell back, but the troupe of possibilities that seemed to come crowding in behind him, tumbling and leaping invisibly about the hall. He saw himself in a dazzle of light, heroic and absurd, and the hallway might have been the pass at Roncesvalles. I should not sneer: I too in secret have always fancied myself a hero, dying with my face to Spain, though I suspect no ministering angel or exaltation of saints will come to carry me off as I cough out my heart's last drops of blood.

Felix was describing how the boat had run aground. Daintily with finger and thumb he hoisted skirt-like the legs of his trousers to show a pair of skinny, bare, blue-white ankles and his shoes dark with wet. Head on one side, and that comical, self-disparaging grin.

'Professor Kreutznaer,' Licht said in a sort of hapless desperation, 'Professor Kreutznaer is . . . busy.'

Felix was regarding him keenly with an eyebrow lifted.

'Busy, eh?' he said softly. 'Well then, we shall not disturb him, shall we.'

The others had shuffled across the bridge by now, dragged forward reluctantly in the wake of Felix's rapid ascent to the house, as if they were attached to him at a distance somehow; they loitered, waiting for a sign. Sophie sat down on a rock and kneaded the foot she had twisted. Hatch was clutching his stomach and rolling his eyes in a dumbshow demonstration of hunger, while Pound snickered and Alice smiled doubtfully. Have we met Alice? She is eleven. She wears her hair in a shiny, fat, brown braid. She is not pretty. Sophie considered the elfin Hatch without enthusiasm, his narrow, white face and red slash of a mouth; there is one clown in every company.

'After the war,' she said to him, 'when I was younger than you are now, we had no food. Every day for months, for months, I was hungry. My mother rubbed the top of the stove with candle grease – ' with one hand she smoothed large, slow circles on the air ' – and fried potatoes in it, and when the potatoes were eaten she fried the peelings and we ate those, too.'

Hatch with a tragic look embraced himself and did a dying fall on to the grass and lay there twitching.

'Oh, leave them alone, Countess,' Croke said waggishly, wagging his head at her. 'This is not old Vienna.'

She eyed him coolly. When he grinned he showed a large set of yellowed, horsey teeth, and the skin over his cheekbones tightened and the skull under the taut skin seemed to grin as well, but in a different way. Countess: he had started calling her that last night in the hotel bar when he was tipsy, winking at her and trying to get her drunk; she suspected gloomily it would stick.

'So funny you are,' she said. 'All of you, so funny.'

The boys laughed – how quickly the grown-ups could irritate each other today! – but they were uneasy, too. Sophie already was an object of deep and secret speculation to them, this moody woman in black who was as old as a mother would be but unlike any mother they had ever known, the hungry way she smoked cigarettes, the way she sat with her knees apart, like a man, not caring (Hatch on the ground was trying to look up her skirt), the fascinating tang of sweat she left behind her on the air when she passed by.

Croke, still leering at her toothily, sang under his breath, in a quavery voice:

Wien, Wien, nur du allein!

When he laughed he coughed, a string of phlegm twanging in his throat, and Alice glared at him. She disapproved of Croke, because of his coarseness, and because he was old.

'I am not even Viennese,' Sophie said ruefully, frowning at her foot.

'But you should be, Countess,' Croke said, with what he thought was gallantry. 'You should be.'

Flora had moved away carefully with her eyes lowered. Sophie watched her narrowly. Flora was wearing an affected, far-off look, as if she thought there might be unpleasantness that she would have to pretend not to notice. How beautiful she was, like one of Modigliani's girls, with that heavy black hair, those tilted eyes, that hesitant, slightly awkward, pigeon-toed grace. Sophie suspected she had been with Felix last night. Sanctimonious little twat.

Vienna. God! She lit a cigarette. Her foot was callused and the nail on the little toe had almost disappeared into the flesh. She closed her eyes. She was sick of herself. Why had she said that nonsense about the potato peelings? For whom was she playing this part that she had to keep on making up as she went along? A comedy, of course, all a horrible comedy. Out there in the flocculent, moth-laden darkness an invisiblc audience was splitting its sides at her. She rose, suddenly angry, at herself and everything elsc, and, carrying her shoes and stepping warily, set off up the pathway to the house, where Felix had reappeared and was waiting for them on the porch with a proprietorial air, his hands like a brahmin's joined before him, a man brimming with secrets, smiling.

He might have been master of the house so warmly did he welcome them, touching an elbow here, patting a shoulder-blade there, winking gaily at the boys, who had carried up his black bag between them. And to their surprise as he ushered them in they all, even Sophie, felt a rush of gratitude for his ministering presence; they remembered the awful, sickening lurch when the boat had keeled over, things falling and a big crate sliding off the deck into the water and the drunken skipper cursing, and it came to them that after all they were survivors, in a way, despite the festive look that everything insisted on wearing, and suddenly they were full of tenderness for themselves and pity for their plight. Licht hovered in the dimness of the doorway, smiling helplessly, nodding to them and mouthing wordless greetings as they entered.

'Hello, Harpo,' Hatch said brightly, and Pound behind him spluttered.

The hall was wide and paved unevenly with black and white tiles. There was a pockmarked mirror in a gilt frame and an umbrella stand with an assortment of walking canes and a broken shooting-stick. The walls up to the dado were clad with embossed wallpaper to which repeated layers of varnish had imparted a thick, clammy, toffee-coloured texture, while above the rail stretched shadowy grey expanses that had once, long ago, been white. There was a smell of apples just starting to rot. And an air now of polite shock, of a hand put to mouth in amazement at all this noise, this intrusion. Licht was beside himself.

They stood uneasily in a huddle and did not know what to do next.

And then something happened, I am not sure what it was. They were all crowded together there, uncertain whether to advance or wait, and this uncertainty produced a ripple amongst them, a restless stirring, as when the day darkens suddenly and a gust of wind from nowhere blows through the trees, shaking them. Nice touch of the Virgilian, that. Croke, squinting up at something on the ceiling, stepped backwards and trod on Sophie's foot, the one that she had twisted. She shrieked, and her shriek brought an immediate and solemn silence and everyone went as still as a statue. I could leave them there, I could walk away now and leave them there forever. The silence lasted for the space of half a dozen heartbeats and then slowly, as if she were slowly falling, Alice began to cry.

'Oh,' Licht said in distress, 'my poor . . . my dear . . .'

He touched a tremulous hand to her shoulder but she twisted away from him violently with a great slack sob. She did not know what was the matter with her. The boys stared at her with frank interest.

'Christ,' Pound said in happy disgust, 'there she goes.'

Alice cries easily.

Licht led them into the kitchen, a big, high-ceilinged room with a scrubbed pine table and mismatched wooden chairs and a jumble of unwashed crockery in the sink. An enormous, gruel-coloured stove with a black chimney squatted in a blackened recess. The window looked out on sloped fields and the tree-clad rise, so that they had a curious sense of submersion, and felt as if they were looking up through the silvery water-light of a deep, still pool. Licht leaned down at the stove and opened the little door of the firebox and looked inside.

'Out, of course,' he said disgustedly and shouted: 'Stove!' but no one answered. He turned up to them an apologetic smile. 'Are you wet?'

They were wet. They were tired. They said nothing. They had got on board a boat at first light to take a little pleasure trip and now here they were stranded in a strange house on this island in the middle of nowhere.

Licht was still leaning at the stove gazing up at them, the smile forgotten on his face. They might have walked straight out of his deepest longings. Days he had dreamed of an invasion just such as this, noise and unfamiliar voices in the hall and the kitchen full of strangers and he amongst them, grinning like a loon. He left the stove and busied himself with making them sit and taking their wet shoes and offering them tea, scurrying here and there, hot with happy fear that they might at any moment prove a figment after all and vanish. Sophie was asking him something about the ruins in the hills, but he could not concentrate, and kept saying yes, yes, and smiling his unfocused, flustered smile. When Flora at the table looked up at him weakly and handed him her wet, warm shoes he felt a sort of plunge inside him, as if something had dropped in the hollow of his heart and hung there bobbing lightly on its elastic. She felt strange, she told him, strange and sort of shivery. Her voice was soft. She looked at him from under her long lashes, helpless and at the same time calculating, he could see it, how she was measuring him; he did not care, except he wished that he were younger, taller, altogether different. He stood before her holding her shoes, one in each hand, and a swarm of impossible yearnings rose up in him drunkenly. He brought her upstairs to rest and lingered in the doorway of the bedroom, twisting and twisting the doorknob in his hand. She sat down slowly on the side of the bed and folded her arms tightly around herself and looked emptily at the floor.

'Are you on a holiday?' he said tentatively.

'What?' She continued to stare before her in dull bewilderment, frowning. She roused herself a little and shook her head. 'No. I'm taking care of them.' She gestured disdainfully in the direction of downstairs. 'Supposed to be, anyway.' She gave a soft snort.

'Oh?'

She glanced up at him impatiently.

'The children,' she said. 'It's only a summer job, at the hotel.' She bit her lip and looked sullen.

'Ah,' he said. Some sort of skivvy, then; he felt encouraged. He waited for more, but in vain. 'Did that boat,' he said after a moment, 'did that boat really run aground?'

She did not seem to be listening. She was staring blankly at the floor again. Behind her an enormous, lead-blue cloud was edging its way stealthily into the window, humid and swollen, the very picture of his own muffled desires. She was so lovely it made him ache to look at her, with her slender, slightly turned-in feet and enormous eyes and faint hint of moustache. A memory stirred in his mind, the sense of something sleek and smooth and faintly, tenderly repulsive. Yes: the hare's nest in the grass that he had found one day on the dunes when he was a child, the two baby hares in it lying folded around each other head to rump like an heraldic emblem. He had brought them home under his coat but his mother would not let him keep them. How tinily their hearts had ticked against his own suddenly heavy heart! That was him all over, always on the look-out for something to love that would love him in return and never finding it. Or hardly ever. Poor mama. When he went back to look for the nest he could not find it and had to leave the leverets under the shelter of a rock, with leaves to lie on and grass and dandelion stalks to eat. Next day they were gone. Not a trace. The stalks untouched. Gone. And yet how little he had cared, standing there in the grey of morning contemplating that absence, while the sea beyond the dunes muttered and the wind polished the dark grass around him. Now he sighed, baffled at himself, as always.

'I think I want to lie down,' Flora said.

'Of course, of course.'

'Just for a little while.'

'Of course.'

He was torn between staying there, leaning sleepless on his shield, and rushing downstairs again to reassure himself that the others had not disappeared. Instead, when she had stretched herself out on the bed, yawning and sighing, and he had shut the door behind him lingeringly, he found himself wandering in a sort of aimless, apprehensive rapture about the upper storeys, stopping now and then to listen, he was not sure for what: for the crackle of wing-cases, perhaps, for the sounds of the new life breaking out of its cocoon. From the stairs he caught a glimpse through the half-closed lavatory door of Sophie sitting straight-backed on the stool with her skirt hiked up and her pants around her knees, gazing before her with a dreamy, stern stare as her water tinkled freely into the bowl beneath her. He hurried past with eyes averted, red-faced, smiling madly in embarrassment, muttering to himself.

Oh, agog, agog!

THE SEAGULLS wake me early. I hear them up on the chimney-pots beating their wings and uttering strange, deep-throated cries. They sound like human babies. Perhaps it is the young I am hearing, not yet flown from the nest and still demanding food. I never was much of a naturalist. How lovely the summer light is at this time of morning, a seamless, soft grey shot through with water-glints. I lie for a long time thinking of nothing. I can do that, I can make my mind go blank. It is a knack I acquired in the days when the thought of what was to be endured before darkness and oblivion came again was hardly to be borne. And so, quite empty, weightless as a paper skiff, I make my voyage out, far, far out, to the very brim, where a disc of water shimmers like molten coin against a coin-coloured sky, and everything lifts, and sky and waters merge invisibly. That is where I seem to be most at ease now, on the far, pale margin of things. If I can call it ease. If I can call it being.

An island, of course. The authorities when they were releasing me had asked in their suspicious way where I would go and I said at once, Oh, an island, where else? All I wanted, I assured them, was a place of seclusion and tranquillity where I could begin the long process of readjustment to the world and pursue my studies of a famous painter they had never heard of. It sounded surprisingly plausible to me. (Oh yes, guv, says the old lag, standing before the big desk in his arrowed suit and twisting his cap in his hands, this time I'm going straight, you can count on it, I won't let you down!) There is something about islands that appeals to me, the sense of boundedness, I suppose, of being protected from the world – and of the world being protected from me, there is that, too. They approved, or seemed to, anyway; I have a notion they were relieved to get rid of me. They treated me so tenderly, were so considerate of my wishes, I was amazed. But that is how it had been all along, more or less. They had worse cases than me on their hands, fellows who in a less squeamish age would have been hanged, drawn and quartered for their deeds, yet they seemed to feel that I was special. Perhaps it was just that I had confessed so readily to my crime, made no excuses, even displayed a forensic interest in my motives, which were almost as mysterious to me as they were to them. For whatever reason, they behaved towards me as if I had done some great, grave thing, as if I were a messenger, say, come back from somewhere immensely difficult and far, bringing news so terrible it made them feel strong and noble merely to be the receivers of it. It may be, of course, that this solemn mien was only a way of hiding their hatred and disgust. I suspect they would have done violence to me but that they did not wish to soil their hands. Maybe they had been hoping my fellow inmates would mete out to me the punishments they were loth to administer themselves? If so, they were disappointed; I was a man of substance in there, ranging freely as I might among that hobbled multitude. And now I had done my time, and was out.

I was not at all the same person that I had been a decade before (is the oldster in his dotage the same that he was when he was an infant swaddled in his truckle bed?). A slow sea-change had taken place. I believe that over those ten years of incarceration – life, that is, minus time off for good, for exemplary, behaviour – I had evolved into an infinitely more complex organism. This is not to say that I felt myself to be better than I had been – the doctrine of penal rehabilitation broke against the rock of my inexpungible guilt – nor did it mean I was any worse, either: just different. Everything had become more intricate, more dense and pensive. My crime had ramified it; it sat inside me now like a second, parasitic self, its tentacles coiled around my cells. I had grown fat on my sin; I seemed to myself to wallow along, bloated and empurpled, like a mutated species of jellyfish stuffed full with poison. Soft, that is, formless, malignant still, yet not so fierce as once I had been, not so careless, or so cold. Puzzled, too, of course, still unable to believe that I had done what I did do. I make no pleas; it is the only thing I can boast of, that I never sought to excuse myself for my enormities. And so I had come to this penitential isle (there are beehive huts in the hills), seeking not redemption, for that would have been too much to ask, but an accommodation with myself, maybe, and with my poor, swollen conscience.

They tell me I am too hard on myself; as if such a thing were possible.

I was brought, or perhaps transported is a better word: yes, I was transported here by boat. It was charming. I had expected to find myself standing outside the gates some desolate grey morning with a brown-paper parcel under my arm, whey-faced and baffled before a prospect of enormous streets, yet here I was, skimming gaily over the little waves with the breeze in my face and the tarry smell of the sea in my nostrils. The morning was sunny and bright, the light like glass. Shadows of clouds raced towards us across the water, darkened the air around us for a second, and swept on. When we got into the lee of the island the breeze dropped and the skipper cut the engine and we glided smoothly forward into a vast, flat silence. The water with the sun on it was wonderfully clear, I could see right down to the bottom, where there were green rocks and opulent, coffee-coloured weeds, and shoals of darting fish, mud-grey, with now and then a flash of platinum-white. The little jetty was deserted, the strand, too, and the green hill behind. On the quayside there was a jumble of tumbledown stone houses with holes in the roofs; at the sight of them, I do not know why, I experienced one of my moments of black fright. I have almost got used to these attacks, these little tremors. They last only an instant. There are times, especially at night, when I mistake them for stabs of physical pain, and wonder if something inside me is diseased, not a major organ, not heart or liver, but the spleen, perhaps, or the gall-bladder, something like that, some bruised little purple plum or orchidaceous fold of malignant tissue that might one day be the thing that would do me in to the accompaniment of exquisite torments.

I heard then for the first time that strange, soft, bellowing sound the island makes, it came to me clearly across the water, a siren voice.

'Like music,' I said. 'Like . . . singing.'

When I asked the skipper what it was he shrugged.

'Ah, don't mind that,' he said. 'There must be an old blowhole somewhere that the tide pushes out the air through. Don't mind that, at all.'

Then that teetering moment of slide and sway and the soft bump of the boat against the dock: landfall.

I liked the island straight away, finding its bleakness congenial. It suits me well. It is ten miles long and five miles wide (or is it five miles long and ten miles wide? – this matter of length and breadth has always puzzled me), with cliffs on one side and a rocky foreshore on the other. The seas round about are treacherous, running with hidden currents and rip-tides, so that yachts and pleasure boats for the most part steer clear of us, with the happy result that we are not troubled by day-trippers, or hearty people in caps and rugged jumpers tramping about the harbour demanding grog and talking incomprehensibly about jibs and mizzens and all the rest of it. The place overall is gratifyingly lacking in the picturesque. It is true, there are whitewashed cottages and dry-stone walls, and sheep, and even here and there a tweed-clad shepherd. We have the bigger stuff as well, the rolling hills and ocean views and shimmering, lavender distances, and at night there is the light-thronged firmament. What is missing is that look of stony fortitude – storms withstood, privations endured – which a real island turns upon the outside world and which fills the casual visitor with an equal mixture of awe and irritation. The fact is, the place is not like an island at all, more like a bit of the mainland that has recently come adrift. There are patches of waste ground, and mysterious, padlocked sheds smelling of diesel oil, and tarred roads that set off determinedly into the hills as if great highways awaited them out there like destiny. The village, though it lies no more than a mile inland from the harbour, hidden in the fold of a hill, has the forlorn look of a place lost in the midst of the plains. It seems to be inhabited entirely by idiots. (I should move there, I could be the village savant; imagine a mournful chuckle.) There is a shop, a post office, and a pub the door of which I do not darken. It is mostly the old who live here now, the young having fled to what I suppose they imagined would be the easier life of the mainland. I had thought, when I first arrived, of opening a little school, like poor Ludwig on the Snow Mountain, to teach the few children that remain, but nothing came of it, as was the case with so many of my projects. I, a school-teacher! What an idea. Still, the thought was benevolent, I do not have many such. The island services in general are meagre. The nearest doctor is a slow and sometimes erratic boat-journey away on the mainland. So when I arrived I felt at once as if somehow I had come home. Will that seem strange, to say I felt at home in such seemingly uncongenial surroundings? But the poverty, you see, the dullness and lack of emphasis, these might have been a form of subtlety, after all. Drama was the last thing I wanted, unless it be seagulls wheeling above oaks, or a boat stuck on a sandbank, or a woebegone band of strangers struggling up the dunes one day and spying an old house standing on the side of a hill.

From my copious reading – what else had I to do, in those first days of so-called freedom, except to read and dream? – I gleaned the following: *I have an habitual feeling of my real life having passed, and that I am leading a posthumous existence.* I had burned my boats, the years were strewn like ashes on the water. I was at rest here, in the calm under the great wave of the world. Yes, I felt at home – I, who thought never again to feel at home anywhere. This does not mean I did not at the same time feel myself to be an outsider. The place tolerated me, that's all. I had the impression of a certain disdain, of everything leaning carefully away from me with averted gaze. The house especially had a frowning, tight-lipped aspect. Or perhaps I am wrong, perhaps what I detected was not contempt, or even disapproval, but something quite other: tactfulness, for instance – inanimate objects seem ever anxious not to intrude – or just a general wish to preserve the forms. Yet wherever I went, even when I walked into an empty room, I had an uncanny sense of things having fallen silent at my approach. I know, of course, that this was all foolishness, that the place did not care a damn about me, really, that I could have vanished into the air with a *ping!* and everything would have gone on in its own sweet way as if nothing had happened. Yet I could not rid myself of the conviction that somehow I was – how shall I put it? – required.

And I was alone, despite the presence of the others. How to be alone even in the midst of the elbowing crowd, that is another of those knacks that the years in captivity had taught me. It is a matter of inward stillness, of hiding inside onself, like an animal in cover, while the hounds go pounding past. Oh, I know only too well how this will seem: that I had retreated into solitude, that I was living in a fantasy world, a world of pictures and painted figures and all the rest of it. But that is not it, no, that is not it at all. It is only that I was trying to get as far away as possible from everything. I had tried to get away from myself, too, but in vain. The Chinese, or perhaps it was the Florentines of Dante's day – anyway, some such fierce and unforgiving people – would bind a murderer head and toe to the corpse of his victim and sling this terrible parcel into a dungeon and throw away the key. I knew something of that, here in my oubliette, lashed to my ineluctable self, not to mention . . . well, not to mention. What I was striving to do was to simplify, to refine. I had shed everything I could save existence itself. Perhaps, I thought, perhaps it is a mistake: perhaps I should be shouldering the emcumbrances of life instead of throwing them off? But no, I wanted not to live – I would have others to do that for me – but only endure. True, there is no getting away from the passionate attachment to self, that I-beam set down in the dead centre of the world and holding the whole rickety edifice in place. All the same, I was determined at least to try to make myself into a – what do you call it? – a monomorph: a monad. And then to start again, empty. That way, I felt, I might come to understand things, in however rudimentary a fashion. Small things, of course. Simple things.

But then, there are no simple things. I have said this before, I shall say it again. The object splits, flips, doubles back, becomes something else. Under the slightest pressure the seeming unit falls into a million pieces and every piece into a million more. I was myself no unitary thing. I was like nothing so much as a pack of cards, shuffling into other and yet other versions of myself: here was the king, here the knave, and here the ace of spades. Nor did it seem possible to speak simply. I would open my mouth and a babble would come pouring out, a hopeless glossolalia. The most elementary bit of speech was a cacophony. To choose one word was to exclude countless others, they thronged out there in the darkness, heaving and humming. When I tried to mean one thing the buzz of a myriad other possible meanings mocked my efforts. Everything I said was out of context, necessarily, and every plunge I made into speech inevitably ended in a bellyflop. I wanted to be simple, candid, natural – I wanted to be, yes, I shall risk it: I wanted to be *honest* – but all my striving provoked only general hoots of merriment and rich scorn.

My case, in short, was what it always had been, namely, that I did one thing while thinking another and in this welter of difference I did not know what I was. How then was I to be expected to know what others are, to imagine them so vividly as to make them quicken into a sort of life?

Others? Other: they are all one. The only one.

Not to mention.

And yet it all went on, went on without stop, and every moment of it had to be lived, used up, somehow; not a lapse, not the tiniest falter in the flow; a life sentence. Even sleep was no escape. In the mornings I would get up exhausted, as if part of me had been out all night roving in the dark like a dog in rut. Such dreams I had, immense elaborations, they wore me out. What were they for, I wondered? They were like alibis, fiendishly intricate versions of an event the true circumstances of which I dared not admit, even to myself, that I remembered. To whom was I offering these implausible farragos, before what judge was I arraigned? Not that I imagined I was innocent, only I would have liked to see the face of my oneiric accusers. I remember the first dream I had, the very first night I slept here. I have no idea what it signified, if it signified anything. I was somewhere in the Levant, at the gates of a vast, grey, crumbling city, at evening, with my mother. She was nothing at all like her real self as I recalled it, but very brisk, very much the intrepid traveller, rigged out in tweeds and a broad-brimmed hat and wielding a stout stick. She kept stopping and hectoring me, the laggard son stumbling at her heels in his city shoes and sag-arsed trousers, overweight and sweating and risibly middle-aged. When we entered the city we found ourselves at once in a high, narrow alleyway lined with stalls. There were many people and a great hubbub of voices and eastern music and the mellifluous shrillings of merchants crying their wares. This is the gold market, my mother said to me, speaking very loudly close to my ear. There was a sumptuous shine in the air, as if the light were coming not from the sky but rising spontaneously from the countless precious things laid out around us, the ornaments and piled plates and great beaten bowls. We pressed on through the winding streets, into the heart of the town. There were mosques and minarets and arched gateways and houses with latticed windows giving on to courtyards where lemon trees grew in enormous stone pots. Everything was made of the same grey stone, a sort of pumice only darker, which was wrong, it should have been something hard and smooth and almost precious, like marble, or porphyry, whatever that is. Evening was coming on, and now there was no one to be seen, and our footsteps echoed along the little streets. It is Ramadan, my mother said softly. At that moment suddenly under a dim archway before us two boys appeared, slender, barefoot, honey-skinned, wearing faded robes that swirled about them loosely as they moved. They crossed the archway at a dancing run from left to right, lithe and swift as monkeys, bearing above their heads a gleaming shell of beaten gold the size and shape of an inverted coracle but so delicate and light it seemed to float on the tips of their fingers. They laughed, making soft, trilling noises deep in their throats. Were they playing a game, or was it some marvellous, ritual task they were performing? I saw them only for a second and then they were gone, and my mother too was gone from my side, and it was all so real, so fraught with mysterious significance, that I began to cry in my sleep, and woke up sobbing my heart out, like a child.

There are the nightmares too, of course, the recurring ones, lit with a garish, unearthly glow, in which the dead speak to me: flesh, burst bone, the slow, secret, blue-black ooze. I shall not try to recount them, these bloodstained pageants. They are no use to me. They are only a kind of lurid tinkering that my fancy indulges in, the crackles and jagged sparks thrown off by the spinning dynamo of my overburdened conscience. It is not the dead that interest me now, no matter how piteously they may howl in the chambers of the night. Who, then? The living? No, no, something in between, some third thing.

Dreams, then waking. At times it was hard to tell the difference; I would drift out of riotous slumber and get up and walk around in a hazy, shallow state that seemed only a calmer, less tormented form of sleep than that which had gone before. I tramped the roads in the chill of dawn while a white sun came up tremblingly out of the sea. Everything is strange at that hour, stranger than usual, I mean: the world looks as I imagine it will look after I am dead, wide and empty and streaked with long shadows, shocked somehow and not quite solid, all odd-angled light and shifting façades. These open vistas – so much sky! – alarmed me. I was permanently dizzy, clinging for dear life to our flying island,

and there was constantly a sort of distant ringing in my ears. It felt like early morning all day long, there was that fizzing in the blood, that taste of metal in the mouth. The days hung heavy, falling towards night. We watched in silence the unremitting, slow advance of time. Here on Devil's Island we are not allowed the illusion of highs and troughs, of sudden speedings up, of halts and starts. There is only the steady, glacial creep that carries all along with it. Sometimes I fancied I could feel the planet itself hurtling ponderously through space in its bubble of bright air. I had my moments of rebellion, of course, when I would scramble up from the slimed flagstones and rattle my shackles in rage, shouting for the non-existent jailer. Mostly, though, I was content, or calm, at least, with the febrile calm of the chronic invalid. That's it, that's what this place is most like, not a prison or a pilgrimage isle, but one of those sanatoriums that were so numerous when I was a child and half the world had rotting lungs. Yes, I see myself up here in those first weeks and months immured behind a wall of glass, peering out in a feverish daze over serried blue pines while a huge sun declined above a distant river valley. Heights, I have always sought the heights, physical if not moral. It is not grandeur I crave, not the mossy crag or soaring peak, but the long perspective, the distance, the diminution of things. I had hardly arrived here before I found myself tramping up the fields behind the house to the oak ridge. Wonderful prospect from this lofty crest, the near green and the far blue and that strip of ash-white beach holding up an enormity of sea and sky, the whole scene clear and delicate, like something by Vaublin himself, a background to one of his celebrated *pélerinages* or a delicate *fête galante*. From this vantage I could make out in the fields around me a curious, ribbed pattern in the turf. I wondered if vines perhaps had grown here once (vines, in these latitudes! – what an ignoramus I am), but the spinster who runs the post office in the village put me right.

'Potato drills,' she told me, shouting because for some reason she took me for a foreigner (which, when I think of it, I suppose I am). 'From before the famine times, that was.' A thousand souls lived here then. I picture them, in their cawbeens and their shawls, straggling down the path to the beach and the waiting black ship, the men fixed on something distant and the women looking back out of huge, stricken eyes. Cythera, my foot. Such suffering, such grief: unimaginable. No, that's not right. I can imagine it. I can imagine anything.

I bring the household rubbish up here on to the ridge to burn it. I like burning things, paper especially. I think fire must be my element; I relish the sudden flare and crackle, the anger of it, the menace. I stand leaning on my pitchfork (a wonderful implement, this, the wood of the shaft silky from use and the tines tempered by flame to a lovely, dark, oily opalescence), in my boots and my old hat, chewing the soft inside of my cheek and thinking of nothing, and am excited and at the same time strangely at peace. At times I become convinced I am being watched, and turn quickly to see if I can catch a glimpse of a foxy face and glittering, mephitic eye among the leaves; I tell myself I am imagining it, that there is no one, but I am not persuaded; I suppose I want him to be here still, someone worse than me, feral, remorseless, laughing at everything. The heat shakes the air above the fire and makes the trees on the far side of the clearing seem to wobble. Between the trunks I can see the sea, deep-blue, unmoving, flecked with white. The stones banked around the fire hum and creak, big russet shards with threads of yellow glitter running through them. I recall as a child melting lumps of lead in a tin can, the way the lead trembled inside itself and abruptly the little secret shining worm ran out. I used to try to melt stones, too, imagining the seams of ore in them were gold. And when they would not break nor the gold melt I could not understand it, and would fly into a rage and want to set fire to everything, burn everything down. Timid little boy though I was, I harboured dreams of irrestible destruction. I imagined it, the undulating sheets of flame, the red wind rushing upwards, the rip and roar. Fire: yes, yes.

I have other chores. I draw wood, of course, and tend the stove, and check that the water pump is running freely and that the septic tank is functioning. These used to be Licht's jobs; he took a great satisfaction in handing them over to me as soon as I arrived. I had not the heart to let him see how I enjoyed the work that he thought would be a burden. I could rhapsodise about this kind of thing – I mean the simple goodness of the commonplace. Jail had taught me the quiet delights of drudgery. Manual work dulls the sharp edges of things and sometimes can deflect even the arrows of remorse. Not that convicts are required any more to do what you would call hard labour. I have a theory, mock me if you will, that modern penal practice aims not to punish the miscreant, or even to instil in him a moral sense, but rather seeks to emasculate him by a process of enervation. I know I had ridiculously old-fashioned notions of what to expect from prison, picked up no doubt from the black-and-white movies of my childhood: the shaved blue heads, the manacled, ragged figures trudging in a circle in the exercise-yard, the fingernails destroyed, like poor Oscar's, from picking oakum – why, even leg-irons and bread and water would not have surprised me – instead of which, what we had was ping-pong and television and the ever-springing tea-urn. I tell you, it would soften the most hardened recidivist. (Perhaps when I am finished with Vaublin I shall produce a monograph on prison reform: here as elsewhere, though it may be slower, the spread of liberal values goes unchecked and cannot but do harm to the moral fibre of the race, which needs its criminals, just as it needs its sportsmen and its butchers, for that vital admixture of strength, cunning and freedom from squeamishness.) Of course, in prison there were deprivations, and they were hard to bear, I will not deny it. I had thought it would be women I would want when I got out, women and silk suits and crowded city streets, all that rich world from which I had been isolated for so long, but here I was, pottering about in this rackety house on a crop of rock in the midst of a waste of waters. I had my books, my papers, my studies, playing the part of Professor Kreutznaer's amanuensis, supposedly aiding him in the completion of his great work on the life and art of Jean Vaublin for which the world, or that part of it that cares about such things, has grown weary of waiting. The fiction that I was no more than his assistant was one that, for reasons not wholly clear to me, it suited us both to maintain; the truth is, before I knew it he had handed over the task entirely to me. I was flattered, of course, but I did not deceive myself as to his opinion of my abilities; it is true, I have a capacity to take pains, learned in a hard school, but I am no scholar. It was not regard for me but a growing indifference to the fate of his life's work that led the Professor to abdicate in my favour. No, that's not right. Rather it was, I think, an act of expiation on his part. He like me had sins to atone for, and this sacrifice was one of the ways he chose. Or was it, on the contrary, as the weasel of doubt sometimes suggests to me, was it his idea of a joke? Anyway, no matter, no matter. My name will not appear on the title page; I would not want that. A brief acknowledgment will do; I look forward to penning it myself, savouring in advance the reflexive thrill of writing down my own name and being, even if only for a moment, someone wholly other. If, that is, it is ever to be finished. I am happy at my labours, happier than I expected or indeed deserve to be; I feel I have achieved my apotheosis. My time is wonderfully balanced between the day's rough chores and those scrupulosities and fine discriminations that art history demands, this saurian stillness before the shining objects it is my task to interrogate. In these soft, pale nights, while a grey-blue effulgence lingers in the window, I work at the kitchen table at the centre of a vast and somehow attentive silence, doing my impression of a scholar, sorting through sources, reading over the Professor's material, in Licht's exuberant typewriting, and writing up my own notes; collating, imbricating, advancing by a little and a little. It is a splendid part, the best it has ever been my privilege to play, and I have played many. I am in no hurry; the lamplight falls upon me steadily, my bent head and half a face, my hand inching its way down the pages. Now and then I pause and sit motionless for a moment, a watchman testing the night. I have a gratifying sense of myself as a sentinel, a guardian, a protector against that prowler, my dark other, whom I imagine stalking back and forth out there in the dark. Where can he be hiding, if he is still here? Could he have got back into the house, could he be skulking somewhere, in the attic, or in some unused room, nibbling scraps purloined from the kitchen and watching the day gradually decline towards darkness, biding his time? Is he in the woodpile, perhaps? If he is here it is the girl he is after. He shall not have her, I will see to that.

So anyhow: I came here, and I settled down, if that is the way to put it. I was content. This was a place to be. I did not travel to the mainland. No one had said I might not do so, but I seemed to feel an unspoken interdiction. If there was such a rule it must have been of my own making, for I confess I had no desire to realight from Laputa into the land of giants and horses. Yes, I was happy to bide here, with my catalogues and my detailed reproductions, polishing my *galant* style in preparation for the great work that lay before me impatient for my attentions. Ah, the little figures, I told myself, how convincingly, how gaily they shall strut!

Did I pin too many of my hopes on this work, I wonder? Could I really expect to redeem something of my fouled soul by poring over the paintings – over the reproductions of the paintings – of a long-dead and not quite first-rate master? We know so little of him. Even his name is uncertain: Faubelin, Vanhoblin, Van Hobellijn? Take your pick. He changed his name, his nationality, everything, covering his tracks. I have the impression of a man on the run. There is no early work, no juvenilia, no remnants of his apprenticeship. Suddenly one day he starts to paint. Yes, a manufactured man. Is that what attracts me? Something in these dreamy scenes of courtly love and melancholy pantomime appeals to me deeply, some quality of quietude and remoteness, that sense of anguish they convey, of damage, of impending loss. The painter is always outside his subjects, these pallid ladies in their gorgeous gowns – how he loved the nacreous sheen and shimmer of those heavy silks! – attended by their foppish and always slightly tipsy-looking gallants with their mandolins and masks; he holds himself remote from these figures, unable to do anything for them except bear witness to their plight, for even at their gayest they are beyond help, dancing the dainty measures of their dance out at the very end of a world, while the shadows thicken in the trees and night begins its stealthy approach. His pictures hardly need to be glazed, their brilliant surfaces are themselves like a sheet of glass, smooth, chill and impenetrable. He is the master of darkness, as others are of light; even his brightest sunlight seems shadowed, tinged with umber from these thick trees, this ochred ground, these unfathomable spaces leading into night. There is a mystery here, not only in *Le monde d'or*, that last and most enigmatic of his masterpieces, but throughout his work; something is missing, something is deliberately not being said. Yet I think it is this very reticence that lends his pictures their peculiar power. He is the painter of absences, of endings. His scenes all seem to hover on the point of vanishing. How clear and yet far-off and evanescent everything is, as if seen by someone on his death-bed who has lifted himself up to the window at twilight to look out a last time on a world that he is losing.

Twice a week I report to Sergeant Toner, the island's only civic guard, a taciturn and stately figure. His dayroom in the barracks reminds me strangely of the schoolrooms of my childhood: the dusty floorboards, the inky smell, the wood-framed clock up on the wall ticking away the slow, sunstruck afternoons. Sergeant Toner moves with vast deliberation, rising from his desk in a rolling motion, as if he were shouldering great soft weights, nodding to me in sober salutation. A kind of monumental decorum marks these occasions. We speak, when we speak, mainly of the weather, its treacheries and unexpected beneficences. The Sergeant leans at his counter, his meaty shoulders hunched and his pink scalp gleaming through the stubble of his close-cropped, sandy hair, and writes my name into the daybook with the stub of a plain, sweat-polished pencil tethered to the counter on a piece of string; that pencil must have been here since the days when he was still a recruit. He breathes heavily, so heavily that once in a while, seemingly without his noticing it, a slurred word will surface, a fragment of his inner musings which he involuntarily extrudes in a sort of rasping sigh. *Ah, dear Christ*, he will murmur, or *Wednesday*, or, on one memorable occasion, *Puddings* . . . He honours the niceties of our predicament, maintaining a careful distance between us. In the beginning I had worried that he would be impressed with me, in a professional way, that he might look on me as a sort of celebrity to be watched over and shown off – after all, it is not every day a man of my notoriety swims into his ken – but the very first time when, nervous as a schoolboy, I came to report to him, he repeated my name to himself thoughtfully a couple of times and then – though he had been expecting me, of course, and knew all about me, having been thoroughly briefed, as they say, by the authorities – he asked gently, with that fastidiousness and sense of tact which I have come so much to admire in him, if I would please spell it for him. When I had done so, and he had carefully written it into his book, we observed a brief silence, with eyes downcast, in acknowledgment I suppose of the solemnity of the occasion. 'Ah yes,' he said then with a sigh, 'yes: life means life, right enough.' This is something that has been dinned into me over the years, yet coming from him, and the way that he put it, it had a certain weight, a certain grandeur, even, and for a moment I saw myself as a person of consequence; a serious person, deeply flawed and irremediably damaged, it is true, but someone, all the same: definitely someone.

I need these people, the Sergeant, and Mr Tighe the shopman in the village, even Miss Broaders, she of the pink twinsets and tight mouth, who presides over the post office. I needed them especially in the early days. They had substance, which was precisely what I seemed to lack. I held on to them as if they were a handle by which I might hold on to things, to solid, simple (yes, simple!) things, and to myself among them. For I felt like something suspended in empty air, weightless, transparent, turning this way or that in every buffet of wind that blew. At least when I was locked away I had felt I was definitively there, but now that I was free (or at large, at any rate) I seemed hardly to be here at all. This is how I imagine ghosts existing, poor, pale wraiths pegged out to shiver in the wind of the world like so much insubstantial laundry, yearning towards us, the heedless ones, as we walk blithely through them.

Time. Time on my hands. That is a strange phrase. From those first weeks on the island I recall especially the afternoons, slow, silent, oddly mysterious stretches of something that seemed more than clock time, a thicker-textured stuff, a sort of sea-drift, tidal, surreptitious, deeper than the world. Look at this box-kite of sunlight sailing imperceptibly across the floor, listen to the scrape of the curtain as it stirs in the breeze, see that dazed green view framed in the white window, the far, narrow line of the beach and beyond that the azure sea, unreal, vivid as memory. This is a different way of being alive. I thought sometimes at moments such as this that I might simply drift away and become a part of all that out there, drift and dissolve, be a shimmer of light slowly fading into nothing. It was coming into the season of white nights, I found it hard to sleep. Extraordinary the look of things at dusk then, it might have been another planet, with that pale vault of sky, those crouched and hesitant, dreamy distances. I wandered about the house, going softly through the stillness and shadows, and sometimes I would lose myself, I mean I would flow out of myself somehow and be as a phantom, a patch of moving dark against the lighter darkness all around me. The night seemed something on the point of being spoken. This sense of immanence, of things biding their time, waiting to occur, was it all just imagination and wishful thinking? Night-time always seems peopled to me; they throng about me, the dead ones, yearning to speak.

The house has a nautical feel to it. Sea breezes make the timbers shift and groan, and the blue, salt-laden light in the windows is positively oceanic. The air reeks of brine and the floors when the sun comes in give off a tang of pitch. Then there is that faint smell of rancid apples everywhere: I might be Jim Hawkins, off on a grand venture. When I came down at last on that morning of their arrival the kitchen was like a ship's cabin. I felt at first a certain sullen indignation, tinged with fear: this was my place and they were invading it. And yet, although I had only been here a few weeks, like Licht I too was eager already for change, for disorder, for the mess and confusion that people make of things. It was simple, you see, no matter how much of a mystery I may make the whole thing seem. Company, that was what we wanted, the brute warmth of the presence of others to tell us we were alive after all, despite appearances. They were crowded at the long pine table nursing mugs of the tea that Licht had made for them and looking distinctly queasy. Their shoes were lined up on top of the stove to dry. It was still early, and outside a flinty sun was shining and piled-up vastnesses of luminous silver and white clouds were sailing over the oak ridge. When I came in from the hall the back door flew open in the wind and everything flapped and rattled and something white flew off the table, and poor Licht waded forward at an angle with one arm outstretched and his coat-tails flying and slammed the door, and all immediately subsided, and our galleon ploughed serenely on again.

'This milk is sour,' said Pound.

I forget: is he the comedian or the fat one with the specs? I can see I shall have trouble with these two.

You would think I would have asked myself questions, as characters such as I are expected to do: for instance, Who can they be? or, What are they doing here? or, What will this mean to me? But no, not a bit of it. And yet I must have been waiting all along for them, or something like them, without knowing it, perhaps. Biding my time, that is the phrase. It has always been thus with me, not knowing myself or my velleities, drifting in ignorance. Now as I stood there gazing at them in dull wonderment, with that eerie sense of recognition that only comes in dreams, a memory floated up – though memory is too strong a word, and at the same time not strong enough – of a room in the house where I was born. It is a recurring image, one of a handful of emblematic fragments from the deep past that seem mysteriously to constitute something of the very stuff of which I am made.

It is a summer afternoon, but the room is dim, except where a quartered crate of sunlight, seething with dustmotes, falls at a tilt from the window. All is coolness and silence, or what passes for silence in summer. Outside the window the garden stands aghast in a tangle of trumpeting convolvulus. Nothing happens, nothing will happen, yet everything is poised, waiting, a chair in the corner crouching with its arms braced, the coiled fronds of a fern, that copper pot with the streaming sunspot on its rim. This is what holds it all together and yet apart, this sense of expectancy, like a spring tensed in mid-air and sustained by its own force, exerting an equal pressure everywhere. And I, I am there and not there: I am the pretext of things, though I sport no thick gold wing or pale halo. Without me there would be no moment, no separable event, only the brute, blind drift of things. That seems true; important, too. (Yes, it would appear that after all I am indeed required.) And yet, though I am one of them, I am only a half figure, a figure half-seen, standing in the doorway, or sitting at a corner of the scrubbed pine table with a cracked mug at my elbow, and if they try to see me straight, or turn their heads too quickly, I am gone.

'That skipper,' Felix was saying. 'What a fellow! *Listing?* I said to him, *listing?* More like we are in danger of turning tortoise, I believe!' And he laughed his laugh.

I was thinking how strangely matters arrange themselves at times, as if after all there were someone, another still, whose task it is to set them out just so.

Licht from across the room gave me one of his mournfully accusing glares.

'It's all right,' he called out loudly, 'it's all right, don't trouble yourself, I'll light the stove.'

Professor Kreutznaer in his eyrie sat for a long time without stirring, hearing only the slow beat of his own blood and the spring wind gusting outside and now and then the hoarse baby-cry of a gull, startlingly close. Strain as he might he could hear nothing from downstairs. What were they doing? They had not left, he would have seen them go. He pictured them standing about the dim hallway, magicked into immobility, glazed and mute, one with a hand raised, another bending to set down a bag, and Licht before them, stalled at the foot of the stairs, nodding and twitching like a marionette, as usual.

He fiddled with the telescope and sighed. Surely he had been mistaken, surely it was not who he thought it was?

He went to the door. It had a way of sticking and was hard to open quietly. Sure enough it gave its little *eek!* and shuddered briefly on its hinges. A flare of irritation made his heart thud hotly. He stood a moment on the landing with an ear cocked. Not a sound. Out here, though, he could feel them, the density of their presence, the unaccustomed fullness in the air of the house. His heart quietened, settling down grumpily in his breast like a fractious babe. The stairs at this level were narrow and uncarpeted. On the return a little circular window, greyed with dust and cobwebs, looked out blearily on treetops and a bit of brilliant blue, it might be sea or sky, he could never decide which. Again he found himself listening to his own heartbeat, with that occasional delicate tripping measure at the systole that made him think of rippling silk. If he were to pitch headlong down these stairs now would he feel it, his face crumpling, knees breaking, his breastbone bumping from step to step, or would he be gone already, a bit of ectoplasm floating up into the dimness under the ceiling, looking back with detached interest at this sloughed slack bag of flesh slithering in a comic rush on to the landing? When he was young he had thought that growing old would be a process of increasing refinement by which the things that mattered would fall away like little lights falling dark one by one, until at last the last light winked out. And it was true, things that had once seemed important had faded, but then others had taken their place. He had never paid much attention to his body but now it weighed on him constantly. He felt invaded by his own flesh, squatted upon by this ailing ape with its pains and hungers and its traitorous heart. And he was baffled all the time, baffled and numb.

He began cautiously to descend the stairs, wincing on each step as the boards squeaked. If it was Felix, how had he found his way here? Chance? He smiled to himself bitterly. Oh, of course – pure chance. He could feel the past welling up around him, a smoking, sulphurous stuff.

At the window on the first-floor landing he paused again and looked out at the distant sea. How clear it was today: he could see the burnished tufts of grass on the slopes of the dunes tossing in the wind. He liked mornings, the cold air and immensities of light, the raw, defenceless feel of things. This was the time to work, when the brain was still tender from the swoons and mad alarms of sleep and the demon flesh had not yet reasserted its foul hegemony. Work. But he no longer worked. He could feel the wind pummelling the house, pounding softly on the window-panes. On the sill a fly was buzzing itself to death, fallen on its back and spinning madly in tiny, spiralling circles. He leaned against the window-frame and at once the old questions rose again, gnawing at him. How can these disparate things – that wind, this fly, himself brooding there – how can they be together, continuous with each other, in the same reality? Incongruity: disorder and incongruity, the grotesqueries of the always-slipping mask, these were the only constants he had ever been able to discern. He closed his eyes for a moment, taking a tiny sip of darkness. Stay here, never stir again, gradually go dry and hollow, turn into a brittle husk a breath of wind would blow away. He imagined it, everything quiet and the light slowly changing and evening coming on, then the long dark, then rain at dawn and the gull's wing, then shine again, another bright day declining towards dusk, then another night, endlessly.

Suddenly there was a muffled cataclysm and the door behind him opened and Flora came out. At first he saw her only as a silhouette against a haze of white light in the lavatory window at her back. She shimmered in the doorway as if enveloped in some dark, flowing stuff, an angled shape flexing behind her shoulder like a wing being folded.

'Oh,' she said, and, so it seemed to him, laughed.

She closed the door behind her with one hand while with the other she held up her long hair in a bundle at the nape of her neck. He touched a hand to his crooked bow-tie. A hairpin fell to the floor and she crouched quickly to retrieve it. He looked down at her knees pressed tightly together, pale as candle-wax, and saw the outlines of the frail bones packed under the skin and caught for a second her warm, dark, faintly urinous smell. She was barefoot. As she was rising she swayed a little and he put out a hand to steady her, but she pretended not to notice and turned from him with a blurred, stiff smile, murmuring something, and went away quickly down the stairs, still holding up the flowing bundle of her hair. When she was gone the only trace of her was the borborygmic grumbling of the cistern refilling, and for a moment he wondered if he might have dreamed her. Suddenly the image of his mother rose before him. He saw her as she had been when he was a child, turning from shadow into light, a slight, small-boned woman in a black dress with a bodice, her heavy dark hair, which gave her so much trouble and of which she was so vain, done up in two braided shells over her ears and parted down the middle with such severity he used to think it must hurt her, the white weal scored from brow to nape like a bloodless wound. *Das Mädel*, his father used to call her, with a bitter, mocking smile, *das kleine Mädel*. Father in his white suit standing under the arbour of roses, idly drawing figures on the pathway with the tip of his cane, gay and disappointed and dreamily sinister, like a character out of Chekhov. Where was that? Up on the Baltic, the summer house. In the days when they had a summer house. The past, the past. He faltered, as if he had been struck a soundless blow, and closed his eyes briefly and pressed his fingertips to the window-sill for support, and a sort of hollow opened up inside him and he could not breathe.

Licht came up the stairs. 'What's wrong?' he said, sounding annoyed. 'What's wrong with you?'

The Professor blinked. 'What?'

'She said you were . . .'

They looked at each other. Licht was the first to turn away his eyes.

'Who is that,' the Professor said after a pause.

'Who?'

'That girl.'

Licht shrugged and hummed a tune under his breath, tapping one foot. The Professor lifted his weary eyes to the window and the shining day outside. The wind was still blowing, the fly still buzzed. He turned to Licht again.

'What did you say to them?' he said. 'Have they asked to stay?'

Licht frowned blandly and went on humming as if he had not heard, picking with a fingernail at a patch of flaking paint on the wall in front of him. The Professor descended a step towards him menacingly and paused. He could feel it suddenly, no mistaking it, the tiny but calamitous adjustment that had been made in their midst.

Felix, then: it must be Felix.

Licht spoke a word under his breath.

'What?' the Professor said.

'Flora,' Licht answered and looked up at him defiantly. 'That's her name. Flora.' Then he turned and skipped off swiftly down the stairs.

The room that Flora found herself in was small and had a low ceiling; everything in it seemed made on a miniature scale, so that she felt huge, with impossible hands and feet. Also the floor sloped; when she got up from the bed and walked to the window it was as if she were toppling backwards in slow motion. One of the panes in the little window was broken and a piece of cardboard was wedged in its place. Down in the sunlit yard a few scrawny chickens were picking half-heartedly in the dust and a fat old dog was asleep under a wheelbarrow. When she leaned down she could see fields and, beyond them, that sort of long ridge with trees on it. There was a fire going up there, weak flitters of white smoke were whipping in the wind above the treetops. She waded back to the narrow bed and sat down carefully with her arms pressed to her sides and her hands gripping the edge of the mattress. She could still feel the sway of the sea, a flaccid, teetering sensation, as if her limbs were brim-full of some heavy, sluggish liquid. She was not well, she did not want to be in this house, on this island. When Licht had brought her up here the bed had still been warm from someone sleeping in it. She had lain on top of the covers – a fawn blanket with a suspicious-looking stain in the middle of it and a sheet made, she was convinced, from old flour sacks – not daring to pull them back. The mattress sagged in the middle as if a heavy corpse had been left lying on it for a long time. On the little pine dressing-table there was a hairbrush with a few thin strands of reddish hair tangled in the bristles. A speckled mirror leaned from the wall at a watchful angle, reflecting a mysterious shimmer of grey and blue. She thought of searching the chest of drawers – she liked to poke about in other people's stuff – but she had not the energy. A coloured reproduction of a painting torn from a book was tacked to the wall beside the mirror. She looked at it dully. Strange scene; what was going on? There was a sort of clown dressed in white standing up with his arms hanging, and people behind him walking off down a hill to where a ship was waiting, and at the left a smirking man astride a donkey.

Felix opened the door stealthily and put in his narrow head and smiled, showing a glint of jagged tooth.

'Are you decent?'

She did not answer. She felt detached from things. Everything around her was sparklingly clear – the tilted mirror, the window with its sunny view, that little brass globe on the bedpost – but it was all somehow small and far away. She might have been standing at the back of a deep, narrow tunnel, looking out. Felix closed the door behind him and moved in that sinuous way of his to the window, seeming not to touch the floor but rather to clamber smoothly along the wall. He did not look at her but kept smiling to himself with a show of ease. Why had she let him into her room last night? She knew nothing about him, nothing; he had just turned up, suddenly there, like someone she had known once and forgotten who now had come back. That was the strange thing, that there had seemed nothing strange about it when he smiled at her in the hotel corridor and put a hand on the door to stop her shutting it and glanced all around quickly and stepped into the room sideways with a finger to his lips. He could have been anyone: anything could have happened. He was horrible with his clothes off, all skin and bone and sort of stretched, like a greyhound standing up on its hind legs. How white he had looked in the dark, coming towards her, glimmering, with that huge thing sticking up sideways like something that had burst out of him, blunt head bobbling and one slit eye looking everywhere for a way in again. He had squirmed and groaned on top of her, jabbing at her as if it were a big blunt knife he was sticking into her. When she moaned and rolled up her eyes she had felt him stop for a second and look down at her and give a sort of snicker and she knew he knew she was pretending. His hair down there was copper-coloured and crackly, like little tight coils of copper wire.

'Nice view,' he said now and for some reason laughed. 'Lovely prospect. Those trees.'

He came towards her, and his reflection, curved and narrow and tinily exact, slid abruptly over the rim of the polished brass ball on the bedpost beside her. She sat without moving and looked at him and a pleasurable surge of fear made her throat thicken; it was like the panicky excitement she would feel as a little girl when in a game of hide-and-seek some surly, bull-faced boy was about to stumble on her in her hiding-place. She saw that Felix was going to try to kiss her and she stood up quickly, lithe as a fish suddenly, and twisted past him.

'It's hot,' she said loudly. 'Isn't it hot?'

Her voice had a quaver in it. He would think she was frightened of him. A voice said mockingly in her head, *You are, you are.* She leaned down and tried to open the little window. He came up behind her and tapped the frame with his knuckles.

'Painted shut,' he said. 'See?' She could feel him thinly smiling and could smell his grey breath. He reached up and deftly plucked out a hairpin and her hair fell down; he took a thick handful of it and tugged it playfully and put his mouth to her ear. 'Poor Rapunzel,' he whispered. 'Poor damsel.'

She closed her eyes and shivered.

'Are you frightened?' he whispered. 'You must not be frightened. There is no danger. Everything is safe and sound. We have fallen flat on our feet here.'

In the yard the chickens scratched among the cobbles, stopped, stepped, scratched again. The dog was gone from under the wheelbarrow. Felix breathed hotly on her neck. Everything felt so strange. Her skin was burning.

'Hmm?'

'So strange,' she said. 'As if I . . .'

He let fall her hair and, suddenly full of tense energy, turned away from her and paced the little room, head down, his hands clasped behind his back.

'Yes yes,' he said impatiently. 'Everyone feels they have been here before.'

She heard the dog somewhere nearby barking half-heartedly.

'That man,' she said. 'I thought he was going to . . .'

'Who?'

'That old man.'

He laughed silkily.

'Ah, you have met the Professor, have you?' he said. 'The great man?'

'He was standing on the stairs. He – '

'Do you know who he is?' He smiled; he seemed angry; she was frightened of him.

'No,' she said faintly. 'Who?'

'Ah, you would like to know, now, wouldn't you.' He glanced at her slyly. 'He is famous.'

'Is he?'

'Or was, at least,' he said and laughed. 'I could tell you a secret about him, but I do not choose to.'

She pressed her back against the window-frame and folded her arms, cradling herself, and watched him where he paced. Yes, he would do anything, be capable of anything. She wanted him to hit her, to beat her to the floor and fall on her and feed his fill on her bleeding mouth. She pictured herself dressed in white sitting at a little seafront café somewhere in Italy or the south of France, where he had brought her, the hot wind blowing and the palms clattering and the sea a vivid blue like in those pictures, and she so cool and pale, and people glancing at her, wondering who she was as she sat there demurely in her light, expensive frock, squirming a little in tender pain, basking in secret in the slow heat of her hidden bruises, waiting for him to come sauntering along the front with his hands in his pockets, whistling.

Then somehow she was sitting on the bed again looking at her bare feet on the blue and grey rug on the floor and Felix was sitting beside her stroking her hand.

'I can give you so much,' he was saying fervently, in a voice thick with thrilling insincerity. 'You understand that, don't you?'

She sighed. She had not been listening.

'What? she said. 'Yes.' And then, more distantly: 'Yes.'

What was he talking about? Love, she supposed; they were always talking about love. He smiled, searching her eyes, scanning her face all over. Behind his shoulder, like another version of him in miniature in a far-off mirror, the man on the donkey in the picture grinned at her gloatingly.

'Will you be my slave, then, and do my bidding?' he said with soft playfulness. He lifted a hand and gently cupped her breast, hefting its soft weight. 'Will you, Flora?' His dark eyes held her, lit with merriment and malice. It was as if he were looking down at her from a little spyhole, looking down at her and laughing. He had not said her name before. She nodded in silence, with parted lips. 'Good, good,' he murmured. He touched his mouth to hers. She caught again his used-up, musty smell. Then, as if he had tested something and was satisfied, he released her hand and stood up briskly and moved to the door. There he paused. 'Of course,' he said gaily, 'where there is giving there is also taking, yes?'

He winked and was gone.

She looked at her hand where he had left it lying on the blanket. Her breast still felt the ghost of his touch. She shivered, as if a cold breeze had blown across her back, her shoulder-blades flinching like folded wings. The day around her felt like night. Yes, that was it: a kind of luminous night. And I am dreaming. She smiled to herself, a thin smile like his, and pulled back the covers and laid herself down gently in the bed and closed her eyes.

When Professor Kreutznaer came down to the kitchen at last the stove was going and Licht was frying sausages on a blackened pan. The Professor stopped in the doorway. The blonde woman sat with her black jacket thrown over her shoulders and an elbow on the table and her head on her hand, regarding him absently, her camera on the table before her. A cloud of fat-smoke tumbled slowly in mid-air. The smaller of the boys was gnawing a crust of bread, the little girl sat red-eyed with her hands in her lap. And that ancient character in the candy-striped coat, what was he? What were they all? A travelling circus? Felix had outdone himself this time. Licht was saying something to him but he took no notice and advanced into the room and sat down frowningly at a corner of the table. The one in the striped blazer cleared his throat and half rose from his chair.

'Croke's the name,' he said heartily, then faltered. 'We . . .' He looked at Sophie for support. 'Damn boat ran aground,' he said. 'That captain, so-called.'

The Professor considered the raised whorls of grain in the table and nodded. The silence whirred.

'We were in a boat,' Sophie said loudly, as if she thought the Professor might be deaf. 'It got stuck on something in the harbour and nearly capsized.' She pointed to their shoes on the stove. 'We had to walk through the water.'

The Professor nodded again without looking at her. He appeared to be thinking of something else.

'Yes,' he said. 'The tides hereabouts are treacherous.'

'Yes.' She caught Croke's eye and they looked away from each other quickly so as not to laugh.

Licht brought the pan from the stove and forked the charred sausages on to their plates, smiling nervously and nodding all around and making as much clatter as he could. He did not look at the Professor. There was a smell of boiled tea.

Felix came bustling in, rubbing his hands and smiling, and sat down beside Pound and picked up a sausage from the boy's plate and bit a piece off it and put it back again.

'Yum yum,' he said, chewing. 'Good.'

Something tilted wildly for a second. All waited, looking from Felix to the Professor and back again, feeling the air tighten between them across the table. The Professor, frowning, did not lift his eyes. Pound regarded his bitten sausage with sullen indignation.

'Well,' Sophie said to break the silence, 'how is Beauty?'

Felix looked blank for a moment and then nodded seriously.

'She is not well,' he said. 'She has an upset head. A certain dizziness, you know.'

Croke nudged Sophie under the table and whispered hoarsely into her ear:

'Struck down by our friend Poison-Prick.'

Sophie let her lids droop briefly and she faintly smiled.

Suddenly, as if he had been rehearsing it in his head, Felix jumped up and leaned across the table and thrust out his hand to the Professor.

'So good of you to take us in,' he said with a breathy laugh, avoiding the Professor's eye, 'so good, yes, thank you.' The old man looked without expression at the hand that was offered him and after a second Felix snapped it shut like a jack-knife and withdrew it. 'May I introduce – ? This is Mr Croke, and Sophie here, and little Alice, and Patch – '

'Hatch,' said Hatch.

'Hatch I mean. Ha ha! And Pound – Pound? Yes.' A mumbling, a shuffling of feet. He sat down. 'Ouf! what a business,' he said. 'I believe that captain was drunk. I said to him, I did, I said to him, *You will be responsible, remember!* A tour of the islands, we were told; a pleasure cruise. What pleasure, I ask, what cruise? Look at us: we are like the Swiss family Robertson!' He laughed excessively, his shoulders shaking, and paused for a moment, licking his lips with a glistening tongue-tip. 'This house, sir,' he said softly, in an almost confidential voice, 'the garden, those trees up there,' pointing, 'I have to tell you, it is all very handsome, very handsome and agreeable. I hope we do not inconvenience you. We shall be here only for a very little time. A day. Less than a day. An afternoon. Perhaps an evening, no more. Dusk, I always think, is so lovely in these latitudes: that greying light, those trembling shadows. I am reminded of my favourite painter, do you know the one I mean?' He mused a moment, smiling upwards, displaying his profile, then looked at the Professor again and smiled. 'You will hardly know we are here at all, I think. Our wings – ' he made an undulant movement with his hands ' – our wings will scarcely stir the air.'

Another silence settled and all sat very still again, waiting for the Professor to speak. But the Professor said nothing, and Felix shrugged and winked at Sophie and made a face of comic helplessness. Licht turned to the stove with a wincing look, his shoulders hunched, as if something had fallen and he were waiting for the crash. A little leftover breathy sob took Alice by surprise and she gulped, and glanced at Hatch quickly and blushed. Felix drummed his fingertips on the table and softly sang:

Din din!
Don don!

The sun shone in the window, the wind rattled the back door on its latch.

'This milk *is* sour,' Pound said. 'Jesus!'

The lounge, as it is called, is a long, narrow, low-ceilinged, cluttered room with windows looking out to sea. It smells like the railway carriages of my youth. Here, in the unmoving, brownish air, big, indistinct lumps of furniture live their secret lives, sprawled armchairs and an enormous, lumpy couch, a high, square table with knobbled legs, a roll-top desk sprouting dog-eared papers so that it looks as if it is sticking out a score of tongues. Everything is stalled, as though one day long ago something had happened and the people living here had all at once dropped what they were doing and rushed outside, never to return. Still the room waits, poised to start up again, like a stopped clock. I have my place to sit by the window while I drink my morning tea, wedged in comfortably between a high bookcase and a little table bearing a desiccated fern in a brass pot; behind me, above my head, on a bureau under a glass dome, a stuffed owl is perched, holding negligently in one mildewed claw a curiously unconcerned, moth-eaten mouse. From where I sit

I can see a bit of crooked lawn and a rose bush already in bloom and an old rain barrel at the corner of the house.

I think to myself, *My life is a ruin, an abandoned house, a derelict place.* The same thought, in one form or another, has come to me at least once a day, every day, for years; why then am I surprised anew by it each time?

I have my good days and my bad. Guess which this one is.

Tea. Talk about tea. For me, the taking of tea is a ceremonial and solitary pleasure. I prefer a superior Darjeeling; there was a firm of merchants in Paris, I remember – what were they called? – who did a superb blend, an ounce or two of which they would part with in exchange for a lakh of rupees. Otherwise a really fine Keemun is acceptable, at a pinch. Then there is the matter of the cup: even the worst of Licht's stewed sludge will taste like something halfway decent if it is served in, say, an antique fluted gold-rimmed piece of bird's-egg-blue Royal Doulton. I love bone china, the very idea of it, I want to take the whole thing, cup and saucer and all, into my mouth and crack it lingeringly between my teeth, like meringue. Tea tastes of other lives. I close my eyes and see the pickers bending on the green hillsides, their saffron robes and slender, leaf-brown hands; I see the teeming docks where half-starved fellows with legs like knobkerries sticking out of ragged shorts heave stencilled wooden chests and call to each other in parrot shrieks; I even see the pottery works where this cup was spun out of cloud-white clay one late-nineteenth-century summer afternoon by an indentured apprentice with a harelip and a blind sister waiting for him in their hovel up a pestilential back lane. Lives, other lives! a myriad of them, distilled into this thimbleful of perfumed pleasure –

Oh, stop.

The philosopher asks: *Can the style of an evil man have any unity?*

The lounge.

The day outside was darkening. A bundled, lead-coloured cloud burning like magnesium all along its edge had reared up in the window. A crepitant stillness gathered, presaging rain. I wonder what causes it, this expectant hush? I suppose the air pressure alters, or the approaching rain damps down the wind somehow. I should have studied meteorology, learned how it all works, the chaotic flood and flow of things, air currents, wind, clouds, these vast nothingnesses tossing to and fro over the earth.

Flora is dreaming of the golden world.

Worlds within worlds. They bleed into each other. I am at once here and there, then and now, as if by magic. I think of the stillness that lives in the depths of mirrors. It is not our world that is reflected there. It is another place entirely, another universe, cunningly made to mimic ours. Anything is possible there; even the dead may come back to life. Flaws develop in the glass, patches of silvering fall away and reveal the inhabitants of that parallel, inverted world going about their lives all unawares. And sometimes the glass turns to air and they step through it without a sound and walk into *my* world. Here comes Sophie now, barefoot, still with her leather jacket over her shoulders, and time shimmers in its frame.

She stopped inside the door and looked about her at the big dark pieces of furniture huddled in the brownish gloom, and immediately there started up in her head the rattly music of a barrel organ and she saw a little girl standing at a window above a wide avenue, with grey light like this lingering and dead leaves in the wind stealthily scurrying here and there over the pavement. Assailed, she sank down into a corner of the sagging couch, drawing up her legs and folding them under her and gingerly massaging her bruised instep. There were so many things she was tired of remembering, the happy as well as the bad. The apartment on

Kirchenallee, the upright piano by the window where she practised scales through the endless winter afternoons, her fingers stiff from the cold and her kneecaps numb. Smell of almonds and ersatz coffee, of the dust in the curtains where she leaned her head, looking down on the people passing by on the broad, bare pavements of the ruined city, hunched and hurrying, carrying bags or clutching parcels under their arms, like people in a newsreel. Her mother in the kitchen selling silk stockings and American cigarettes from a suitcase open on the table, talking and talking in that high, fast voice that sounded always as if at any moment it might break and fly off in pieces like a shattering lightbulb. The customers were furtive, timid, resentful, Frau Müller who limped, the sweaty, grey-faced man in the tight suit, that skinny girl from the café across the street. They glanced at her guiltily with weak, somehow beseeching smiles as they crossed the living room, hiding their purchases; how quietly, how carefully they would shut the door behind them, as if they were afraid of breaking something. She had thought she had managed to forget all that, she had thought she had banished it all, and now here it was again. The past mocked her with its simplicities, its completedness.

You see how for them too the mirror turns transparent and that silver world advances and folds them in its chill embrace?

She longed to be in her darkroom, in that dense, red, aortic light, watching the underwater figures darken and take shape, swimming up to meet her. Things for her were not real any longer until they had been filtered through a lens. How clear and small and perfectly detailed everything looked inside that little black box of light!

Humbly the first drops of rain tapped on the window.

All out there, oh, all out there.

What if, I ask myself, what if one day I were to wake up so disgusted with my physical self that my flesh should seem no longer habitable? Such torment that would be: a slug thrashing in salt.

Sophie.

Sophie sighed and

Sophie looked at her hands and sighed and closed her eyes for a second. She felt dizzy. There was a sort of whirring in her head. It was as if she had been spinning in a circle and had suddenly stopped. When she was a little girl her father would take her hands and whirl her round and round in the air until her feet seemed to fill with lead and her wrists creaked. It was like flying in a dream. Afterwards, when he let go of her and she stood swaying and hiccuping, everything would keep on lurching past her like a vast, ramshackle merry-go-round. And sometimes she grew frightened, thinking it was the movement of the earth she was seeing, the planet itself, spinning in space. She had never really lost it, that fear of falling into the sky. There were still moments when she would halt suddenly, like an actor stranded in the middle of the stage, lines forgotten, staring goggle-eyed and making fish-mouths. She took a cigarette from the packet in the pocket of her leather jacket and struck a match. She paused, watching the small flame creep along the wood, seeing the tiny tremor in her hand. Corpsing: that was the word. She imagined being in bed here, in an anonymous little room up at the very top of the house, just lying at peace with her hands resting on the cool, turned-down sheet, looking at the sea-light in the salt-rimed windows and the gulls wheeling and crying. To be there, to be inconsequential; to forget herself, even for a little while; to stop, to be still; to be at peace.

She entertained the notion that her father was alive somewhere, a fugitive in the tropic south, on some jungly islet, perhaps; she pictured him, immensely old by now, shrivelled and wickedly merry, sitting at his ease in the shade outside an adobe shack, tended hand and foot by a flat-nosed Indian woman while naked children brown and smooth as mud gambolled at his feet, with the broad, cocoa-coloured river at his back, and beyond that the enormous forest wall, screeching, green-black, impenetrable. She wanted him to have been important, terrible, a hunted man; it was her secret fantasy. They had waited for him day after day in the icy apartment (strange how heavy the cold felt, a sort of invisible, stony substance standing motionless in the air), then week after week, then the weeks became months, the months years, and he did not come. She thought of him as she had seen him for the last time, going down the stairs with a kit-bag on his shoulder. She could not remember his face now, but she recalled how lightly he had skipped down the steps, whistling, his head with its oiled hair and neat white parting sinking from sight. The pain, the outrageous pain of being abandoned had surprised her, the way all pain always surprised her in those days, like news from another world, the big, the real one, where she did not want to go but to which each day brought her a little closer. She was six years old when he left. Her mother lay in bed at night and cried; night after night, Sophie could hear her from across the hall, moaning and gulping, stuffing the pillow into her mouth, trying to stop herself, trying not to be heard, as if it were something shameful she was doing, some shameful act.

There was a scrabbling at the door and Croke came in cautiously, first a big, liver-spotted paw, then bigger head, then knees, then last of all the bowed back. He glanced about the room and did not see her curled up in the shadowed corner of the sofa. He advanced to the window, stepping over the carpet with a camel's ponderous slouch, seeming to lag half a pace behind his legs, his long head swaying on its drooped stalk. The rain was coming down heavily now, like a fall of dirty light. He stood with his hands behind his back and stared out bleakly, his loose lips pursed as if he were trying to remember how to whistle.

'The golden world!' he muttered, in a tone of deep disgust.

He farted, closing one eye and scrunching up his face at the side. At Sophie's soft laugh he started in fright and peered wildly at her over his shoulder.

'Jesus!' he cried. 'Do you want to kill me?' He waggled his fingers at her as if he were sprinkling water. 'Sitting there like a ghost!'

She laughed again. He was a game old brute: when she had stumbled on the bridge and he caught her his big hands had been all over her. She shivered, remembering the feel of his old man's arm, the slippery, fishy flesh inside thc sleeve and beneath it the bone hard and sharp as an ancient weapon. Now he paced agitatedly in a little circle, mumbling to himself and shaking his head. He halted, looking down at his feet.

'My shoes are wringing still,' he said and did his phlegmy laugh. 'Leaky as an unstanched wench. Ha!' He peered at her but she said nothing and he resumed his pacing. He stopped at the window and looked out again balefully at the rain. The world out there had turned to an undulant grey blur.

Silence. Picture them there, two figures in rainlight. Something, something out of childhood.

'I was trying to think,' Croke said, 'of the name of that thing they keep the host in to show it at Benediction. What do they call that? The thing shaped like the sun that the priest holds up. Did you ever see it? What is it, now. I've been trying to remember all morning.' He sighed. 'And I was an altar boy, you know.' He turned to her stoutly, expecting her to laugh. 'I was.'

But she was not listening. She sat and rocked herself in her arms, her eyes fixed on the floor. Croke shrugged and turned away and fiddled with the knobs of a huge, old-fashioned radio standing on a low table beside the window.

The green tuning light came on, a pulsing eye, and as the valves warmed up a distant crackling swelled, as if it were the noise of the past itself that was trapped in there among the coils and the glowing filaments. He spun the dial, and out of the crackling a faint voice emerged, speaking incomprehensible words, distantly. Croke listened slack-eyed for a moment and then switched it off.

Felix came in. When he saw Sophie he hesitated and let his gaze go blank and wander about the room. Croke he ignored.

'What a place!' he said. 'You know there is no telephone?'

She watched him, her eyes narrowed against the smoke of her cigarette. She had heard him creeping about in the hotel corridor last night, until that little bitch had let him in, she was sure of it. She had been using her cupped hand as an ashtray and now she held the swiftly-smoking stub of her cigarette aloft and looked about her with a frown. Felix stepped smartly to the mantelpiece and found a saucer there and brought it to her. He watched with what seemed almost fondness as she leaned forward and crushed out the butt. The last, acrid waft of smoke was like something swift and bitter being said. She raised her eyes briefly and then looked away.

'You know who he is,' he said, 'the Professor? You recognised him?' She shrugged, and he shook his head at her reprovingly. *'O, Fama . . .!'* He heaved a histrionic sigh.

'Tell me, then,' she said, stung. 'Tell me who he is.'

'Someone famous. A famous man.'

She looked sceptical.

'Oh yes?'

He nodded with mock solemnity and laid a finger to the side of his nose. She felt herself flush. She said brusquely:

'Should you not go and see if the Princess is sleeping soundly?'

Still he leaned above her in his buttoned brown suit and

stringy tie, a pent-up, parcelled man, his smile twitching and one eyebrow arched, studying her. She drew the collar of her jacket tight about her throat.

'Am I,' he said, 'the charming Prince, I wonder, or the Beast?' She did not answer and he advanced his smiling face close to hers and softly asked: 'Are you jealous?'

She laughed out loud.

'What, of her?'

He shook his head once.

'I meant of me,' he said.

She opened wide her eyes and looked at him steadily with a formless smile and said nothing. Croke stood motionless with his head lifted as if he were listening to something in the distance, an echo of that voice out of the ether. (That gold thing, like a sort of sunburst, with the big gold knobs on the handle and the big square base, and the price tag still on the instep of the priest's shoe when he genuflected; smell of incense and of candle-grease, the fleshy stink of lilies – *what* was it called?) There was a gust of wind, and the rain whispered softly like blown sand against the glass. Felix turned from Sophie with a flourish and strolled up the room and down again at an equine prance, seeming pleased with himself, humming lightly under his breath and smirking. He stopped to examine the stuffed owl, his narrow head lifted at an angle and his lips pursed. A spot of silver light gleamed in the hollow of his temple. He took a dented, flat gold case from his breast pocket and extracted from it a black cheroot and lit it carefully, holding it clipped between the second and third fingers of his left hand.

'I see you kept your baccy dry, anyhow,' Croke at the window said, and still was ignored.

'We have not had a real talk, you and I,' Felix said to Sophie over his shoulder, making a frowning face at the owl. A ribbon of harsh smoke trickled out at the corners of his mouth. The bird stared back at him with apoplectic fixity. 'We should, I think, don't you?'

Abruptly the rain stopped and the sun came out shakily and everything outside shimmered and dripped.

'Talk?' Sophie said. 'Talk about what?'

'Oh, anything. Everything. I am trying to be friendly, you see.'

Sophie considered his narrow back for a moment thoughtfully.

'Who is he?' she said. 'That old man.'

'What? I told you: a famous person. From the past. A professor of fine arts.' He seemed to find that very funny. 'Oh yes,' he said, laughing without sound, one bony shoulder shaking, 'a great appreciator of the fine arts!'

She studied him with her head held on one side.

'Is that why you came here,' she said, 'because of him?'

He laughed almost shyly this time and touched a hand to his dyed hair.

'No, no,' he murmured happily. 'Chance – pure chance!'

She nodded, not believing him.

'He does not seem to have heard of *you*,' she said.

'He has – oh, he has. But perhaps he prefers to forget.' He cast a smiling glance at her. 'Maybe you will make him famous again?' He took the cheroot from his lips and lifted an invisible camera to his eye. 'Snap-snap, yes? *The great man at his desk*.' He was mimicking her accent.

She rose from the couch, smoothing the lap of her dress, and crossed the room and stood with one hand on the doorknob and the other still holding her jacket closed at her throat.

'What a fraud you are,' she said.

'A fake, yes,' he answered swiftly, pouncing, with his fierce, tight-lipped smile, 'but not a fraud. Ask the Professor: he knows about such things.' He advanced a step towards her eagerly and stopped and stood with his hands in the pockets of his jacket and his head thrown back, looking at her along his nose and smiling genially, the cheroot held in his teeth and his curved mouth oozing smoke. 'What do you say,' he said, 'shall we fight?'

She hesitated, her eyes lowered, looking at the spot where he was standing. She pictured herself striding forward without a word and beating him to his knees, could almost see the blood-dark shadow in her head and feel the irresistible exultation shake her heart; she would cross the space between them at a run, one arm drawn back like a bow, fleet-footed, winged, taking a little skipping step halfway, the floor like firm air under her tread, and then feel the crack of fist on flesh and hear his laughter and his cries as he fell in a clatter with limbs askew, like a wooden doll. She trembled, and turned abruptly and went out, letting the door shut behind her with a ragged click.

Felix turned to Croke with eyebrows raised and empty palms helplessly upturned and lifted his shoulders and sighed.

'Listen,' Croke said, 'you look like a man that would know: that thing at Benediction that the priest holds up, what is that called?'

He demonstrated, lifting clasped hands aloft. Felix studied him carefully and then slowly smiled and wagged a finger in his face.

'Aha,' he said, with a reproving laugh, 'trying to pull the wool from under my feet, eh?'

Flora's dream has darkened. She wanders now in a wooded place at evening. The trees encircle her, stirring their branches and murmuring among themselves like masked attendants at a ceremony. Above her the sky is bright, lit with the smoke-blue, tender glow of springtime, but all is dimness and false shadow where she walks, circling the circle of trees, searching in vain for a way out. People are indistinctly present, posed like statues, Sophie and the children, old Croke in his straw hat, and someone else whose face she cannot see, who stands in the centre of the clearing, motionless and hanging somehow, as if suspended from invisible strings, a glimmering figure clad in white, grief-stricken and in pain, who does not stir or speak. Felix approaches her astride a pantomime donkey, stumping along on his own legs with the stuffed animal clamped between his knees. He puts his face close to hers and laughs and crosses his eyes and flaps his pink, pointed tongue suggestively. She notices that the donkey, though it is made of some sort of thick, furred stuff, is alive; it looks up at her pleadingly and she recognises Licht, sewn up tight inside the heavy fur. She flees, but there is no way out, and she hears Felix at her heels, his laughter and the jingling of buckles and poor Licht's harsh gasps of complaint. At last she runs behind the motionless, white-clad figure and finds that it has turned into a hollow tube of heavy cloth, and there is a little ladder inside it that she climbs, pulling the heavy, stiff tunic shut behind her. There is a musty smell that reminds her of childhood. In the dark she climbs the little steps and reaches the hollow mask that is the figure's face and fits her own face to it and looks out through the eyeholes into the broad, calm distances of the waning day and understands that she is safe at last.

I walked up the fields to the oak ridge. I noticed that my hands were shaking; nothing like a visitation to set the adrenalin coursing through the blood. The rain had stopped but the grass was thick with wet. Another dark cloud stood hugely above the trees like an ogre with arms outstretched. The little wood was green as green, and there were bluebells and wild garlic and even a nosegay of primroses here and there, nodding on a mossy bank or lurking coyly in the rotted bole of a storm-felled oak. The trees were lacily in leaf, at just that stage when Corot loved to capture them. All very pretty, and plausible too, yet I could not help thinking how all of it seemed laid on for someone else, someone milder than I, less tainted, without that whiff of brimstone that I suspect precedes me wherever I go. In the clearing my fire of yesterday was smouldering still; I soon got it back to life. Presently the rain started up again, tentatively at first, pattering on the dead leaves above me and then coming down in whitish swathes, billowing brightly through the trees and hissing in the fire. I stood with my head bowed and my arms hanging at my sides and the rain ran over my scalp and into my eyebrows and trickled down my face like tears and fell in heavy drops from my chin. Sometimes I like to abandon myself to the elements like this. I have never been one to worship nature, yet I recognise a certain therapeutic value in the contemplation of natural phenomena; I believe it has to do with the world's indifference, I mean the way the world does not care about us, about our happiness, or how we suffer, the way it just bides there with uplifted glance, murmuring to itself in a language we shall never understand. Even such a one as I might learn humility from that unfailing example of endurance and small expectations. Nothing surprises nature; terrible deeds, the most appalling crimes, leave the world unmoved, as I can attest. Some find this uncanny, I know, and lash out all round them, raging for a response, though nothing avails, not even the torch. I, on the other hand, take comfort from this universal dispassion –

But stop, stop; I have begun to generalise again. That is what the philosophic mode will do to you. Nature did not exist until we invented it one eighteenth-century morning radiant with Alpine light.

Anyway, I am standing in the rain with my head bowed, in my penitential pose. All at once, though I had noticed no flash, a terrible crack of thunder sounded directly above my head, making the trees rattle. It gave me a dreadful fright. What a thing that would be, to be struck down by a bolt out of the blue, or the grey, at least. So much for the world's indifference then; that would be what you might call a pathetic fallacy, all right. Or perhaps lightning would galvanise me into life, poor inert monster that I am? Then, by God, the world would want to watch out, oh yes.

The rain crashed down and almost at once began to ease. A storm in May; how well that sounds, to say it. I thought how my life is like a little boat and I must hold the tiller steady against the buffeting of wind and waves, and how sometimes, such as this morning, I lose my hold somehow and the sail luffs helplessly and the little vessel wallows, turning this way and that in the swell. Such formulations please me, as if to picture the world in this way were somehow to subdue it. (Subdue? Did I say subdue? Perhaps I am not so insouciant in the face of nature's heedlessness after all.) Yes, a little skiff, and I in it, out over depthless waters.

When the shower had passed and the sun came out again I took off my shirt and strung it between two sticks by the fire to dry. The breeze fingered my bared back, giving me gooseflesh. I looked at myself; I noticed that I was beginning to develop breasts; I laughed, and hunkered down by the fire for warmth. The flames faltered among the wet wood and the smoke stung my eyes. When Hatch and Pound came upon me even Hatch hung back at first, uncertain of this big, half-naked, red-eyed, dripping creature, the wildman of the woods, squatting with his arms wrapped round his knees and watching them from under half-closed lids. Circumspectly then they advanced and stood beside me and we stared all three into the fire. Around us the wind swept wetly through the trees and the leaves dripped and the damp sunlight flickered. Each fresh gust brought with it faintly the sound of the sea: the far, faint thud of waves and the hiss of water running on the shingle. I closed my eyes and the past was like a melody I had lost that was starting to come back, I could hear it in my mind, a tiny, thin, heartbreaking music.

'What's this place called?' Hatch asked.

'The Land of Nod,' I said, and they laughed without conviction and then lapsed again into silence.

I studied them with covert attention. Hatch was sly and unhappy and Pound was sharper than he looked. Pound's mother was supposed to have accompanied them on the boat trip but something had come up. He frowned into the fire, gnawing his lip. I wondered what his mammy would say if she knew her plump little boy was consorting unchaperoned with the ogre himself in the wild wood now. Sometimes I wonder if it was wise of the authorities to free me like this. But perhaps they knew me better than I know myself? I am harmless, I'm sure. Fairly harmless. No longer dangerous, anyway. Or not very.

Hatch said nothing; Hatch had no mother.

A strong gust shook the trees and the wet leaves clattered.

'This is worse than at home,' Pound said with sudden vehemence and kicked the embers at the fire's margin. 'Nothing to bloody do.'

I remembered suddenly how when I was young like them I sat in a hazel wood one winter Sunday by a damply smoking fire like this one as night came on and a boy whose name I cannot recall (Reck, I think it was, or Rice) arrived and told us a woman had been beaten to death in her sweetshop down a lane. I pictured the scene, distorted, wavering, the colours seeping into each other, as if I were looking at it all through bottle-glass, and felt fearful and inexplicably guilty. I have never forgotten that moment, that sudden, blood-boltered vision, intense as if I had been there myself. First such stain on my life.

The boys watched me uncertainly, waiting for me to

speak. I said nothing. They must have thought I was cracked. I am, a little. I must be, surely. It would be a comfort to think so.

A squashy, wet, warm smell rose from the greenery around us as the sun dried out the rain, and suddenly summer stood up out of the undergrowth like a gold man, dripping and ashine. Between the trees the lapis glint of sea. The air was gaudy with birdsong.

I left them and made my way down the hillside, carrying a stick; my shirt, still damp, clung to my back. The wind had grown gay and the sun was hot. The house stood below me, closed on itself. I sat down on a rock under a flowering thorn bush. There are times when my mind goes dead, as if something had switched itself off in my head. Some mornings when I wake I do not remember who I am or what it is I have done. I will lie there for a minute or more, unwilling to stir, basking in the anaesthetic of forgetfulness. It is like being new-born. At such moments I glimpse a different self, as yet unblackened, ripe with potential, a sort of radiant big infant swaddled in shining light. Then it all comes seeping back, spreading like a slow, thick liquid through my mind. Yet sometimes even when I am fully awake, in the middle of the day, I will imagine for a second, as if I were walking in a dark place and suddenly stepped through a patch of sunlight, that none of it had happened, that I am what I might have been, an innocent man, though I know well I have never been innocent, nor, for that matter, have I ever been what could properly be called a man. Still the dream persists, suppressed but always there, that somehow by some miraculous effort of the heart what was done could be undone. What form would such atonement take that would turn back time and bring the dead to life? None. None possible, not in the real world. And yet in my imaginings I can clearly see this cleansed new creature streaming up out of myself like a proselyte rising drenched from the baptismal river amid glad cries.

While I sat there on my hard rock under the may-tree the house below me as I watched over it began to come alive. Licht appeared in the yard with slops for the chickens, and above him, on the first floor, the french windows opened with theatrical suddenness and Sophie stepped out into the sunlight on the balcony with her camera. Dimly at a high-up window I could see Felix loitering, his long swarth face and glittering eye. Alice was climbing the stairs, I saw her on successive landings, a small, solemn figure resolutely ascending, first to the right, then to the left, and then the frosted glass of the lavatory window whitened briefly as she entered there and shut the door behind her. The Professor was pacing the turret room, a moving darkness against the light of the windows all around him, and now, as he turned, the weathervane on the roof turned with him in the breeze, and I smiled at this small coincidence that only I had seen.

It was Flora I was vainly watching for, of course, the rest of them might have been so many maggots in a cheese for all I cared. Oh yes, I had spotted her straight away, with my gimlet eye, the moment I had walked into the kitchen and seen them sitting there barefoot with their mugs of tea. She sprang out from their midst like the Virgin in a busy Annunciation, calm as Mary and nimbed with that unmistakable aura of the chosen. What did I hope for, what did I expect? Not what you think. I have never had much interest in the flesh. I used to be as red-blooded, or red-eyed, at least, as the next man, but for me that side of things was always secondary to something else for which I cannot find an exact name. Curiosity? No, that is too weak. A sort of lust for knowledge, the passionate desire to delve my way into womanhood and taste the very temper of its being. Dangerous talk, I know. Well, go ahead, misunderstand me, I don't care. Perhaps I have always wanted to be a woman, perhaps that's it. If so, I have reached the halfway stage, unsexed poor androgyne that I am become by now. But the girl had nothing to do with any of this. (By the way, why so coy about using her name? Want to rob her of her individuality, eh? – want to turn her into *das Ewig-Weibliche* that will lead you on to salvation, is that it, you sly old Faustus?. . . What have I said?) Sophie would have been more my vintage, with her camera and her fags and her tragic memories, but it was the girl I singled out. It was innocence I was after, I suppose, the innocent, pure clay awaiting a grizzled Pygmalion to inspire it with life. It is as simple as that. Not love or passion, not even the notion of the radiant self rising up like flame in the mirror of the other, but the hunger only to have her live and to live in her, to conjugate in her the verb of being.

Leave me there on my rock, leaning on my staff under may blossom in the rinsed air of May, a figure out of Arcady. Give me this moment.

The Professor paced the narrow round of his glass tower and considered the ruins of his life. When he sat down in his sea-captain's chair the things on the desk before him would not be still, pencils, papers, a teacup in its saucer, all trembled faintly; it puzzled him, until he realised that it was he, his tremulous presence, that was making everything quake like this. He was breathless and a little dazed, as if at the start of a large and perilous exploit. He felt excited, foolish, aghast at himself, as always, at the preposterousness of all that he was and did. Felix. It was Felix, bringing it all back. He seemed to hear the squeal of pipes and the rattle of timbrels, a raucous clamour rising through the bright air; was it the god departing, or returning a last time, to deliver him a last blow to the heart?

'Am I disturbing you?'

Sophie made a show of hesitating on the threshold, leaning

against the door-frame, regarding him with a small, false, enquiring smile. He said nothing, merely looked at her, and she advanced, still smiling. She smelled of smoke and perfume and something sweetly dirty. The expanse of skin above her collarbone was mottled and there were hairline cracks in the make-up around her eyes. Stop at the window, consider the view. The sun shines on a glitter of green and summer strides up the hillside. He watched her where she stood with her back to him and her arms folded, as if she were holding another, slighter self clasped tightly to her. He noticed her poor bare feet with their stringy tendons and the scribble of purplish veins at the backs of her ankles. Once the world had seemed to him a rich, a coloured place, now all he saw was the poverty of things.

'Felix says you are famous,' she said without turning.

'What?'

He was not sure if he had spoken or only imagined that he had. He had got out of the habit of speech.

'He seems to know you,' she said.

He nodded absently, frowning, glancing here and there about the desk as if he were trying to calculate its dimensions.

'That girl,' he said, 'what is her name – ?'

'Flora.'

'Yes. She reminds me of someone.'

'Oh,' she said blankly. 'Who?'

'From long ago.'

A ravelled silence.

'I know what you mean,' she said.

He lifted his head, frowning. 'What?'

'Faces,' she said. 'There are not many; five or six, I think, no more than that.'

He nodded; he had not been listening.

'Dead,' he said. He cleared his throat and gave himself a sort of heave as if he were shifting a weight from one shoulder to the other. Dead, yes; her cold hand in his, like a little bundle of brittle twigs wrapped in tissue paper; how much smaller than herself she had seemed, like a carved figurine, a memento of herself she had left behind. 'My mother,' he said. Sophie turned her face to the view again and stood still. 'A long time ago.' He nodded slowly, thinking. 'Remarkable, that girl . . .'

Another silence, longer this time. With the covert flourish of a conjuror she produced her camera from somewhere under her arm. He fidgeted, and she laughed.

'Don't worry,' she said, 'I have not come to photograph people, only ruins.' She focused on his desk, the back of his chair, the window-sills. He listened with faint pleasure to the repeated grainy slither of the shutter working. 'I am making a book,' she said. '*Tableaux morts*: that is the title. What do you think?'

He had stopped listening again.

'Have you known him for a long time?' he said.

She glanced at him, then shook her head.

'He was at the hotel last night,' she said, 'and afterwards on the boat. Why?'

He shrugged.

'I thought you knew him,' he said. 'I thought . . .'

'No,' she said. 'I do not know him.'

Thus they converse, haltingly, between long pauses. Behind the language that they speak other languages speak in silence, ones that they know and yet avoid, the languages of childhood and of loss. This reticence seems imperative. Both are thinking how strange it is to be here and at the same time to be conscious of it, seeing themselves somehow reflected in each other. That must be how it is with humans, apart and yet together, in their world, their human world.

Far thunder at dead of night, I wake to it, a low rumble along the horizon, the air crumpling. I imagine what it must be like out there, out beyond the land, where the humped sea hugely heaves, black as oilskin, under a bulging, clay-dark sky; I imagine it, and I am there. In these waters there are dolphins, I have seen them; uncanny creatures, with their rubbery grins and little mewling cries. It is said they save men from drowning. Would they save me, I wonder, if I came plummeting down and disappeared under the waves with a hiss? I live amongst ghosts and absences. A nightbird flies past, I hear the rapid whirr of wings, and down in the direction of the stream suddenly something gallops away. A horse? There are no horses here. A donkey, perhaps. I hear it, clear as anything, the unmistakable sound of hoofbeats. Who is the horseman?

Life, life: being outside.
Night and silence and
Oh life!
And I in flames.

I HAD HARDLY been a week on the island before I found myself a widow-woman. At least, I am sure that is how they told it hereabouts, where it seems every other cottage harbours a canny bachelor on the look-out for a secondhand mate, one already well accustomed to the bit, as Mr Tighe the shopman put it to me wheezily the other day, leaning over his counter on one elbow and giving me a large, lewd wink. My widow even had a few acres of land. She lived above us here on the ridge, in a rain-coloured cottage backed up crookedly against the massy darknesses of the oak wood. She kept chickens, and a goat tethered to a post in the front yard. Odd objects lay here and there about the place, as if they had become bogged down on their way elsewhere. There was a bright-red plastic baby-bath, a car tyre, a rusty mangle, and something that looked like a primitive version of a washing machine. The first time I went up there it was a brumous evening, more like November than May, with a solid blare of wind out of the west and the sea lying flat in the distance like a sheet of rippled steel. The front door stood open but there was no one to be seen. I approached cautiously, unnerved by the look of that dark doorway; I am always wary of strange houses. The goat, chewing on something with a rapid, sideways motion, eyed me with what seemed a sardonic smirk, while the chickens gave their goitrous croaks of complaint. I knocked and waited, and had to knock again, and at last there was a scuffling sound and she appeared, rising up suddenly in the dim doorway with her medusa-head of tangled hair and her unnerving, bleached-blue eyes. She said nothing, but stood with her hand on the latch and looked at me with a sceptical air, as if she did not really believe I could be real. She was a tall, spare figure with arthritic hands and a fine, long, ravaged face, handsome and yet curiously indistinct: when I think of her I always see her in profile, upright, archaic, noble, as if on the side of a worn silver coin. Everything about her was faded, her skin, her old skirt, her bird's nest of ash-coloured hair, and I had the notion that if I reached out to touch her my hand would encounter only shadowed air. For a moment I could think of nothing to say, then asked lamely if she would let me have a few eggs, since that was mainly what we were living on here at Château d'If and the hens that week had taken it into their heads to stop laying. She waited a moment, pondering, and then turned without a word and went away to the back of the house. I peered greedily through the open doorway: that's me always, hungering after other worlds, the drabber and more desolate the better, God knows why: so that I can fill them up, I suppose, with my imaginings. There was a table with a plain cloth, a rocking chair, a black stove; the walls and the concrete floor were bare. At the back dimly I could see a lean-to kitchen, with a roof of transparent corrugated plastic from which there sifted down an incongruously lovely, peach-coloured light such as might bathe a domestic interior by one of the North Italian masters. When she returned with the eggs in a paper bag I offered to pay for them but she shrugged and said she had more of them than she could use. Her voice was so distant and light I could hardly hear it, a sort of dry, papery rustling. I was halfway down the hill again before her accent registered.

She was not a native of these parts. Her name was Mrs Vanden. The islanders called her the Dutchwoman, but she might have been South African; I never did find out what her true nationality was. She had lived in many places abroad – her husband had been a colonial official of some sort. She rarely talked about the past, and when she did her voice took on a weary and faintly irritated edge, as if she were a historian describing an important but not very interesting period of antiquity. The late Mr Vanden hardly figured in this all-but-vanished age, and perhaps it was because I know so little about him that he has assumed in my imagination the outlines of a legendary figure, a Stanley or a Mungo Park, with pith helmet and swagger stick and enormous moustaches. How his widow ended up here I do not know. When I ventured to ask her, she said she had come to the island to get away from the noise; I presume she meant noise in general, the hubbub of the world. She was a great one for silence; it seemed a form of sustenance for her, she fed on it, like a patient on a drip. Sometimes when I visited her, as I did with increasing and, it strikes me now, surprising frequency over the weeks that I knew her, she hardly spoke a word. Perhaps Mr Vanden had been a talker? They did not seem rude, these silences. Rather, I took them as a mark of, not friendliness, perhaps – I would not describe our relations as friendly, no matter how close they might have been – but of toleration. She suffered me as she did those things in the yard, the odds and ends that just happened to have come to rest there. I suspect she never did manage to believe that I was entirely real. At times, if I were to say something after a long pause, or otherwise make my presence unexpectedly felt, a look of startlement tinged with dismay would cross her face, as if some comfortably inanimate presence had suddenly sprung to troublesome life before her eyes.

I met her a second time one evening in the oak wood. I had the fire going there; in fact, it was her fire I had taken over, as she had taken it over from some previous tender of the flame; I see a line of us, with our flints and pitchforks, stretching back to the time of the druids. She came wandering through the trees with her head down, in that distracted way she had, weaving a little, as if she were searching for something on the ground. I confess I was not greatly pleased to see her; a good bonfire, like so many things for me in those days, from sex to tea, was best enjoyed in solitude. She did not look at me, and even when she had drifted to a stop by the fire I was not sure if she was fully aware of me. She wore wellingtons and a crooked skirt and a battered hat that surely had seen duty on the veldt. The evening was grey and greyly warm. We stood gazing into the flames. Then she cast a thoughtful, sideways glance at my feet and invited me to come to her house and take tea. I was too surprised to refuse.

Her kitchen smelled of cooking fat and bottled gas and old water. I sat warily at the bare deal table and watched her. She reminded me of a piece of polished bone, or a stick of driftwood, thinned and hardened by the action of the years. I looked for her marks on the room, the impress of her solitary life here, but could find none. Plain chairs, plain pots, plain delft on the dresser. On a nail above my head hung one of Mr Tighe's advertising calendars with a photo on it of an outmoded bathing beauty. My attention was caught briefly by an electric Sacred Heart lamp on a wooden socket fixed to the wall, pink as an iced lolly and tremulously aglow, but when she saw me looking at it she smiled drily and shook her head: it had been here, she said, when she came to the house, and she had not known how to disconnect it.

We ate in ruminant silence. The slow day died and the sun went down in the kitchen window in a gradual catastrophe of reds and golds. As the dusk advanced we talked desultorily of this and that. It was not exactly a conversation, more a sort of laborious, intermittent batting; we were like a pair of decrepit tennis players having a game at close of day, lobbing slow balls high up to and fro through the darkening air. The name Dickie kept coming up, and Mrs Vanden grew almost animated: Dickie was this, and Dickie had done that, and oh, Dickie did have such a fine seat on a horse. I took it she was speaking of her late husband, but when my mistake became apparent an awkward silence fell and she looked at me directly, for the first time, it seemed, with those blank, impenetrable eyes, and it was as if I had come to a stumbling stop on the very lip of a precipice with nothing before me but the vast and depthless sky. No, she said, Dickie was her daughter, her only child, dead this twenty years. I was flustered, and could think of nothing to say, and looked down in confusion at my plate. I ask myself now, did I miss a real opportunity on that occasion? For what? Well, I might for instance have found out all sorts of things about her and her travels with the intrepid Mr Vanden. Perhaps I might even have let my own dead walk abroad for a bit, they who are as palpably present to me as Dickie the phantom horsewoman was to her. But the moment passed and already it was night, and I stood up fumblingly from the table and thanked her and hurried off down the hill through the immense, soft darkness.

How courtly we were, how correctly we conducted ourselves. I think that even if she had been fifty years younger there would have been no more between us than there was. And yet I believe that what there was was much. Does that make sense? There are certain people who seem to know me better than I know myself. To some, I realise, this would be an uncomfortable intrusion on their privacy and their sense of themselves, and it is true, there were occasions when in her presence I was acutely conscious of the pressure upon me of the sagging and unmanageable weight of all she must have known about me and did not say; mostly, though, I felt, well, lightened, somehow, as if I had been given permission to set down for a moment my burden – the burden of my self, that is – and stand breathing, unrequired briefly, in some calm, wide place. There was nothing filial in all of this, and certainly, I am sure of it, nothing maternal – no mother of mine was ever remotely like Mrs Vanden, apart from the Dutch blood – yet there was in it something that must have been very like that tentative, unspoken complicity, that feeling of basking in the knowledge of a secret agreement, that I am told exists between sons and mothers. This is perilous territory, I know; any minute now Bigfoot will come clumping on to the scene, with his sockets streaming. But I don't care, you can do all the cheap psychologising you want, I will still say that I felt when I was with her that I was protected, shielded somehow from at least some of the things that the world had it in mind to do to me; the smaller things, the quotidian inflictions. It is what I had always wanted, someone strong and mute and unknowable behind whose skirts I could hide. Wait, that's a surprise; do I mean that? Sometimes my pen just goes prattling along all by itself and the strangest things come out, things I did not know I was aware of, or of which I would prefer not to be made aware, or not to hear expressed, anyway. *Mute*, now, *unknowable*: is that what I really want, a sort of statue, one of those big Mooreish pieces, all scooped-out hollows and cuppable curves, faceless and tightly swathed, like a bronze mummy (oops! – what a treacherously ambiguous medium our language is)? I was content, at any rate, to be adrift in Mrs Vanden's company, if that is what it can be called, incurious as to the nature of her inner life, her thoughts, her opinions, if she had any.

I should berate myself for my selfishness, I suppose, my incurable solipsism, yet I cannot do it, with any conviction. I have the notion – I hesitate to speak of it, really, knowing how it will sound – that what we achieved, that what we began to achieve, Mrs V. and I, was a new or at least rare form of relation, one that, I realise, I had been aiming for for longer than I can remember. I do not know what to call it, how to describe it; words such as *reticent*, *respectful*, *calm*, these do not begin to suffice. There are men, I know, who prowl the world in search of an ideal woman, one who will indulge their darkest desires and slake for them the hot, half-formed urgings of the blood; I am like that, except that what I lust after is not some sly-eyed wanton but a being made up of stillnesses; not inert, not lifeless, only quiet, like me – yes, quiet, I am quiet, in spite of all this gabble – a pale pool in a shaded glade in which I might bathe my poor throbbing brow and cool its shamefaced fires (I know, I know: the pool, and the lover leaning over it, I too caught that echo). Forgiveness, I suppose; it all seems to come down to that, in the end, though I hate these big words. Forgiveness not for the things I have done, but for the thing that I am. That is the toughest one to absolve: what they used to call, if I remember rightly, a reserved sin.

Anyway, one day a couple of weeks after our first meeting I went up to the cottage and she did not answer my knock, though the door stood open as always, and when, with my heart in my mouth, I had climbed the stairs to what I knew was her bedroom, I found her lying neatly on her back in the narrow bed with the blanket pulled to her chin and her eyes open and all filmed over and a cocky fly strolling across her cold forehead. At first, in my surprise and numbed dismay, I had the crazy thought that it was not she at all, but an effigy of herself she had left behind her to fool me while she made good her escape. (I was not too far off the mark, I suppose.) The fly on her forehead stopped and wrung its hands as if in energetic dismay and then flew off in a bored sort of way, and I leaned over her and closed her eyes – now *there* is a creepy sensation – and quietly withdrew. I discovered that I was holding my breath. At the front door I debated with myself whether or not to shut it, but decided in the end to leave it open, since that was her way; besides, it is the practice in these parts, when someone dies, for the house to be left open to all-comers. Do I imagine it, or did the goat give me a soulful, commiserating look as I walked off down the path?

What I felt most strongly was resentment. It was as if she had played a tasteless practical joke on me, had tricked me, first luring me on and then abruptly vanishing. I had needed her, and she had let me down. But what had I needed her *for*? I brooded on the question without really wanting to find the answer, touching it gingerly, with the barest tips of thought, as if it were one of those lethal lumps the precise depth and dimensions of which I would not care to discover. Forgiveness, as I've said, absolution, I was aware of all that; but that was what I had wanted, not what I had wanted her to represent, as a being separate from me. (Oh God, this is all so murky and confused!) Look, here, let me come clean: I could not rid myself of the belief that she had seemed some sort of hope, not just for me, but for – well, I don't know. Hope. I am well aware how foolhardy it is to say such things, but there you are: it's true, it's what I felt. The trouble with death, I realised, is that it is really not an ending at all; it leaves so much unfinished, and so much unassuaged. You keep thinking that the one who died has just gone away, has walked off in the middle of things and will come back presently and take up where you both left off. I cursed myself for not having searched her house that last day, when I had the opportunity; no one would have known, I could have delved into every corner, investigated every last cranny in the place. However, I know in my heart that I would have found nothing, no cache of family papers, no eyebrow-raising diaries, no bundle of dusty letters done up in a blue ribbon. She had jettisoned everything but the barest essentials. Compared to hers my life was still awash with the flotsam of former, sunken lives. I entertained the hope that someone would turn up and surprise us at the funeral, a leathery old colonial, say, who would talk about kaffirs and gin slings and that time that new chap went mad and shot himself on the steps of the club, but in vain; Sergeant Toner and I were the only mourners. As the priest droned the prayers and shook holy water on her coffin I realised with a start that I had not even known her Christian name.

Another dead one; dear Jesus, I do keep on adding to them, don't I? Well, that's life, I suppose. I think of them like the figures in one of Vaublin's twilit landscapes, placed here and there in isolation about the scene, each figure somehow the source of its own illumination, aglow in the midst of shadows, still and speechless, not dead and yet not alive either, waiting perhaps to be brought to some kind of life. That's it, let us have a disquisition, to pass the time and keep ourselves from brooding. Think of a topic. Ghosts, now, why not. I have never been able to understand why ghosts should be considered something to be afraid of; they might be troublesome, a burden to us, perhaps, pawing at us as we try to get on with our poor lives, but not frightening, surely. Yet, though the fresh-made widow weeps and tears her breast, if she were to come home from the cemetery in her weeds and veil and find her husband's spirit sitting large as life in his favourite armchair by the fire she would run into the street gibbering in terror. It makes no sense. I can think of times and circumstances when even the ghosts of complete strangers, no matter how horrid, would be welcomed. The prisoner held in solitary confinement, for instance, would be grateful surely to wake up some fevered night and find a troupe of his predecessors come walking through the wall in their rags and beards and clanking their chains, while Saint Teresa would have been tickled, I suspect, to receive a visit to her interior castle from some long-dead hidalgo of Old Castile. And what of our friend Crusoe in his hut, would he not have been happy to be haunted by the spirits of his drowned shipmates? The ship's doctor could have advised him on his ague, the carpenter on his fencing, while the cabin boy, no matter how fey, surely would have afforded a welcome change of fare from Friday's dusky charms.

There are ghosts and ghosts, of course. Banquo was a dampener on the king's carousings, and Hamlet's father made what I cannot but think were excessive calls on filial piety. Yet, for myself, I know I would be grateful for any intercourse with the dead, no matter how baleful their stares or unavoidable their pale, pointing fingers. I feel I might be able, not to exonerate, but to explain myself, perhaps, to account for my neglectfulness, my failures, the things left unsaid, all those sins against the dead, both of omission and commission, of which I had been guilty while they were still in the land of the living. But more than that, more important than the desire for self-justification, is the conviction that I have, however preposterous it may sound, that there is an onus on us, the living, to conjure up our particular dead. I am certain there is no other form of afterlife for them than this, that they should live in us, and through us. It is our duty. (I like the high moral tone. How dare I, really!)

Let us take the hypothetical case of a man surprised by love, not for a living woman – he has never been able to care much for the living – but for the figure of a woman in, oh, a painting, let's say. That is, he is swept off his feet one day by a work of art. It happens; not very often, I grant you, but it does happen. The fact that the subject is a female perhaps is not of such significance, although it should be perfectly possible to 'fall in love', as they like to put it, with a painted image; after all, what is it lovers ever love but the images they have of each other? Freud himself remarked that in the passionate encounter of every couple there are four people involved. Or should it be six? – the two so-called real lovers, plus the images they have of themselves, plus the images that they have of each other. What a tangled web Eros weaves! Anyhow. This man, this hypothetical man, finds himself one day in the house of a rich acquaintance, where he is confronted by a portrait of a woman and knows straight away that at once and by whatever means he must possess it. That is what they mean by love, surely? It is not, mark you, that the woman is beautiful; in fact, the model was evidently a plain, pinched person with fishy eyes and a big nose and too much flesh about the lips. But ah, in her portrait she has presence, she is unignorably *there*, more real than the majority of her sisters out here in what we call real life. And our Monsieur Hypothesis is not used to seeing people whole, the rest of humanity being for him for the most part a kind of annoying fog obscuring his view of the darkened shop-window of the world and of himself reflected in it. He tells himself he will steal the picture and hold it for ransom, but really that is just for the purposes of the plot. His true and secret desire – secret even from himself, perhaps – is to have this marvellous object, to have and to hold it, to bathe in the brightness of its perfected, still and immutable presence. He is, or at least has been, let us say, a man of some learning, trained to reason and compute, who in the face of a manifestly chaotic world has lost his faith in the possibility of order. He drifts. He has no moral base. Then suddenly one midsummer day he comes upon this painting and is smitten. Some other object might have done as well, a statue, for example (I feel we shall have something to say on the subject of statues before long; yes, definitely I feel that topic coming on), or a beautiful proposition in mathematics, or even, who knows, a real, walking-and-talking, peeing-and-pouting, big live pink mama-doll. Obviously the need was there all along, awaiting its fulfilment in whatever form chance might provide. It is *being* that he has encountered here, the thing itself, the pure, unmediated essence, in which, he thinks, he will at last find himself and his true home, his place in the world. Impossible, impossible dreams, but for a moment he allows himself to believe in them. He takes the painting.

Here the plot does not so much thicken as coagulate.

He is an inept thief, our lovelorn hypothetical hero. He comes along bold as brass in broad daylight and lifts the lady off the wall, then turns and is confronted at once by a living, flesh-and-blood person (oh yes, lots of flesh, lots of blood), a maidservant, perhaps (pretend this is olden times, when domestics were readily available, not to say expendable), who by bad luck happens at that moment to walk into the room. Well, to shorten a long and grisly tale, without ado he bashes in the maid's head, not because she is a threat to him, really, but because, well, because she is there, or because she is there and he does not see her properly, or – or whatever, what does it matter, for Christ's sake! He kills her, isn't that enough? And he makes his get-away. Such things were commonplace in olden times. Suddenly, however, to his intense surprise and deep chagrin, he discovers that the picture has lost its charm for him. Ashes. Daubs. Mere paint on a piece of rag. He tosses it aside as if it were a page of yesterday's newspaper. What interests him now, of course, is the living woman that he so carelessly did away with. He recalls with fascination and a kind of swooning wonderment the moments before he struck the first blow, when he looked into his victim's eyes and knew that he had never known another creature – not mother, wife, child, not anyone – so intimately, so invasively, to such indecent depths, as he did just then this woman whom he was about to bludgeon to death. Well, he was shocked. Guilt, remorse, fear of capture and disgrace, he had expected these things, welcomed them, indeed, as a token that he had not entirely relinquished his claim to be considered human, but this, this sudden access to another's being, this astonished and appalled him. How, with such knowledge, could he have gone ahead and killed? How, having seen straight down through those sky-blue, transparent eyes into the depths of what for want of a better word I shall call her soul, how could he destroy her?

And how, having done away with her, was he to bring her back? For that, he understood, was his task now. Prison, punishment, paying his debt to society, all that was nothing, was merely how he would pass the time while he got on with the real business of atonement, which was nothing less than the restitution of a life. *Restitution*, that was the word, he remembered it from when he was a child at school and they told him what the thief must do, which is *to make proper restitution*.

Of course, he did not know how to do it, where to begin. He stood aghast before the prospect, baffled and helpless. That moment of ineffable knowing when he had turned on her with the weapon raised was no help to him here, that was a different order of knowledge, the stuff of life, so to speak, while what he needed now was the art of necromancy. The question was how to put into place another's life, but how could he answer, he who hardly knew how to live his own? A life! with all its ragged complexities, its false starts and sudden closures, the summer solitudes and winter woes, the inexplicable exaltations in April weather, the meals to be eaten, the sleeps to be slept, the blood in its courses, the coat that will go one more season, the new shoes, the old shoes, the afternoons, the nights, the bird-thronged dawns, the old dying and the new ones being born, the prime and then in a twinkling the autumnal shadows, then age, and then the proper death. That was what he had taken from her, and now must restore. He would need help. Oh, he would need help. And so he waits for the rustle in the air, for the moment of sudden cold, for the soundless falling into step beside him that will announce the presence of the ghost that somehow he must conjure.

As I say, merely a hypothesis.

Last night I had a dream about my father. This is an unusual occurrence. I rarely think of him, never mind entertain him in my dreams. My mother was a dreadful old brute but we were fond of each other, I believe, in our violent, unforgiving way. For my father, however, I seem never to have felt anything stronger than distaste. I mean, I probably loved him, as sons do love fathers, biologically, as it were, but I had as little to do with him as I could. He was a fearsome little fellow, a constant complainer and prone to sudden, ungovernable rages. I always think of him, God forgive me, as Mr Hyde, in his too-big tweeds, stumping along and snorting and stabbing at things with his stick. He died badly, rotting away before our eyes, shrinking to nothing as if he were consuming himself in his own anger. In my dream we were walking together through a huge and echoing administrative building, a place out of my childhood, a town hall or public library or something, I don't know. Anyway, the light in the dream was the light of childhood, steady and clear and dense with its own insubstantial vastness. Though I could see no one, I could hear distinctly the sounds of the place: the brittle clacking of a typewriter, the laughter of a fellow and a girl larking somewhere, and someone with squeaky shoes walking away very businesslike down a long corridor. Father and I were climbing an interminable, shallow staircase with many turns: I could feel the clammy sheen of the banister rail under my hand and sense the high, domed ceiling far above me. The old man was stamping along at a great rate, a pace in front of me, as usual, head down and elbows going like pistons. Suddenly he faltered, and I, not noticing, came up behind him and collided with him, or perhaps it was that he fell against me, I do not know which it was. Anyway, for an amazing moment I thought he was assaulting me. What I noticed most strongly was his smell, of hair oil and serge and cigarette smoke, and something else, something intimate and sour and wholly, shockingly other. He clung to me for a second to steady himself, fixing iron fingers on my wrist in a grip at once infirm and fierce, and I seemed to feel a sort of oscillation start up suddenly, as if some enormous, general and hitherto unnoticed equilibrium had collapsed. A clerk put his sleek head out of an office doorway below us and quickly withdrew it again. My father thrust me aside with what seemed revulsion. *I tripped!* he snarled, as if expecting to be contradicted, and glared at the banister, white with fury. He searched his pockets and produced a handkerchief and wiped his hands. We stood panting, as if we had indeed been engaged in a scuffle. A telephone rang nearby, a raucous jangling, like metallic laughter, and someone picked it up and began to speak at once in a low voice, urgently, as if trying to placate the machine itself. And I realised that what we had come there for was my father's death certificate; this seemed perfectly natural, of course, as such things do in dreams. We went on up the long stairs, and he was very brisk now, cheery, almost, in a pitiful sort of way, trying to pretend nothing of any note was happening, and I was embarrassed for him because I understood that he had already started to die and that death was something that would be shameful for him as a man, like being cuckolded, or going bankrupt. I was hoping that no one would see us there together, for if we got away without being seen we could pretend I did not know that he was doomed and that way he would save face. Then came a confused and hectic digression which I shall not bother with: how strange, the people that pop up in dreams, like the figures that loom at the shrieking travellers in a ghost train, springing out of the surrounding murk for a gesticulating, mad moment before being jerked away again on their strings. Anyway, after that wild interval my father and I found ourselves presently in an enormous room full of people rushing about in all directions, shouting, waving bits of paper at each other, demanding, beseeching, cursing. Father plunged at once, terrier-like, into the thick of this mêlée, shoving and shouting with the best of them, with me after him, desperately trying to keep up. He was outraged that the officials among the throng were not marked off somehow from the rest, and he kept stopping random passers-by, grasping them by the upper arms and rising on tiptoe and roaring in their faces. You don't understand, he would yell at them, I'm here for my chit, dammit, I'm here for my chit! But no one listened, or even looked at him, so busy were they craning to look past him, trying to glimpse whatever it was they were searching for with such fierce determination. Somehow I lost him, and now I in my turn found myself running here and there in desperation, shouting out his name and plucking at people and demanding if they had seen him. And then all at once, like smoke clearing, the crowd dispersed and I was left alone in the enormous room. After a long, panicky search I found a little door built flush to the wall and so well camouflaged that it could hardly be distinguished from the panelling, though by some means I knew it had been there for me to find. When I went through I was in another, much smaller room, with a barred window looking out on a sunlit, classical landscape of meadows and hills and bosky glades, dotted about with statuary and marble follies and dainty, sparkling waterfalls. My father was sitting crookedly on a chair in the middle of the bare floor with an air of bewilderment, stooped and crumpled, peering up fearfully as if expecting a blow; it was obvious that he had been thrust hurriedly on to the chair as I was about to enter. Behind him a group of silent men in starched high collars and black morning-coats and striped trousers stood about in attitudes of stern pensiveness, frowning at their fingernails, or gazing fixedly out of the window. Father had been weeping, his face was blotched and his nose was runny. All his fierceness was gone. It's *you*, he said to me, in a mixture of accusation and pleading, *you* have to serve your term before they'll do anything! At that the group of gentlemen behind him sprang at once into action and came forward hurriedly and picked him up, still seated, and bustled him chair and all out of the room, negotiating the narrow door with difficulty, muttering directions to each other and tut-tutting irritably. When I opened my eyes and sat up in the dawn light I was lost for a moment in that half-world between sleep and waking, and was convinced I had not been dreaming at all, but remembering; all day there has lingered the uneasy sense of an opportunity missed, of some large significance left unacknowledged. Certain dreams do that, they seem to darken the very air, crowding it with the shadows of another world.

Dreams bring remembrance, too; perhaps that is what they are for, to force us to dredge up those dirty little deeds and dodges we thought we had succeeded in forgetting. These half-involuntary memories are a terrible thing. There are days like this when they course through me from morning until night like pure pain. They leave me gasping, even the seemingly happy ones, as if they were the living record of heinous yet immensely subtle sins I had thought were covered up forever. And always, of course, there is the unexpected: although last night's dream was about my father, all day today I have been thinking mainly of my mother. After father died I was surprised by the depth of her grief. It made of her something ancient and elemental, a tribal figure, sitting dry-eyed draped in black, bereft, unmoving, monumentally silent, like a pelt-clad figure in a forest clearing watching over the smouldering ashes of a funeral pyre. Had I misjudged her, thinking she was made of sterner stuff? I believe that was for me the beginning of maturity, if that is the word, the moment when I realised it was too late to readjust my notions of her; too late for atonement, too (there is that word again). I tiptoed around her, now knowing what to say, fearful of intruding on this primitive rite. The house wore the startled, doggy air of having been undeservedly rebuked. I knew the feeling.

INHABITANTS OF THIS PLACE. What a peculiar collection we must seem, the Professor and Licht, the girl and I, disparates that we are, thrown together here on this rocky isle. The girl has complicated everything, of course. Before her coming things had settled down nicely; even Licht, who at first had been so resentful of me, had reconciled himself to my presence. Yes, without her we might have pottered along indefinitely, I at my art history and Licht at his schemes – he is a great one for schemes – and the Professor doing whatever it is the Professor does. Now we have grown restless, and chafe under the imposed languor of these summer days; time, that before seemed such a calm medium, has grown choppy as a storm-threatened sea. If the others had remained, I mean Sophie and Croke and the children, if they too had stayed behind they might have become a little community, might have formed a little fold, and I could have been the shepherd, guarding them against the prowling wolf. Idle fancies; forgive me, I get carried away sometimes.

Inevitably of course there has grown up a half-acknowledged divide, with the Professor and Licht on one side, the girl and I on the other, and behind that again there is yet another grouping in which the girl stands between Licht and me, a pair of ragged old rats scrabbling in the dirt and showing each other our sharpest teeth. Licht thinks he is in love with her, of course, and resents what he considers the excessive attentions I pay to her. Her silences torment him and strike him mute in his turn; he creeps up and stands behind her tongue-tied and quivering, or sits and stares at her across the dinner table, rabbit-eyed, his pink-rimmed nostrils flared and his hands trembling. He devises sly, round-about ways of talking about her, deprecating as Mr Guppy, introducing her name with elaborate casualness into the most unlikely topics and employing laboriously cunning circumlocutions. He is heartsick, mooning about the house with the agonised look of a man nursing an unassuageable toothache. At least it has made him smarten himself up a bit. He runs a comb now and then through that fright-wig of hair, and bathes more frequently than he used to, if my nose is any judge. I suppose she has become associated in his mind with the dream he has of leaving here and finding some more fulfilling life elsewhere; I see them, as in one of those old silent films, in a bare room with a square table, he sitting head in hands and she smiling her Lulu smile at the mustachioed and leering landlord who beckons to her suggestively from the doorway.

She is a singular creature, or seems so to me, at any rate. She claims to be twenty-one but I think she is no more than eighteen or nineteen. She will not tell me about her life, or at least does not: I mean maybe if I knew how to ask, if I knew the codes that everyone else has been privy to since the cradle, she would prattle away non-stop about her mammy and her daddy and schooldays and the job she did at the hotel and all the rest of it. As it is she wears the dulled, frowning air of an amnesiac. There are times when I catch her studying me with that remote stare that she has as if I were something that had suddenly appeared in her path, like a rock, or a fallen branch, or an unfordable blank span of water. Probably she finds me as baffling a phenomenon as I find her, my songless Mélisande. She trails about the house in an old raincoat of Licht's that she uses for a dressing-gown, with her lank hair and wan cheeks. I am startled anew each time I encounter her. I am like an anthropologist studying the last surviving specimen of some delicate, elusive species long thought extinct. I am assembling her gradually, with great care, starting at the extremities; I ogle her bare feet – the little toe is curled under its neighbour like a baby's thumb – her hard little hands, the vulnerable, veined, milk-blue backs of her knees. Sometimes at night she comes and sits in the kitchen while I work. I do not know if she is lonely, or afraid, or if the kitchen is just one of a series of stopping-places in her fitful wanderings; she has a way of touching things as she passes them by, tapping them lightly with her fingertips, like a child touching the markers of a secret game. She is tense, restless, preoccupied, always poised somehow, as if at any moment she might unfurl a set of hidden wings and take flight out of the window into the darkness and be gone. It will happen; some morning I will wake and know at once that she has flown, will feel her absence like a jagged hole in the air through which the wind pours without a sound. What shall I do then, when my term is ended?

Felix she does not mention.

I tell her about the painter Vaublin, what little is known of him. She listens, large-eyed, nodding faintly now and then, taking it all in or thinking of something else, I do not know which. Perhaps I am talking to myself, telling myself the same story all over again. Listen –

Who does not know, if only from postcards or the lids of superior chocolates boxes, these scenes suffused with tenderness and melancholy that yet have something harsh in them, something almost inhuman? *Le monde d'or* is one of those handful of timeless images that seem to have been hanging forever in the gallery of the mind. There is something mysterious here beyond the inherent mysteriousness of art itself. I look at this picture, I cannot help it, in a spirit of shamefaced interrogation, asking, What does it mean, what are they doing, these engimatic figures frozen forever on the point of departure, what is this atmosphere of portentousness without apparent portent? There is no meaning, of course, only a profound and inexplicable significance; why is that not enough for me? Art imitates nature not by mimesis but by achieving for itself a natural objectivity, I of all people should know that. Yet in this picture there seems to be a kind of valour in operation, a kind of tight-lipped, admirable fortitude, as if the painter knows something that he will not divulge, whether to deprive us or to spare us is uncertain. Such stillness; though the scene moves there is no movement; in this twilit glade the helpless tumbling of things through time has come to a halt: what other painter before or after has managed to illustrate this fundamental paradox of art with such profound yet playful artistry? These creatures will not die, even if they have never lived. They are wonderfully detailed figurines, animate yet frozen in immobility: I think of the little manikins on a music-box, or in one of those old town-hall clocks, poised, waiting for the miniature music that will never start up, for the bronze bell that will not peal. It is the very stillness of their world that permits them to endure; if they stir they will die, will crumble into dust and leave nothing behind save a few scraps of brittle lace, a satin bow, a shoe buckle, a broken mandolin.

I admire the faint but ever-present air of concupiscence that pervades all of this artist's work. Viewed from a certain angle these polite arcadian scenes can seem a riotous bacchanal. How lewdly his ladies look out at us, their ardent eyes shiny as marbles, their cheeks pinkly aglow as if from a gentle smacking. Even the props have something tumescent about them, these smooth pillars and thick, tall trees, these pendulous and smoothly rounded clouds, these mossy arbours from within which there seem to issue the sighs and soft laughter of breathless lovers. Even in *Le monde d'or*, apparently so chaste, so ethereal, a certain hectic air of expectancy bespeaks excesses remembered or to come. The figure of Pierrot is suggestively androgynous, the blonde woman walking away on the arm of the old man – who himself has a touch of the roué – wears a wearily knowing air, while the two boys, those pallid, slightly ravaged putti, seem to have seen more things than they should. Even the little girl with the braided hair who leads the lady by the hand has the aura of a fledgling Justine or Juliette, a potential victim in whom old men might repose dark dreams of tender abuse. And then there is that smirking Harlequin astride his anthropomorphic donkey: what sights he seems to have seen, what things he knows!

I pause to record an infestation of flies, minute, glittering black creatures with disproportionately large yet impossibly delicate wings shaped like sycamore seeds. I think they must be newly hatched. What is a blow-fly? That is what I thought when I saw them: blow-flies. Is there something dead around here that has not yet begun to stink? I cannot discover where they are coming from; they just appear in the light of the lamp, attracted by the warmth, I suppose, and fly up against the bulb and then drop stunned on the table and flop about groggily until I sweep them away with my sleeve. They have got into my papers, too, I lift a page and find them squashed flat there, tiny black and crimson bursts of blossom stuck with wing-petals. It is eerie, even a bit alarming, yet I am almost charmed. It is like something out of the Bible. What does it portend? I have become superstitious, the result no doubt of living for so long with ghosts. Down here in the underworld things give the uncanny impression of being other things, all these Pierrots and Colombines in their black masks, and even flies, looked at in a certain light, can seem celestial messengers. When they first began to appear I did not feel repugnance, only a sort of pleased surprise. I sat for a long time watching them, head on hand, lost to myself and inanely smiling, like one of those bewhiskered dreamers fluttered about by fairies in a Victorian engraving. I know that the reality they inhabit is different from mine, that for them this world they have blundered into is all struggle and pain and sudden, inexplicable fire – they are only flies after all, and I am only I – yet as they rise and fall, fluttering in the light, they might be a host of shining seraphim come to comfort me.

Today in my reading I chanced upon another jewel: *Hard beside the woe of the world, and often upon its volcanic soil, man has laid out his little garden of happiness.* Yes, you have guessed it, I have taken up gardening, even in the shadow of my ruins. It is a relaxation from the rigours of scholarship. (Scholarship!) But no, no, it is more than that. Out here among these greens, in this clement weather, I have the irresistible sensation of being in touch with something, some authentic, fundamental thing, to which a part of me I had thought atrophied responds as if to a healing and invigorating balm. So many things I have missed in my life; there are moments, rare and brief, when I think it might not be too late after all to experience at least some of them. My needs are modest; a spell of husbandry will do, for now. (Later will there come the tree of knowledge, Eve, the fatal apple, and all the rest of it, Cain included?) Perhaps I shall make a little statue of myself and grind it up and mix it with the clay, as the philosopher so charmingly recommends, and that way come to live again through these growing things.

I found down at the side of the house the remains of what must once have been a kitchen garden. Everything was choked with weeds and scutch grass, but the outlines of bed and drill were still there. I cleared the ground and found good black soil and put in vegetables – runner beans, mainly, I'm afraid, for I love their scarlet flowers. Already the first fruits have appeared (shall I hear the voice of the turtle, too?). I cannot express the excitement I felt when these tender seedlings began to come up. They were so fragile and yet so tenacious, so – so valiant. I have a great fondness for the stunted things, the runts, the ones that fail to flower and yet refuse to die, or are beaten down by the wind and still put out blossoms on the fallen stems. I have the notion, foolish, I know, that it is because of me that they cling on, that my ministrations, no, simply my presence gives them heart somehow, and makes them live. Who or what would there be to notice their struggles if I did not come out and walk among them every day? It must mean something, being here. I am the agent of individuation: in me they find their singularity. I planted them in neat rows, just so, and gave each one its space; without me only the madness of mere growth. Not a sparrow shall fall but I . . . how does it go? I have forgotten the quotation, the misquotation. Just as well, I am getting carried away; next thing I shall be hearing voices. It is just that there are days when, like Rameau's nephew, I have to reflect: it is an affliction that must run its course.

Where was I? My garden, yes. I entertain high hopes of a bumper crop. What shall I do with such abundance, though? Perhaps Mr Tighe will take some of it to sell in his shop? If not, what matter. Let it all go to waste. Life, growth, this tender green fighting its way up through the dirt, that's all that interests me. Obvious, of course, but what do I care about that? The obvious is fine, for me. Sometimes, anyway.

And then there are the weeds; I know that if I were a real gardener I would do merciless and unrelenting battle against weeds, but the fact is I cherish them. They seem to me even more fiercely alive than the planted things they flourish among. Cut them down today and tomorrow they will be back; tear them out of their holes and leave the merest thread of root behind and they will come shouldering their way up again, stronger than ever. Compared to these ruffians even my hardiest cabbages are namby-pambies. How cunning they are, too, how cleverly they choose their spot, growing up slyly beside those cultivated plants they most resemble. Against whom are they adopting this camouflage? Pests do not seem to eat them, having my more tender produce to gorge upon, and birds leave them alone. Is it me they fear? Do they see me coming, with my boots and blade? I wonder if they feel pain, experience terror, if they weep and bleed, in their damp, vermiculate world, just as we do, up here in the light? I look at the little sprigs of chickweed trembling among the bean shoots and I am strangely moved. Such steadfastness, such yearning! They want to live too. That is all they ask: to have their little moment in the world.

A robin comes to forage where I dig, a tough-looking type. It watches me with a glint and darts under my feet after its prey. Seagulls swoop and blackbirds fly up at a low angle, fluting shrilly. This morning when I was hoeing between the potato beds a rat appeared, nosing along under the whitewashed wall that separates my garden from the yard. It must have been sick: when it saw me it did not run away, only sat up on its hunkers and looked at me in weary surprise. (Where is that dog?) I thought of Alba Longa, of course, of Carthage in flames, all that. What a mind I have, stuffed with lofty trivia! After a moment or two the thing turned and made off, going at a sort of sideways wallow and dragging its fat pink tail over the clay. Trust me: the quick all around and I find myself face to face with a rat dying of decrepitude. I suppose I should have killed it. I am not so good at killing things, any more. Will it come back? In dreams, perhaps.

All this, the garden and so on, why does it remind me so strongly of boyhood days? God knows, I was never a tow-haired child of nature, ensnared with flowers and romping on the grass. Cigarettes and dirty girls were my strongest interests. Yet when I trail out here with my hoe I feel the chime of an immemorial happiness. Is it that the past has become pastoral, as much a fancy as in my mind this garden is, perpetually vernal, aglow with a stylised, prelapsarian sunlight such as that which shines with melancholy radiance over Vaublin's pleasure parks? That is what I am digging for, I suppose, that is what I am trying to uncover: the forfeited, impossible, never to be found again state of simple innocence.

So picture me there in this still-springlike early summer weather, in my peasant's blouse and cracked brogues, delving among the burdocks, an unlikely Silvius, striving by harmless industry to do a repair job on what remains of my rotten soul. The early rain has ceased and the quicksilver air is full of flash and chill fire; a surprise, really, this drenched brilliance. There is a sort of ringing everywhere and everything is damp and silky under a pale, nude sky. We had a wet winter, summer has made a late start, and the clay is sodden still, a rich, dark stuff that heaves and slurps when I plunge my blade into it. All moves slowly, calmly, at a mysteriously ordained, uniform pace; I have the sense of a vast clock marking off the slow strokes, one by one by one. I pause and lean on the handle of the hoe with my face lifted to the light, ankles crossed and feet in the clay (which is their true medium, after all) and think of nothing. There is a tree at the corner of the garden, I am not sure what it is, a beech, I believe, I shall call it a beech – who is to know the difference? – a wonderful thing, like a great delicate patient animal. It seems to look away, upward, carefully, at something only it can see. It makes a restless, sibilant sound, and the sunlight trapped like bright water among its branches shivers and sways. I am convinced it is aware of me; more foolishness, I know. Yet I have a sense, however illusory, of living among lives: a sense, that is, of the significance, the ravelled complexity of things. They speak to me, these lives, these things, of matters I do not fully understand. They speak of the past and, more compellingly, of the future. They are urgent at times, at times so weary and faded I can scarcely hear them.

I have discovered the source of those flies: a bunch of flowers that lovelorn Licht left standing for too long on the window-sill above the sink. Another attempt to brighten the place; that is his great theme these days, the need to 'brighten up the place'. Chrysanthemums, they were, blossoms of the golden world. Among the petals there must have been eggs that hatched in the sun. The water they were standing in has left behind a sort of greeny, fleshy smell. But imagine that: flies from flowers! Ah Charles, Charles – wait, let me strike an attitude: there – Ah, Charles, *mon frère mélancholique!* You held that genius consists in the ability to summon up childhood at will, or something like that, I can't remember exactly. I have lost mine, lost it completely. Childhood, I mean. Versions of it are all I can manage. Well, what did I expect? Something had to be forfeited, for the sake of the future; that is where I am pinning my hopes now. The future! Ah.

Flora is sleeping on her side with one glossy knee exposed and an arm thrown out awkwardly, her hand dangling over the side of the bed. See the parted lips and delicately shadowed eyelids, that strand of damp hair stuck to her forehead. A zed-shaped line of sunlight is working its imperceptible way towards her over the crumpled sheet. She murmurs something and frowns.

'Are you all right?' Alice says softly and touches her lolling arm.

'What?' Flora sits up straight and stares about her blankly with wide eyes. 'What?'

'Are you all right?' People waking up frighten Alice, they look so wild and strange. 'They sent me up to see if you were better.'

Flora closed her eyes and plunged her hands into her hair. She was hot and damp and her hair was hot and damp and heavy. She took a deep breath and held it for a moment and then sighed.

'I'm not better,' she said. 'I feel shivery still. I must have got a chill. Will you bring me a drink of water?'

She flopped back on the bed and stared vexedly at the ceiling, her dark hair strewn on the pillow and her arms flung up at either side of her face. The undersides of her wrists are bluish white.

'It was raining but it's lovely now,' Alice said.

'Is it?' Flora answered from the depths. She was trying to remember her dream. Something about that picture: she was in that picture. 'Yes,' she said, staring at the print pinned on the wall beside her, that strange-looking clown with his arms hanging and the one at the left who looked like Felix, grinning at her.

Alice had the feeling she often had, that she was made of glass, and that anyone who looked at her would see straight through and not notice her at all. She is in love with Flora; in her presence she has a sense of something vague and large and bright, a sort of painful rapture that is all the time about to blossom yet never does. She wished now she could think of something to say to her, something that would make her start up in excitement and dismay. She could hear the wind thrumming in the chimneys and the gulls crying like babies. She thought of her mother. A cloud switched off the sunlight. In the sudden gloom she began to fidget.

'That man made sausages for us,' she said.

A faint smell of frying lingered.

'Who?' Flora said. Not that she cared. She lifted her knees under the blanket and hugged them; she reclined there, coiled around the purring little engine of herself, with the restless and faintly aggrieved self-absorption of a cat. Suddenly she sat up and laughed. 'What?' she said, 'Did *he* cook – Felix?'

Alice put her hands behind her back and swivelled slowly on one heel.

'No,' she said witheringly. 'The one that lives here. That little man.'

The sunlight came on again and everywhere there was a sense of running, silent and fleet. Flora pulled the coarse sheet over her breast and snuggled down in the furry hollow of the mattress, inhaling her own warm, chocolatey smells. She no longer cared whose bed it was, what big body had slept here before her. Blood beat along her veins sluggishly like oil.

'Tell them I'm all right,' she said. 'Tell them I'm asleep.' The soft light in the window and the textured whiteness of the pillow calmed her heart. She was sick and yet wonderfully at ease. She closed her eyes and listened to the sounds of the day around her, birdsong and far calls and the wind's unceasing vain attempt to speak. She was a child again, adrift in summer. She saw the sun on the convent wall and the idiot boy on the hill road making faces at her, and below her the roofs shimmering, the harbour beyond, and then the sea, and then piled clouds like coils of dirty silver lying low on the hot horizon. 'Tell them I . . .'

*

Outside the door Alice paused. Through the little window above the landing she could see the shadows of clouds skimming over the distant sea and the whitecaps that from here looked as if they were not moving at all. Outside the window on the next landing there was a big tree that shed a greenish light on the stairs. She glanced down through the shifting leaves and thought she saw someone in the garden looking up at her and she turned hot with fright. Hatch had said this place was surely haunted. She hurried on.

The kitchen had the puzzled, lost look of a place lately abandoned. Only Licht was there, sitting at the strewn table with his head lifted, dreaming up into the wide light from the window. At first when he saw her he did not stir, then blinked and shook himself and sat upright.

'She said to say that she's asleep,' she said. He nodded pleasantly and smiled, quite baffled. 'Flora,' she said with firmness.

'Ah. Flora.' Nodding. 'Yes.' His gaze shied uncertainly. He was thinking there was something he should think. The noise of the wind had made him feel dizzy, as if a crowd had been shouting in his ear for hours, and he could not clear that awful buzzing sensation in his head. For an instant he saw himself clearly, sitting here in the broad, headachey light of morning, an indistinct, frail figure. Over the oak wood a double rainbow stood shimmering, one strong band and, lower down, its fainter echo. 'Flora,' he said again. Dimly in the dark of his mind the lost thought swirled.

Alice imagined taking him by the shoulders and shaking him; she wondered if his head would rattle.

'She said to say she's still not well,' she said.

'Oh?' Childe Someone to the dark tower came. 'I hope she . . .'

The unwashed crockery was still in the sink, the breakfast things were on the table.

'Will we wash up?' Alice said.

Licht shook his head.

'No,' he said, 'leave that, that's someone else's job.' He looked at her sidelong with a crafty smile. 'We had a maid one time who had a dog called Water, and when my mother complained that the plates were dirty, Mary always said, *Well, ma'am, they're as clean as Water can make them.*' He laughed, a sudden, high whoop, and slapped the table with the flat of his hand and then grew solemn. 'Poor mama,' he murmured. He stood up. Hop, little man, hop. 'Come,' he said, 'I'll show you somethng.'

The rainbows were fading already in the window.

The house was quiet as they climbed up through it and she imagined figures lurking unseen all around her with their hands pressed to their mouths and their eyes slitted, trying not to let her hear them laughing. She walked ahead of Licht and had a funny sensation in the small of her back, as if she had grown a little tail there. She could hear him humming busily to himself. The thought of her mother was like a bubble inside her ready to burst. Everything was so awful. On the boat that morning Pound had come into the lavatory when she was there and offered her sweets to pull down her pants and let him look at her. She was a little afraid of him, but she felt sorry for him, too, the way he bared his front teeth when he frowned and had to keep pushing his glasses up on his sweaty nose. His breath smelled of cheese.

On the first landing Licht stopped and cocked his head and listened, his smile fixed on nothing. Who did he look like, in that long sort of frock-coat thing and those tight trousers? 'All clear!' he whispered, and winked and shooed her on. The White Rabbit? Or was it the March Hare. For she was Alice, after all.

'Tell me,' he said, 'was the boat trip nice?'

She was not sure what she should answer. She thought he might be making fun of her. He was walking beside her now, leaning around so that he could look into her face.

There were little webs of wrinkles at the corners of his mouth and eyes, very fine, like cracks in china.

'It was all right,' she said carefully. 'Then it ran on to that sandbank thing and we all fell down. I think – '

'Ssh!'

They crept past the room where Flora was asleep. He wondered if she had taken off her clothes. A slow, dull ache of longing kindled itself anew in his breast.

Again he stopped and listened.

All clear.

They gained the topmost storey.

In the turret room Alice stood with her hands clasped before her and her lips pressed shut. Everything tended upwards here. The windows around her had more of sky in them than earth and huge clouds white as ice were floating sedately past. Something wobbled. She had a sense of airy suspension, as if she were hovering a foot above the floor. She imagined that as well as a tail she had sprouted little wings now, she could almost feel them, at ankle and wrist, little feathery swift wings beating invisibly and bearing her aloft in the glassy air. She could see all around, way off to the sea in front and behind her up to the oak wood. It seemed to her she was holding something in her hands, a sort of bowl or something, that she had been given to mind.

'This is Professor Kreutznaer's room,' Licht said, with a hand on his heart, panting a little after the climb. 'This is his desk, see – and his stuff, his books and stuff.'

She advanced a step and bent her eyes dutifully to the muddle of yellowed papers with their scribbled hieroglyphs and the big books lying open with pictures of actors and musicians and ladies in gold gowns. It all seemed set out, arranged like this, for someone to see. There was dust on everything.

'Does he look at the stars?' she said.

'What?' He had turned his head and was gazing out of the windows into the depths of the sky.

'The stars,' she said, louder. 'At night.'

Reluctantly he came back from afar. Alice pointed to the telescope.

'I suppose so,' he said. 'And the sea.' He gestured vaguely. 'The clouds.'

She stood before him, blank and attentive, waiting. He touched a fingertip to the back of the swivel chair and it flinched.

'He used to only look at pictures,' he said, frowning. 'He was an expert on provenance.'

She nodded.

'Providence,' she said. 'Yes.'

'No no: *provenance*. Where a painting comes from, who owned it, and so on. You have to know that sort of thing to prove it's not a fake. The painting, I mean.'

'Oh.'

A helpless silence fell. Faintly from the garden below came the sound of voices; in a rush both stepped at once to the window and peered down, their foreheads almost touching. The boys were down there, wrestling half-heartedly on the grass.

'Look at them,' said Alice softly, with soft contempt.

Licht from the corner of his eye studied her in sudden wonderment. He had not been able to look at her this closely before now. She might have been a new species of something that had alighted at his side. He could hear her breathing. Each time that she blinked, her eyelashes rested for an instant on the soft rise of her cheek. She had a smell like the mingled smell of milk and pencil shavings. Distinctly they heard Hatch say, *Oh, fuck!* Silence, dark woods, that wind again, like a river running through the glimmering leaves. He closed his eyes. A nerve was twitching in his jaw.

'Do you ever think,' he said softly, 'that you are not here?

Sometimes I have the feeling that I have floated out of myself, and that what's here, standing, talking, is not me at all.' He turned his troubled eyes away from her and bit his lip. Alice gazed intently down through the glass, hardly breathing. Something swayed between them and then gently settled. He sighed. Of late he had been experiencing the strangest things, all sorts of strange noises and reverberations in his head, pops and groans and sudden, sharp cracks, as if the world were surreptitiously disintegrating around him. One night when he was on the very brink of sleep something had gone off with a bang and a flash of white light, like a pistol being fired inside his skull, and he had started awake in terror but there was nothing, not the faintest sound or echo of a sound. 'I wonder,' he said, 'I wonder is there something the matter with my brain.' He saw himself elsewhere, running down a street, or crouched at a school desk in dusty sunlight under a ponderously ticking clock. 'Do you think we just die, Alice?' he murmured. 'That everything just . . . ends?'

The shadow of a bird, stiff-winged and plunging, skimmed slantwise across the window.

'I think that captain really was drunk,' she said suddenly, still looking down through the glass.

'What?'

'The captain of the boat. He had a bottle under a shelf. First he cursed and then laughed and told that Felix fellow to go to hell.'

She sighed.

'Is that right?' he said. He watched her as she stood on tiptoe peering down through the window, the shell-pink rim of one ear showing through her hair and a tongue-tip touching her upper lip.

'I'm staying in a hotel, you know,' she said. She gestured in the direction where she thought the mainland lay. 'My mammy . . .'

A tremulous frown passed over her face and he was afraid she was going to cry again.

'Come on,' he said.

Outside the turret room three deep steps led up to a door so low that even Alice had to stoop going through it. Here is the attic, a long, broad, tent-shaped, shadowed place with a dazzling pillar of sunlight suspended at an angle from a grimy mansard window in the roof. Smell of dust and apples and the sweetish stink of decaying timbers. It is hot up here under the roof and the air is thick. There were things piled everywhere, bits of furniture, old bottles, croquet mallets, an antique black bicycle, all standing like their own ghosts under a soft, furry outline of dust. 'The Emperor Rudolf,' Licht was saying, 'the Emperor Rudolf . . .' but the odd acoustics of the place took the rest of his words and made of them an unintelligible booming. They stood a moment, struck, listening to the echoes ricochet and fall like needles. A draught came in from the stairs and a door somewhere cried tinily on its hinges. The heat pressed on their eardrums. Unseen pigeons murmured lasciviously in the eaves and a mouse under the floorboards softly scurried. I have been here before.

'A great collector,' Licht said softly, as if someone else might be listening. 'Did you ever hear of him?'

Alice glanced sideways worriedly at his knees. 'I don't think so,' she said slowly.

'He had such things! – a magic statue, for instance, that sang a kind of song when the sun shone on it.' He looked uncertain for a moment. 'At least, that's what I read in a book somewhere.'

She turned and took a step away from him carefully, teetering. The thing she seemed to be holding in her hands now felt as if it were brimming over with some precious, volatile stuff. Suddenly he laughed behind her and the echoes flew up.

'Listen,' he said, 'listen,' and came forward with a finger lifted. 'What shape is a dead parrot?' She made a pretence of thinking hard. He watched her gloatingly, nodding, his eyebrows rising higher and higher. 'Give up?' She got ready to laugh. 'A polygon!' He quivered with glee, teeheeing soundlessly. She smiled as hard as she could, nodding. She had heard it before.

In a corner the floor was strewn with shrivelled apples. When his eye fell on them Licht grew morose.

'My pippins,' he said. 'I forgot about them.' He picked one up and sniffed it wistfully. 'Gone.' He gave her a mournful smile. 'Like poor Polly.'

He knelt before a brassbound chest. There were costumes in it, he told her, fancy-dress things from long ago, ball-gowns and helmets and an officer's uniform with a cocked hat. He tugged at the catches but could not get them undone. After a brief effort he gave up; leave them, leave them there, the gaudy centuries. He sat down on the lid of the chest and rocked himself back and forth, hugging one knee, while Alice stood, swaying a little, looking away. Another cloud swept over and the sunlight in the window above their heads died abruptly with a sort of click.

'He was famous, you know,' Licht said. 'Oh yes. He was in books, and people came from all over the world to get his opinion on pictures.' His face darkened and he looked like a vexed child. 'Then they said that he – ' He paused and lifted a warning finger, listening.

Eek.

The sunlight returned. Distantly they heard again from the garden the raucous voices of the boys.

'Where was he emperor of?' Alice said.

Licht looked at her and blinked. 'Eh? No, no, not him – I mean Professor Kreutznaer.'

'Oh.'

He looked more vexed than ever. He stood up from the

chest and paced the floor moodily with his hands at his back and the corners of his mouth pulled down. Alice felt the invisible bowl tilting in her hands.

'I was his assistant, you know,' he said airily, pointing to the papers on the desk. 'I used to type up what he wrote.' He waggled his fingers, tapping invisible keys. 'I was the only one who could read his handwriting.'

He stood and frowned, scratching his head with one finger.

'Did they write about you in the books, too?' she asked.

He glanced at her sharply. 'Of course not!' he snapped, and she felt the ghost of a quicksilver splash fall at her feet. He broke off and lifted a hand again, frowning, his rabbity nostrils flared. A stair creaked; then silence. (The Professor is out there, poised like a voyeur, listening.) I watch them, outlined in dusty sunlight against the soft dark, an emblem of something, and my heart contracts.

'What is it?' Alice whispered.

'What? Oh, I thought I heard – ssh!'

They listened. No sound. Licht shrugged and started to speak, but suddenly Alice turned to him and said:

'I'm afraid!'

And as soon as it was said it ceased to be true. Licht stepped back, staring, cradling in his startled palms the invisible vessel she had handed him.

When Alice had run off down the stairs and Licht came stooping through the little doorway Professor Kreutznaer was there at the landing window with his fists sunk in the sagging pockets of his old black jacket. Licht flushed angrily.

'What are you doing?' the Professor said.

'Nothing!' Licht cried. It came out as a squeak. He cleared his throat and tried again. 'Nothing. What do you mean? Are you spying on me?'

From below came the abrupt thud of the front door slamming; the house quivered and after a second a ghostly draught came wafting up the stairs.

'I told you you shouldn't let them stay,' the Professor said. 'Why did you let them in?'

Licht strode past him to the window and stood looking out. Tears of anger and resentment welled up in his eyes.

'Why do you blame me?' he cried. 'You blame me for everything, and spy on me, creeping around and listening at doors. It's you they're after, it's you that fellow came to find!' How gay and carefree everything outside seemed, the sun on the dunes and the grass waving and the unreal blue of the sea in the distance. At moments such as this he felt the world was rocking with laughter, jeering at him. He beat his fists softly on the window-sill and wept, his shoulders shaking. 'I have to get away from here,' he said as if to himself and heaved a juicy sob, shaking his head slowly from side to side, and a big bubble of spit formed on his blubby lips and burst with a tiny plop. 'I have to get away!'

The Professor regarded him in silence, frowning. Licht, pawing at his eyes and muttering something, pushed past him and blundered away down the stairs.

The front door banged again and the Professor felt the tiny tremor under his feet. He waited and presently he heard another sound, closer at hand, and when he looked over the banisters he saw Felix on the landing below, leaning at the door of the bedroom there with one hand in the pocket of his jacket and his head inclined, smiling to himself, listening for a sound from within. The Professor drew back quickly, his heart joggling, but too late. For a moment there was silence and then from below he heard Felix laugh softly and softly sing up the stairwell:

'Helloo-oo!' Pause. 'Professor?' Pause; again a laugh. 'Are you there, Truepenny?'

The Professor closed his eyes briefly and sighed. There

were things he did not wish to recall. Black nights by the river, the lamps on the quayside shivering in the wind and the gulls wheeling in the darkness overhead like big, blown sheets of paper, and the boys standing in the shadows, all silk and sheathed steel, shuffling their feet in the cold, the tips of their cigarettes flaring and their soft cat-voices calling to him as he walked past them on the pavement for the third or fourth time, trying to appear distracted, trying to look like what at other times he thought himself to be. *How are you, hard? Are you looking for it, are you?* They all had the same, quick eyes, like the eyes of half-tamed animals. He was frightened of them. And yet behind all the toughness and the insolent talk how tentative they were; alone with him at last in a dark doorway or down a back lane they laughed self-consciously and ducked their heads, avoiding his furtive, beseeching eyes, pretending not to be there, just like him. It was that mixture of menace and vulnerability he found irresistible. And then stumbling away through the rain-slimed streets, light-headed, shaking with a sort of sated glee. Never again! he would cry out in his heart, never, I swear it! addressing a phantom version of himself that stood over him with arms folded and lips shut tight in terrible accusal. And Felix there always, lord of the streets, popping up out of nowhere, horribly knowing, making little jokes and smiling his malign, insinuating smile. They all knew Felix, with his cartons of contraband cigarettes off the boats and his little packets of precious powder. *The Pied Piper, Professor, that's me.* And that laugh.

'Coo-ee!' he called now, in soft singsong. He was leaning out over the banisters, his face upturned, with a wide, lipless grin. *There* you are. Don't be shy, Professor, it's only me.'

Professor Kreutznaer slowly descended the stairs; Felix, still grinning, stood and watched him approach, beating out a little rhythm on the banister rail with his fingertips. How silent the house seemed suddenly.

'What – ' the Professor said, and had to clear his throat and start again. 'What are you doing here?'

Felix expelled a gasp of laughter and pressed spread fingers to his breast and assumed an expression of startled innocence.

'You mean here?' he said, pointing to the floor under his feet. 'Why, nothing. Loitering without intent.'

'I mean on the island,' the Professor said.

Felix merely smiled at that and moved to the window and leaned there looking out brightly at the sunlit scene: the sloped lawn and the bridge over the stream and the grassed-over dunes in the distance and the far strip of sea. He sighed. 'What a pleasant place you have here,' he said. 'So peaceful.' He glanced over his shoulder and winked. 'Not like the old days, eh? Although I suppose there is the odd fisher-lad to bring you up your kippers.' He took out his dented gold case and lit a cheroot and placed the spent match carefully on the window-sill. He nodded thoughtfully, smoking. 'Yes,' he said, 'a spot like this would do me very nicely, I must say.'

The Professor stood and listened to the unsteady beating of his heart, thinking how fear always holds at its throbbing centre that little, thin, unquenchable flame of pleasure.

'Why have you come here,' he said.

Felix blew a big stream of smoke and shook his head in rueful amusement.

'I told you,' he said. 'The captain was drunk, our boat ran aground. We are castaways!' And lightly laughed. 'It's true, really. A happy chance. Are you not pleased to see me?'

The Professor continued to fix him with a dull glare.

'How did you know where to find me?' he said.

Felix clicked his tongue in mock annoyance.

'Really,' he said, 'I don't know why you won't believe me!' He chuckled. 'Have I ever lied to you?'

At that the Professor produced a brief bark of what in him passed for laughter. They eyed each other through a swirl of lead-blue smoke. The Professor raised his eyes and Felix touched a hand shyly to his dyed hair.

'I thought you'd never notice,' he said and put on a coy look and batted his eyelashes. 'You know me, Professor, mutability is my middle name.'

'What do you want from me?' the Professor said.

'Want? Why, nothing. What did I ever want? Amusement. Diversion. The company of a great man.'

Felix turned away smilingly and put his face close against the window and peered down at the garden. The wind swooped outside, the sunlight flickered.

'Tell me,' he said, 'how is the art market behaving these days? Volatile, is it?'

There was the sense of something beating in the air, as if after the tolling of a bell.

'I think I'm dying,' the Professor said.

He heard himself say it and took a step backwards in surprise and a sort of gulped dismay, as if from the windy edge of a high place. Felix at the window glanced at him absently over his shoulder.

'What?' he said. 'Dying? Yes, well.' He turned to the window again and smoked in silence for a long moment. 'This truly is a grand spot,' he said. 'I really do like it. In fact, I like it so much I think I'll stay for a while.'

Again that bell-tone beating in the air.

'No,' the Professor said.

Felix was peering hard out at the hillside where a bedraggled figure was sitting under a tree in blossom. '*Montgomery!*' Felix cried out softly, '*why has your man got pointed ears?*' He turned to the Professor smartly, with a bright smile. 'No, did you say?' he said. 'My my, that's not very hospitable. I only mean to stay for a little while. Until I find my feet again – I've had a few reverses lately. Nothing serious, you understand; nothing on the scale of some I could mention.'

They stood and contemplated each other, Felix with his meaning smile and the Professor grimly staring.

'You can't stay here,' the Professor said.

'Oh, come,' Felix cried, 'we shall fleet the time carelessly as we did in the golden world – oops!' He clapped a hand to his mouth and raised his eyebrows high in mock dismay. 'What have I said? – dear me, Professor, you've grown quite pale.' He put his head on one side and contemplated with pursed amusement the old man standing hunched and scowling before him. 'By the way, I went down to Whitewater the other day,' Felix said pleasantly. 'The daughter is in charge there now – quite the chatelaine. You pay a pound and they let you wander around at will. Very trusting, I must say – but then, they always were, weren't they. I wanted to see if the gilt was still on the Golden World. What an amazing work it is – never ceases to surprise me. It's so – ' his voice sank softly ' – so convincing, I always think.' His cheroot had died; he placed the butt beside the spent match on the window-sill. 'I spoke to the lady of the house. She was most kind, most helpful.'

The Professor nodded grimly.

'She told you where I was,' he said. Felix only smirked. The Professor heard himself breathing and felt that silken ripple in his breast. 'You can't harm me,' he said.

Felix reared back with an astonished smile.

'Harm you?' he cried. 'Why would I want to harm you? No: you are going to be my golden goose, after all.'

He winked then and turned briskly and set off down the stairs, skipping swiftly; halfway down the flight he paused and turned back. 'By the way,' he said, 'I hope you appreciate how discreetly I've behaved here, though you wouldn't even condescend to shake my hand.' He wagged his head reprovingly and chuckled and went on down the stairs.

When he was gone, the Professor stood motionless, suspended for a moment, as so often these days, waiting for something that did not come. Idly he tried the bedroom door. It was locked.

CROKE, NOW, try Croke, he is the real thing, the *homo verus* of myth and legend. He stepped out on the sunlit porch and stopped with a sour look and sniffed the day. Sea stink and the thick pungency of drenched grass and a sort of buttery smell that he supposed must be the smell of gorse. He did not much care for the countryside, trees and weather and suchlike. He was a city man, born and bred. A walk by the canal of an October morning, swans gliding on their own reflections and the sun on the gasworks and the air delicately blued with petrol fumes, that was enough of outdoors for him. He descended the porch steps and turned right along the flagged path past the rose bush and the rain barrel and the bluebottle-coloured mound where the coal-ash from the kitchen stove is dumped. Stunted apple trees grow here, standing in lush grass, and there are fruit bushes and a thick clump of nettles jostling greenly to attention, their webbed ears pricked up. Smell of roses, then of lilac, then of something sweetly dead. A cloud abruptly palmed the sun. Water was dripping nearby, or was it a bird, making that *plip, plip* noise? He arrived at the iron gate that led from the corner of the lawn into the yard behind the house. The cobbles were still wet in patches. He watched his hand grasp the bar of the gate and for a moment he was held, staring at that withered claw he could hardly believe was his. Nowadays he avoided looking at himself too closely, not caring to see the dewlapped neck and grizzled chest, the sagging tits, the quaking, varicosed legs. The years had worn his skin to a thin, translucent stuff, clammy and smooth, like waxed paper, a loose hide within which his big old carcass slipped and slid. He would not need a shroud, they could just truss him up in himself like a turkey and fold over the flaps and tie a final knot. He smiled grimly and the gate opened before him with a clang. A wash of sunlight swept the yard and as he stepped forward falteringly into this sudden weak blaze the god unseen anointed him and he felt for a moment an extraordinary happiness.

A hen was picking over bits of straw, sharp eye agleam, looking for something among the slimed cobbles. It paused thoughtfully and dropped behind it a little twirled mound of shit, chalk-white and olive-green. Croke stared in mild disgust: what in the name of God is it they eat? The dog emerged from its bed under the wheelbarrow and advanced lopsidedly a pace or two and halted, gasping. 'Here, old fellow,' Croke said and was startled at the loudness of his voice, how hollow it sounded, how unconvincing. He saw himself there, a comic turn, in his candy-stripes and sopping shoes and ridiculous straw hat. 'Here, boy,' he said gruffly. 'Here, old chap.'

The dog, a black and white spaniel with something awful coming out of its eyes, turned disdainfully and waddled back to its lair.

Croke walked on and came to another, wider iron gate. Beyond it were the fields sloping up to the oak ridge. He took off his hat and looked at it, feeling the air suddenly cool on his forehead.

What is it called, that thing, that gold thing?

Under the gate there was a patch of churned-up mud (are there cows?) with little puddles of sky-reflecting water in it like shards of glass. He stepped across the mud-patch shakily but the ground beyond too was boggy and the wet grass clutched at his feet alarmingly. He kept going, though, clambering up the uneven slope and treading on his own squat shadow lurching along in front of him.

> *Unless to see my shadow in the sun,*
> *And* something *on mine own deformity.*

Not that he was ever let play the king. All he ever got to do was stand around in sackcloth trews and a tunic that smelled of someone else's sweat, trying not to yawn while a fat queer in a paper crown strode up and down, ranting. Pah. In his heart he despised the whole business, dressing up and pretending to be someone else. It was a pity no one did revues any more. He used to like revues, the old-fashioned kind, before everything got smart and smutty. He had been a great straight-man, because of his size, probably: a big, slow, shiny-faced gom with slicked-back hair standing up there in suit and tie with his brow furrowed while the little fellow ran rings around him, what could be funnier? Strange, he had never minded looking foolish like that. The funny men thought they were the ones in control; wrong, of course; that was the secret. Nasty little tykes, the lot of them, jealous, tightfisted, throbbing with grievances – and chasers too, God, yes, anything in a skirt.

He found himself thinking of Felix. He did not trust that joker, with his dyed hair and his dirty smile. Very sallow, too: was he a jewboy? Got his hands on the girl straight away, of course. They always do. That girl, now –

Oh!

He reared back in fright as a bird of some sort flew up suddenly out of the grass with burbled whistlings and shot into the sky. A lark, was it? He stood with his head thrown back, leering from the effort, and watched the tiny creature where it hung above him, pouring out its thick-throated song. After a minute it got tired, or perhaps the song was finished, and it sank to earth in stages, dropping from one steep step of air to another, and disappeared into the grass again. Croke walked on. Long ago, when he was a child, someone had kept a canary; he remembered it, perched in its cage in a sunny window. Who was that, who would have kept a singing-bird? He could see it all clearly, the cage there, and the net curtain pulled back, and the window with the little panes and the yellow light streaming in. He sighed. Melancholy, thick and sweet as treacle, welled up in his heart.

He went on, up the slope. This last part was steep and there was mud and dead leaves to make the going treacherous. He smelled wet smoke. Above him the trees were making a troubled, rushing sound. He paused to rest for a moment, leaning forward with his hands on his knees and breathing with his mouth open. His lungs pained him. What was he doing, climbing up here, what craziness had got hold of him? He could die like this, keel over like a tree and die, be here for days and no one would find him. He turned his darkening gaze to the fields falling away behind him, to the house down there, to the beach and the distant sea. White clouds sailed above his head. He seemed for a moment to be airborne, and he felt light-headed. Behind him someone started to sing.

Oh
He came off twice
In a bowl of rice
And called it tapioca

It was one of the boys. He was squatting in the middle of a clearing beside the remains of a fire, poking at the smouldering embers with a stick. He looked up at Croke without surprise. His no-colour hair was wet and plastered to his skull. His eyes were an eerie, washed-out shade of blue.

'Which one are you?' Croke said, still wheezing from the climb. 'Are you Hatch?' It occurred to him he should carry a cane, it would lend him authority, pointing with it and so on. Hatch went on looking at him with detachment; he might have been looking in through the bars of a cage. Croke, disconcerted by the child's unwavering regard, tried another tack and pointed to the fire. 'Go out on you?' he said.

Hatch shrugged. 'Pound pissed on it.'

'I did not,' Pound said, stepping out of the trees. Pound was the fat one: glasses, cowlick, shoes like boats. 'He pissed on it himself.'

Unnerved, Croke grinned weakly. He opened his mouth but could think of nothing to say, and stood irresolute, feeling exposed and somehow mocked. He was secretly a little afraid of these two. Hatch in particular alarmed him, with his pixie's face and violet eyes and pale little clawlike hands.

Pound came and stood by the fire and kicked at the ashes with the toe of his shoe. He cast a sidelong glance in Croke's direction. 'He must be gone,' he said to Hatch. 'I can't see him.'

'Gone to ground,' Hatch said and laughed.

A gust of wind blew across the clearing, lifting dry husks and the lacy skeletons of last year's leaves. In the silence Croke had a dreamy sense of slow, weightless toppling.

'Someone up here, was there?' he said.

Hatch stuck his stick into the ashes.

'That fellow,' he said.

'Which fellow?'

'Tarzan the apeman.'

This time Pound laughed, a fat bark. Croke looked from

one of them to the other, the fey one squatting on the ground and fatty with his swollen cheeks and infant's pasty brow. He tried again to think of something to say that would confound them, something harsh and funny, but in vain, and turned instead with an angry gesture and walked away, willing himself to saunter, the back of his neck on fire. Children and animals, children and animals: he should have known better.

He came to the edge of the trees and had to scramble down the first few yards of the slope at a crouch. He felt odd: *wall-falling*, his father used to say: *I'm wall-falling*. The ground seemed more uneven than it had when he was coming up, and the grass hid holes in which he was afraid he would twist an ankle (there must be cows, then – or horses, perhaps there are horses, after all). The house was clear to see below him but somehow he kept listing away from it, as if there were a hidden tilt to things, and when he got down to level ground the roof and even the little turret sank from view off to the left behind a steep, grassy bank riddled with rabbit burrows and he found himself toiling along a broad, sandy path with high dunes on either side.

The sea was before him, he could hear it, the hiss and rush of it and the gritty crash of the waves collapsing on the shingle. The sun shone upon him thickly. He stopped and stood there dully in the sun, his head bowed. What had happened to him? He could not understand it. A minute ago he had been up there on the ridge and now he was down here, sunk in this hot hollow. He looked about. The boys were behind him, standing on a dune, watching him. He could not see them very well; were they laughing? He felt dizzy again and something was buzzing in his head.

He went on. Sweat dimmed his sight. The band of his hat was greasy and hot and there was sand in his waterlogged shoes, hard ridges of it under his arches and wedged against his toes, making his corns pain him. The way grew steeper, the smooth slope rising before him like a wall; up there on the crest of the rise the wind was lifting fine swirls of sand and the sky beyond was a surprised, dense blue. A thick stench assailed him. A dead sheep lay crumpled in the sand, the head twisted sideways and the dainty black hoofs splayed. It must have lost its footing and tumbled down the dunes and broken its neck. Something had eaten out the hindquarters; the empty fleece, still intact, flapped in the wind, so that the dead thing seemed to be shuddering in pain and struggling to yank itself to its feet. He passed it by, trying not to breathe the smell, and caught the shine of a glazed muzzle and the black hole of an eye-socket. He coughed, spat, groaned. He hardly knew where he was any more, there was only this slope and the dazzling glitter of sunlight and the burning sand squirming under his feet. He wanted to get to the sea; he would be all right if only he could get to the sea. He heard the music the island makes, the deep song rising out of the earth, and thought he must be imagining it. He stumbled on, his heart wobbling in its cage and the salt air rasping in his lungs. After a dozen paces he halted again and turned. The boys were still behind him, keeping their distance. They stopped when he stopped and stood impassive, watching him. He shouted and shook his fist at them. Why would they not help him? Surely they could see he was in need of help. He was frightened. He thought he was going to cry. There was sand in his mouth now. What is that word? Anabasis. No. Descant. No, no, that thing, that gold thing, what is it! As if in a dream he watched his leaden feet slog through the sand, one sinking as the other rose, then that one sinking in its turn. How had he come to this, what had gone wrong, and so quickly? He saw the canary again, the light in the window of the cramped front room and the old man in the big high bed. Yes, yes, that was it, she had bought the bird for him at the end, to keep him company – *To pipe me out!* the old man would shout, laughing and coughing, amused and furious. He heard again the harsh laugh and the voice weary with contempt: *My son, the comedian.* Down the narrow stairs, the years falling away and suddenly he was a child again, the hall with the lino gleaming and that worn quarter-circle inside the door where the flap dragged, and out into the square, hand in her hand, the drinking trough and the cherry trees in blossom in their wire cages, and then the big, wide, echoing corridor ablaze with grainy light and the tall nun's rapid step on the bumpy tiles – never see their feet – and her thin, high voice saying something about prayers and being good.

Mother! Hold me!

He gained the crest of the slope and stood for a moment swaying, looking out in slack-jawed amazement over the beach and the blue-green vasts of water, smelling the stink of sand and wrack. The wind blew his hat off and bowled it down the slope behind him. He set off across the beach at a stumbling run, yearning towards the ocean, his long arms swinging and his knees going out sideways. At the margin of the waves he halted. Above him the sun was a wafer of white gold shaking and slipping at the centre of the huge blue. He stretched out his arms. He was laughing or crying, he did not know which.

That gold

That thing that gold

He shut his eyes and it was as if a door had slammed shut inside his head.

The boys appeared over the brow of the dunes in time to see him rise up slowly on one leg, like a big old dying bird, his arms clutching helplessly at hoops of air. He wavered a moment, then slowly toppled over and collapsed full-length upon the sand.

*

I dreamed last night that – No, no, I can't. Some dreams are too terrible to be told.

Pain in my breast suddenly. Ah! it pains. Perhaps I am the one who is dying of his heart. That would be a laugh, for me to die and leave them there, trapped, the tide halted, the boat stuck fast forever. End it all, space and time, one huge flash and then darkness and a blessed silence as the babble stops. Serve them right. Serve us all right. We are the dangerous ones, no other species like us, all of creation cowering before us, the death-dealers. I see a forked beast squatting on the midden of the world, red-eyed, regardant, gnawing on a shinbone: poor, dumb destroyer. Better without us, better the nothing than this, this shambles we have raised. Yes, have done with it all: one universal neck and I the hangman. In the end. Not yet. In the end.

Vaublin's double. Curious episode. (See how quicky I recover my poise?) All the experts, Professor Kreutznaer included, agree that it was all a delusion, a phantasm spawned by fever and exhaustion in that last, desperate summer of the painter's brief life. I am not so sure. The deeper I look into the matter the stranger it becomes. He was living on the Île de la Cité, last resting place in his fitful wanderings at the end, in big rooms high above the Seine. He was thirty-seven; his lungs were ruined. The paintings from that period, hurried dreamscapes bathed in an eerie, lunar radiance, have a shocked look to them, the motionless, inscrutable figures scattered about the canvas like the survivors of a vast calamity of air and light. What he is seeking here is something intangible, some pure, distilled essence that perhaps is not human at all. He speaks in one of his last letters of coming to the realisation that the centre of a painting, that packed point of equilibrium out of which every element of the composition flows and where at the same time everything is ingathered, is never where it seems it should be, is never central, or obviously significant, but could be a patch of sky, the fold of a gown, a dog scratching its ear, anything. The trick is to locate that essential point and work outwards from it. By now he had given himself up entirely to theatricality. The actors from the Comédie-Française sat for him in costume, all the leading figures, Paul Poisson, La Thorillière, the tragedienne Charlotte Desmares, Biancolelli whose Pierrot was the talk of the season. They were perfect for his purposes, all pose and surface brilliance. They would strike an attitude and hold it for an hour without stirring, in a trance of self-regard. He was drawing too on his memories of the *fêtes* and staged *spectacles* years before in the great gardens of the city. Those green and umber twilights of which he was so fond are surely recollections of the Duchesse de Maine's *grands nuits* at Sceaux, the soft shadows among the trees, the music on the water, the masked figures strolling down the long lawns as the last light of evening turned to blackening dusk and the little bats came out and flittered in the darkening air. The melancholy that was always his mark is mingled in these final scenes with a kind of shocked hilarity. The luminance in which they are bathed seems always on the point of being extinguished, as if it had its source in the little palpitant flame of the painter's own enfeebled, failing life.

When the notion came to him of a shadowy counterpart stalking him about the city he thought the thing must be a joke, an elaborate hoax got up perhaps by someone with a grudge against him – he had always been of a suspicious nature. In the street an acquaintance would stop and stare in surprise, saying he had seen him not five minutes ago walking in the opposite direction and wearing a black cloak. He was not amused. Then he began to notice the pictures. There were *fêtes galantes* and *amusements champêtres*, and even theatre scenes, his speciality, the figures in which seemed to look at him with suppressed merriment, knowingly. They were executed in a style uncannily like his own, but in haste, with technical lapses and scant regard for quality of surface. This slapdash manner seemed a gibe aimed directly at him and his pretensions, mocking his lapses in concentration, the short-cuts and the technical flaws that he had thought no one would notice. When he tried to get a close look at this or that piece somehow he was always foiled. He would glimpse a *Récréation galante* being carried between two aproned porters out of a dealer's shop, or a gold and green *Île enchantée*, which for a dizzy second seemed surely his own work, hanging over the fireplace of a fashionable salon just as he was being ushered from the room. Who was this prankster who could dash off imitation Vaublins with such assurance, who knew his secret flaws, who could imitate not only his strengths but his weaknesses too, his evasions, his failures of taste and technique? He tells in a letter to his friend and obituarist, the collector Antoine de La Roque, of having a feeling constantly of being hindered; some days, he says, he has almost to fight his way to the easel, as if indeed there were an invisible double there before him, crowding him aside, and when he steps to the canvas another, heavier arm seems to lift alongside his. *I seem to hear mocking laughter*, he wrote, *and someone is always standing in the corner behind me, yet when I turn there is no one there.*

He had begun work on *Le monde d'or*, hastening while his strength lasted. The summer was hot. I see him aloft in his attic rooms, all doors and windows open to the air and the noises of the city, the breezes and sudden smells and shimmering water-lights. His hands shake, everything shakes, flapping and straining as if the house were a great, lumbering barquentine in full sail. He tells La Roque, *I have embarked for the golden world.* He wants to confess to something but cannot, something about a crime committed long ago; something about a woman.

STEALTHILY THE DAY BURGEONS, climbing towards noon. The wind has died. On the ridge the oaks are motionless, dark with heat, and the air above the fields undulates like a blown banner. The hens have departed from the yard, fleeing the sun, the old dog is asleep again under the wheelbarrow. The beech tree at the corner of the garden stands unmoving in the purple puddle of its own shadow. Something squeaks and then is still. Hushed, secret world! The back door is open, an up-ended box of soft black darkness; glide through here, light as a breeze, touch this and that, these dim things, with a blindman's feathery touch. The narrow passageway beside the stairs smells of lime, the hall is loud with light. Voices. Upstairs a door opens and rapid footsteps sound. Listen! they are living their little lives.

In the kitchen Sophie stood with one haunch perched on the edge of the table taking photographs of Alice, who sat before her on a chair with her little wan face meekly lifted up to the lens, intent and motionless, like a flower holding itself up to the light. Felix came in from the hall, with Licht, rabbit-eyed and shaky, trotting worriedly at his heels. Sophie held up a hand to them and they stopped in the doorway, watching.

'Don't move,' she said to Alice softly and with soft

intentness turned the camera this way and that, softly crushing the shutter-button.

Felix came up behind her and she lowered the camera but did not turn to him. Alice smiled up at her anxiously.

'I thought you only take pictures of things that are dead,' Felix murmured.

Sophie did not reply. She could feel the faint heat of his presence behind her; she put down the camera and rose abruptly and crossed to the window and stood with her hands braced on the cool, fat rim of the sink. She looked down at her face in the bit of broken mirror propped on the window-sill and hardly recognised her own reflection, all glimmering throat and hooded, unfamiliar eyes, like a burnished metal mask. When she turned back Felix was looking at her knowingly, with sly amusement, his head on one side and his lips pursed, and she felt herself flinch, as if she had brushed against some thrillingly loathsome, lewd and cloying thing.

A shadow fell in the doorway and Croke came in blunderingly, carrying his straw hat and laughing in distress.

'Jesus!' he said.

He stood swaying and looked about him in a kind of wonderment, smiling dazedly, his mouth open. The brim of his hat was crushed on one side and there were patches of wet sand on his blazer and his white trousers were stained and wet again at the cuffs. Hatch and Pound appeared behind him, one on either side, with the cerulean air of noon between them, bored and dully frowning. 'What?' Croke said sharply, as if someone had spoken. He shook his head and lumbered forward and sat down heavily at the table beside Alice. He seemed to have aged and yet at the same time looked impossibly young, with his face lifted listeningly and his hands hanging between his knees, a big, ancient, bewildered babe. His sunken jaw was stubbled and there were flecks of spit at the corners of his mouth; his hair stood up in a cowlick over one ear, when he tried to smooth it flat it sprang up again.

'Fell down,' he said, gesturing. 'Like that: bang, down on my arse.'

He shook his head, bemused and laughing; he picked up a fork from the table and fiddled with it distractedly and put it down again. The boys sidled in and he heaved himself round on his chair and pointed a quivering finger at them accusingly. 'And as for these two – !' He laughed again and coughed and thumped himself in the chest with his fist, then turned back to the table and frowned, licking salt-cracked lips. The world was luminous around him. Everything shone out of itself, shaking in its own radiance. There was movement everywhere; even the most solid objects seemed to seethe, the table under his hands, the chair on which he sat, the very walls themselves. And he too trembled, as if his whole frame had been struck like a tuning fork against the hard, bright surface of things. The others looked at him, stilled for a moment, staring. He imagined himself as they would see him, a shining man, floating in the midst of light. He turned his head quickly and peered up, thinking he had heard a voice behind him call out his name. No one was there.

'Jesus!' he said again softly, with a soft, whistling sigh.

Licht went to the stove and pushed the pots and pans this way and that. A spill of sunlight from the window wavered in the murky recess above the stove, a roiling, goldened beam. He closed his eyes for a second and saw himself free, flying up without a sound into the blue, the boundless air. He crossed to the meat-safe on the wall and took out a white dish on which was draped a scrawny, plucked chicken with rubber-red wattles and scaly, yellow claws.

'Look at that,' he said in disgust. 'Tighe didn't clean it again.'

He put the bird on the table and took off his coat.

'When my father died,' Croke said to no one in particular, 'he was younger than I am now.'

He looked about him with an empty smile, his clouded stare sliding loosely over everything. Alice stared with faint revulsion into the whorl of his huge, hairy ear. She thought of a picture she had seen when she was little of an old beggarman standing at a street corner and a tall angel with long golden hair and broad gold wings bending over him solicitously. She wondered idly if Croke was dying. She did not care. She picked up Sophie's camera and was surprised by its weight. She liked the feel of it, its hard heaviness and leathery, stippled skin, the silky coolness of its steel underparts. She pictured the film rolled up tight inside, with her face printed on it over and over, dozens of miniature versions of her, with ash-white hair and black skin, strangely staring out of empty eye-sockets, and she shivered and felt something approach in the shadowed, purplish air and touch her.

'So he breaks into the laundry,' Hatch was saying furtively, 'and fucks them all and then runs off, and the headline in the paper next day says: *Nut Screws Washers and Bolts.*' He laughed wheezily, his colourless lips drawn back and his sharp little teeth on show. He cocked an eye at Licht and said: "At'sa some joke, eh, boss?'

Licht pretended not to hear; Hatch turned to Alice.

'I suppose you don't get it,' he said.

Pound, slumped at the table with his chin on his fat hands, snorted. Light flashed on his glasses and made it seem as if he had no eyes. Hatch kicked him casually under the table and said:

'How's your diet?' He winked at Alice. 'His ma has him on a diet, you know.'

'Shut up,' Pound said listlessly. 'You eat your snot.'

Felix laughed and clipped the fat boy playfully on the ear and said:

'Bunter, you are a beast.'

'Ow!'

Hatch's violet eyes glittered and he kicked Pound again on the shin, harder this time.

'Damn you,' Licht said to the chicken through clenched teeth and hacked off its head.

Felix went and stood beside Sophie at the sink and peered at her closely, putting on a look of grave concern.

'You seem down in the doldrums, *contessa*. What is it – crossed in love?'

And he chuckled.

She studied his long, laughing face and merrily malicious eye. When he laughed he slitted his eyes and the pointed, pink, wet tip of his tongue came flicking out.

'Will the *principessa* be joining us?' she asked.

He shrugged.

'*Quella povera ragazza!*' he said, and shook his head and heaved a heavy sigh. 'She sleeps.'

'Yes,' Sophie said. 'I know.'

It took him a moment. He laughed, and wagged a finger at her playfully.

'*Ah, crudèle!*' he trilled.

He went and stood in the back doorway and contemplated happily the sunlit yard, a hand inserted in the side pocket of his tight jacket and his narrow back twisted. A robin alighted at his feet.

'Oh!' Alice stood up quickly from the table. 'I was supposed to bring her a drink of water.'

She went hurriedly to the sink and rinsed a smeared glass and filled it under the tap. Felix produced a key from the pocket of his jacket and held it negligently aloft.

'You will need this,' he said. Sophie stared in scorn and he shrugged. 'A man must protect what is his,' he said, smirking.

Alice took the key and put it in the pocket of her dress and went out, holding the glass carefully in both hands and watching the water sway under its shining, tin-bright, tense meniscus, her grave little face inclined.

Without warning Hatch and Pound leaped up from the table, like a pair of leaping fish, and Hatch in an amazing rage went at the fat boy with fists flailing. Pound stood suspended like a punchbag, with a mild expression, almost diffident, frowning in a kind of puzzlement as the punches sank in. Hatch leaned against him with his head down, hitting and hitting, as if he were trying to fight his way into Pound's fat chest. The others looked on, mesmerised, until Croke struggled up and grasped Hatch by his skinny shoulders and lifted him into the air, where the boy, incoherently in tears, squirmed and swore, thrashing his arms and legs like a capsized beetle. Croke set him on his feet with a thump and the boy sat down and gathered himself into a huddle, biting his knuckles and furiously sobbing.

'I only said,' Pound said dully, 'I only said . . .'

Alice came back and sat down and folded her hands in her lap. Felix lifted an eyebrow at her.

'How is the patient?' he asked.

Alice did not look at him.

'She says she only wants to rest,' she said and pursed her lips.

Felix came and stood above her, a hand outstretched.

'The key?'

Alice looked sideways at his hand and considered.

'She has it,' she said and smiled a little smile of triumph and for a second she looked like a tiny wizened old woman.

Sophie laughed.

Felix hesitated, then shrugged and walked to the middle of the floor and stood with his feet together and his elbows pressed to his sides, smiling about him and bobbing gently on his toes, like a swimmer effortlessly treading water, borne up in his element. '*Ah, Mélisande, Mélisande!*' he sang softly in thin falsetto, turning heavenwards his stricken eyes. Then he cut a sudden caper, tip and toe, rolling his eyes and waggling his hands limply from the wrists.

The latch of the back door rattled and knuckles tentatively rapped.

Felix, crooning wordlessly and holding himself at breast and back in a tango-dancer's embrace, shimmied to the door and flung it wide. Light from the yard entered and along with it the smell of sun-warmed straw and hen droppings. Soft flurry of wings. A little breeze. The blue day shimmers.

A red-haired, buck-toothed boy in wellingtons stood on the step.

'Aha!' cried Felix, 'there you are! How fares *le bateau ivre*? Gone down, I trust, women and children in the boats, flag still flying and the captain saluting from the poop, all that?'

The boy squinted at him warily and said:

'The skipper says to say the tide will be up before long and youse are to be ready.'

Felix turned back to the room and opened wide his arms.

'Do you hear, gentles?' he said. 'The waters are rising.'

Sophie was winding the film in her camera.

'Are you not coming with us?' she asked.

But Felix only smiled.

Easing open the wooden gate Sergeant Toner paused a moment before tackling the steep path up to the house. He lifted his cap and scratched his head with middle and little finger and reset his cap at a sharper angle. The light had thickened to a hot haze over the fields. Housemartins skimmed here and there in the radiant air above him, shooting in swift loops in and out of their nests under the eaves. The Sergeant, large, freckled, mild man, moves in his policeman's deliberate way, thoughtfully, with a sober and abstracted air. He climbed the steps to the porch and knocked loudly on the door and waited, and knocked again, but no one answered, and cupping his hands around his eyes he bent and peered through the ruby panels of the door but could see nothing except the claret-coloured shapes of hall table and umbrella stand and the tensed and somehow significantly unpeopled stairs. He descended the steps and stood with hands on hips and head thrown back and peered up frowningly at the upstairs windows. Behind sky-reflecting glass nothing moved. He turned and put his hands behind his back and with fist clasped in palm walked slowly around by the side of the house. In the yard a high-stepping hen stopped and looked at him sharply and the dog under the wheelbarrow growled but did not rise, thumping its tail half-heartedly in the dust. The back door was open; the kitchen was deserted. The Sergeant leaned in and rapped on the door with his knuckles and called out: 'Shop!' but no answer came except a tiny, ringing echo, like a stifled titter, of his own big voice. He stepped inside and stood a moment listening and then walked forward on creaking soles and pulled out a chair and sat down, removing his cap and setting it on the table beside his elbow, where the shiny dark-blue peak reflected in elongated form a squat milk-jug. He sighed. On the stove a big pot was making muffled eructations and there was the smell of chicken soup. A shimmering blade of sunlight stood broken on the rim of the sink.

Somewhere in the house someone loudly sneezed.

A very large bumble-bee flew in through the back door and did a staggering circle of the room and settled on the window-sill. Sergeant Toner studied it with interest as it throbbed there in its football jersey. He thought how it would feel to be a bee in summertime, drunk on the smell of clover and of gorse, and for a moment his mind reeled in contemplation of the prospect of other worlds.

Licht came hurrying in from the hall and skidded to a stop and stared at the Sergeant and sneezed.

'God bless you!' Sergeant Toner said largely, with broad good humour.

Blinking rapidly and gasping Licht fumbled in his trouser pocket and brought out a greyed handkerchief and stood with his mouth open weakly and his red-rimmed nose tilted back.

'Ah . . . ah . . . ahh,' he said expectantly on a rising scale, but this time nothing happened and amid a general sense of anti-climax he put away his handkerchief. 'Getting a cold,' he said thickly. He looked as if he had been weeping. He lifted the lid of the simmering pot on the stove and peered squintingly through the steam.

The bee with an angry buzzing rose up from the window-sill and flew straight out the door and was gone.

'I was just passing by,' the Sergeant said, quite at his ease.

'Oh,' Licht said flatly and nodded, avoiding the other's eye. He sniffed. 'Will you take something?'

The Sergeant considered.

'Glass of water?' he said, without conviction.

Licht centred the big black kettle on the hob; a thread of steam was already rising from the spout. Sergeant Toner watched him as he had watched the bumble-bee, with interest, calmly. Licht's hands were unsteady. He let fall a spoon and tried to catch it and knocked over the tea caddy and spilled the tea. The spoon bounced ringingly on the tiles. The kettle came to the boil.

'I think we're in for a fine spell,' the Sergeant said.

Licht nodded distractedly. He paused with the grumbling kettle in his hand and frowned at the wall in front of him.

'I spend my life making tea,' he said darkly to himself.

Sergeant Toner nodded seriously but made no comment. Licht picked up the spoon from the floor and wiped it on his trousers and spooned the tea into the pot and poured the seething water over the leaves and banged the lid back on the pot, then carried pot and a cracked white mug to the table and set them down unceremoniously beside the Sergeant's hat. Milk, sugar, the same spoon. The Sergeant surveyed the table hopefully.

'A heel of bread would be the thing,' he said, 'if you had it.'

Licht, unseen by the Sergeant, cast his eyes to the ceiling and went to the sideboard and came back with a biscuit tin and opened it and put it on the table with a tinny thump. The fawn smell of biscuit-dust rose up warmly on the air. Sergeant Toner smiled and nodded thanks. Judiciously he poured the tea, raising and lowering the pot with a practised hand, watching with satisfaction the rich, dark flow and enjoying the joggling sound the liquid made filling up the mug. Licht fetched cutlery from a drawer and began to set out places at the table while the Sergeant looked on with placid gaze.

'Visitors?' he said. Licht did not answer. From the dresser he brought soup bowls and dealt them out. The Sergeant idly counted the places, his lips silently moving. 'Do you remember,' he said, 'the time we had the devil-worshippers?' He glanced up enquiringly. His white eyelashes were almost invisible. 'Do you remember that?'

Licht looked at him blankly in bafflement.

'What?' he said. 'No.'

'Your mother, God rest her, was still with us then.'

The Sergeant lifted the brimming mug with care and extended puckered lips to the hot brim and took a cautious slurp. 'Ah,' he said appreciatively, and took another, deeper draught and then put down the mug and turned his attention to the biscuit tin, rising an inch off the chair and peering into the mouth of the tin with lifted brows. 'A bad lot, they were,' he said. 'They used to cut up cats.'

Licht went to the sink, where the line of sunlight, thinned to a rapier now, smote him across the wrists. The sink was still piled with unwashed crockery; he stood and looked helplessly at the grease-caked plates and smeared cutlery.

'Locals, were they?' he said absently.

The Sergeant was biting gingerly on a ginger nut. 'Hmm?'

Licht sighed. 'Were they locals, these people?'

'No, no,' the Sergeant said. 'They used to come over on the boat from the mainland when their feast days or whatever they were were coming up. The solstices, or whatever they're called. They'd start off by making a big circle of stones down on the strand, that's how I'd know they were here. Oh, a bad crowd.'

Licht plunged his hands into the greasy water.

'Did you catch them?' he asked.

Sergeant Toner smiled to himself, drinking his tea.

'We did,' he said. 'We always get our man, out here.'

The Professor came in. Seeing the Sergeant he stopped and stood and all went silent. The Sergeant half rose from his chair in respectful greeting and subsided again.

'I was just telling Mr Licht here about the devil-worshippers,' he said equably.

The Professor stared.

'Devil-worshippers,' he said.

'They killed cats,' Licht said from the sink, and snickered.

'Oh, more than cats,' said the Sergeant, unruffled. 'More than cats.' He lifted the teapot invitingly. 'Will you join me in a cup of this tea, Professor?'

Licht came forward bustlingly and put the lid back on the biscuit tin, ignoring the Sergeant's frown of weak dismay.

'We're a bit busy,' Licht said pointedly. 'I'm making the lunch.'

Sergeant Toner nodded understandingly but made no move to rise.

'For your visitors,' he said. 'That's grand.'

For a moment all three were silent. Licht and the Professor

looked off in opposite directions while the Sergeant thoughtfully sipped his tea.

'I seen the ferry out on the Black Bank, all right,' he said. 'Ran aground, did it?' He paused. 'Is that the way they came?' Then, softly: 'Your visitors?'

Licht lifted a streaming plate from the sink and rubbed it vigorously with a dirty cloth.

'The skipper was drunk, apparently,' he said. 'That ferry service is a joke. Someday somebody is going to be drowned.' It sounded a curiously false note; too many words. He rubbed the plate more vigorously still.

The Sergeant nodded, pondering.

'I was talking to him, to the skipper,' he said. 'The eyes were a bit bright, right enough.' He nodded again and then sat still, thinking, the mug lifted halfway to his mouth. 'And where would they be now, tell me,' he said, 'these castaways?'

Licht looked at the Professor and the Professor looked at the floor.

'Oh,' Licht said with a careless gesture, 'they're around the house, getting ready.'

The Sergeant frowned. 'Ready?'

'To leave,' Licht said. 'They're waiting for the tide to come up.'

He could feel his voice getting thick and his eyes prickling. He wished now they had never come, disturbing everything. Blast them all. He thought of Flora.

'Just over for the day, then, were they?' the Sergeant said.

Licht turned away and muttered something under his breath.

'Beg pardon?' Sergeant Toner said pleasantly, cupping a finger behind his ear.

'I said,' Licht said, 'maybe they came to say a black mass.'

A brief chill settled. Sergeant Toner was not a man to be

mocked. Licht turned to the sink again, head down and shoulders hunched.

The Professor cleared his throat and frowned. The Sergeant with a musing air inspected a far corner of the ceiling.

'Was there a chap with them,' he said, 'thin chap, reddish sort of hair, foreign, maybe?'

Licht turned from the sink.

'Red hair?' he said. 'No, but – '

'No,' the Professor said heavily, and Licht glanced at him quickly, 'there was no one like that.'

Sergeant Toner nodded, still eyeing the ceiling. From outside came the faint buzz of a tractor at work far off in the fields. Licht dried his hands, not looking at anyone now. The Sergeant made a tube of his fist and confided to it a soft, biscuity belch, then poured himself another cup of tea. The sun had left the window but the room was still drugged with its heat.

'Grand day,' the Sergeant said. 'A real start to the summer.'

The Professor looked on as the Sergeant put two spoonfuls of sugar into his tea, hesitated, added a third, and picked up the mug in both large hands and leaned back comfortably on his quietly complaining chair. 'Did you ever wonder, Professor,' he said, 'why people do the things they do?' The Professor raised his eyebrows and said nothing. 'I see a lot of it,' the Sergeant went on, 'in my line of work.'

The Professor regarded him with a level stare.

'A lot of what?' he said.

'Hmm?' The Sergeant looked up at him smilingly with his head at an enquiring tilt. 'Oh, anything and everything.' He drank the last draught of tea and set down the mug firmly on the table and looked at it, smiling to himself. 'People think we're out of touch out here,' he said. 'That we don't know what's going on in the big world. But I'll tell you now, the fact is we're no fools at all.' He looked up laughing in silence. 'Isn't that so, Mr Licht?'

Licht, at the stove peering into the soup-pot, pretended not to hear.

The Professor turned aside slowly, like a stone statue turning slowly on a pivot. The Sergeant made a show of rousing himself. He slapped himself on the knees and took up his cap and stood up from the table.

'I'll be on my way now,' he said, firmly, as if someone were seeking to detain him. He walked heavily to the back door and paused to set his cap carefully on his large head. Before him the afternoon stood trembling in the yard. 'If you do see that chap,' he said, 'the one I mentioned, tell him I'm on the look-out for him.' He glanced back over his shoulder. 'You know the one I mean?'

The Professor was looking away at nothing. Licht turned from the stove and nodded and did not speak.

'Well,' the Sergeant said, hitching up his belt, 'good day to you both.'

He tipped a finger to the peak of his cap and made his way almost daintily down the back step. They listened to the noise of his boots crossing the yard. The dog growled.

Licht halted on the landing and sneezed hugely, bending forward at the waist and spraying his shoes with spit. 'Bugger!' he cried, fumbling for his handkerchief. He waited, peering slackly before him, hankie at the ready, and then sneezed again and shuddered. Perhaps it was Flora's cold he had caught. The thought brought him a crumb of melancholy comfort. Heavy footsteps sounded below him and presently the Professor appeared, rising up in the stairwell dark-browed and brooding, like an effigy, being borne aloft on unseen shoulders. When he saw Licht he stopped with his foot on the top step and they stood confronting each other with a sort of weary animosity. Suddenly Licht understood that something had happened, that something had shifted, that things would never be again as they had been before. He experienced a pang of regret. He had wanted change and escape but this felt more like an end than a beginning.

'Well,' he said, 'what was all that about?'

He could even hear the new note in his voice, that touch of imperiousness and impatience. The Professor turned aside and looked hard out of the window at the dunes and the far sea.

'I think I may have to leave,' he said, in a distant voice, as if in his mind he were already on his way.

'Yes?' Licht said, surprised at himself, at how cold his own voice sounded. The Professor opened his mouth to speak, fumbling the words as if they were coin, but in the end said nothing and shrugged and moved past Licht and went on up the stairs. Licht looked after him as he ascended, like a bundled, flying figure on a painted ceiling, and watched until he was gone from sight, and then listened until his footsteps were no longer to be heard, and even then he lingered, gazing upwards almost wonderingly, imagining the old man rising steadily through higher and still higher reaches of luminous, washed-blue air, and dwindling to a point, and vanishing.

Listening at the door of what already he thought of as Flora's room Licht could hear no sound. As the grave. The shadows on the landing seemed to gather about him like other, ghostlier listeners. He tried the doorknob; the tumblers played a sinister phrase on their tiny clavier: locked. He listened again and then tapped a knuckle gently on the wood. He wanted to say her name but did not dare. He knocked again and leaped in fright when at once a muffled voice spoke directly behind the door.

'Who's there?'

He looked about him wildly, thrilled with panic. It was as if he had put his hand into a trap and had been invisibly seized and held.

'It's me,' he said squeakily. 'Licht.' She said nothing. He stood listening to his heart beating itself against the bars of its cage. He felt foolish and at a loss, and inexplicably expectant. 'Are you all right?'

There came a sigh and then a faint, silky slithering; when she spoke, her voice was at the level of his knees; she must be sitting on the floor, or kneeling there, perhaps, with her forehead against the door.

'What do you want?' she said.

He squatted on his heels and lost his balance and had to steady himself. Clearly, yet with a curious, dreamy sense of inconsequence, and not for the first time, he saw his life for what it was. In the end nothing makes sense.

'There was a guard here,' he said.

Briefly he entertained an image of Sergeant Toner marching off down the hill, thumbs hitched in his belt and his big feet splayed, a wind-up, mechanical man with cheery painted cheeks and fixed grin and a huge key slowly rotating between his shoulder-blades.

'A guard?' Flora said dully through the door.

'Yes. A policeman. He was looking for . . . he was looking for someone.'

She said nothing for a long time. He waited and presently she asked him what time it was. He heard her sigh and rise and walk away from the door, her bare feet making a fat, slow little slapping patter on the floorboards, and then the mattress-springs jangled and after that there was stillness again. Shakily he stood up, stiff-kneed and grimacing. He listened for another moment, then sighed and went on down the stairs.

*

Everywhere was silence. She lay still and listened but could hear nothing except the far soft gasping of the sea and the gulls crying and that strange booming in the distance. The day glared with a brassy radiance. She felt shaky; her mind was vague yet she had an impression of openness and clarity, as of light falling into a vast, empty room. She remembered Licht coming to the door; was there another after him or had she dreamed it, the timid little knock, the whisperings, the soft noise of breathing as whoever it was stood out there, listening? Alice, was it, or someone else again? Now there was only this silence and a sort of hollowness everywhere. She had made a journey through a dark place: water, sea-surge and sway, a dull, repeated rhythm, then a reddening, and then the sudden astonishment of light. Sticky-eyed, with a coppery taste in her mouth and her skin smeared, she struggled from the bed and stood trembling, looking about her at nothing she could recognise, the hot key clutched in her damp hand. Something was starting up, she could sense it. Someone was waiting for her, content to wait, biding his time. She unlocked the door and stepped on to the landing, a blanket clutched about her, and paused a moment to listen again. She heard a step below her on the stairs and drew back, waiting, half in fear and half in fascinated, breathless expectation.

Nothing could have prepared me for it. After all these weeks, out of nowhere, as if, as if, I don't know. This morning, not half an hour ago, I, that is Flora and I, that is Flora, when I . . . Easy. Go easy. What happened, after all, except that she began to talk? Yet it has changed everything, has transfigured everything, I don't know how. Let me try to paint the scene, paint it as it was and not as it seemed, in washes of luminous grey on grey. The kitchen, midsummer morning, eight o'clock. Grey is not the word, but a densened whiteness, rather, the sky all over cloud and the light not falling but seeming to seep out of things and no shadows anywhere. Think of the particular thick dulled shine on the cheek of a tin teapot. Breakfast time. Frail smoke of morning in the air and a sort of muffled hum that is not sound but is not silence either. An ordinary day. My mind does not work very well at that early hour; that is to say, it works, all right, but on its own terms, as if it were independent of me, as if in the night it had broken free of its moorings and I had not yet hauled it back to shore. So I am sitting there at the old pine table, in that light, with the breakfast things set out and a mug of strong tea in one hand and a book in the other and my mind rummaging idly through its own thoughts. Licht and the Professor are still abed – they are late risers – and I am, I suppose, enjoying this hour of solitude, if enjoyment is the word for such a neutral state of simple drift. Enter Flora. She was barefoot, with her shoulders hunched as usual and her hands buried deep in the pockets of Licht's old raincoat. She sat down at the table and in dumb show I offered her the teapot and she nodded and I poured her out a mug of tea. The usual. We often meet like this at breakfast time; we do not speak at all. How eloquent at these times the sounds that humble things make, the blocky slosh of tea being poured, the clack and dulled bang of crockery, the sudden silver note of a spoon striking the rim of a saucer. And then without warning she began to talk. Oh, I don't know what about, I hardly listened to the sense of it; something about a dream, or a memory, of being a child and standing one summer afternoon on a hill road under a convent wall and looking across the roofs of the town to the distant sea while a boy who was soft in the head capered and pulled faces at her. The content was not important – to either of us, I think. What interested her was the same thing that interested me, namely . . . namely what? How the present feeds on the past, or versions of the past. How pieces of lost time surface suddenly in the murky sea of memory, bright and clear and fantastically detailed, complete little islands where it seems it might be possible to live, even if only for a moment. And as she talked I found myself looking at her and seeing her as if for the first time, not as a gathering of details, but all of a piece, solid and singular and amazing. No, not amazing. That is the point. She was simply there, an incarnation of herself, no longer a nexus of adjectives but pure and present noun. I noticed the little fine hairs on her legs, a scarp of dried skin along the edge of her foot, a speck of sleep in the canthus of her eye. No longer Our Lady of the Enigmas, but a girl, just a girl. And somehow by being suddenly herself like this she made the things around her be there too. In her, and in what she spoke, the world, the little world in which we sat, found its grounding and was realised. It was as if she had dropped a condensed drop of colour into the water of the world and the colour had spread and the outlines of things had sprung into bright relief. As I sat with my mouth open and listened to her I felt everyone and everything shiver and shift, falling into vividest forms, detaching themselves from me and my conception of them and changing themselves instead into what they were, no longer figment, no longer mystery, no longer a part of my imagining. And I, was I there amongst them, at last?

2

Let us regress. Imagine the poor old globe grinding to a halt and then with a cosmic creak starting up again but in the opposite direction. Events whizz past in reverse, the little stick figures hurrying backwards, the boat hauling itself off the sandbank with a bump and putting out stern-first to fasten the unzipped sea, the sun calmly sinking in the east. Halt again, and we all fall over a second time and then pick ourselves up, blinking. The fact is, I did find myself outside the gates one grey morning, I did have a brown-paper parcel under my arm. I had imagined this moment so often that now when it had arrived I could hardly believe in it. Everything looked like an elaborate stage-set, plausible but not real. It was early, there was no one about except a schoolboy, with satchel and one drooping sock, who gave me, the freed man, a resentful, murky stare and passed on. A harsh wind was blowing. I hesitated, uncertain which way to turn. It is a desolate spot, this cobbled sweep where the broad gates give on to the road. I suspect it was a site of execution in former times, it has the shuddery, awed air of a place that has known some dreadful dawns. Minor devils surely hang about here, on the look-out for likely lads. I, of course, am already spoken for, by the boss.

I felt, I felt – oh, what did I feel. Well, fearful, for a start, but in an odd, almost girlish way. For the first minute or two I kept my eyes lowered, shy of the big world. It is laughable, I know, but I was terrified someone would see me there, I mean someone from the old life who would recognise me. And then, my horizons had been limited for so long: high walls make the gaze turn inward. For years I had only been able to see beyond the confines of my sequestered world by looking up. I was the boy at the bottom of the well, peering aloft in awe at the daytime stars. In captivity I had got to know the sky in all its moods, the great, stealthy drifts of light, the pales and slow darkenings, the twilight shoals. Out here, though, this morning, all was wide air and flat, glimmering spaces, and the prospect before me looked somehow tilted, and for a moment I had a bilious sense of falling. A lead-grey plume of smoke flew sideways from a tall chimney and a flock of crows wheeled afar in the wind. I turned up the collar of my jacket and set off shakily down the hill, towards the quays.

Sartorially my situation left a lot to be desired; I had, unwisely, as it now turned out, garbed myself for the occasion in the white – by now off-white – linen suit I had been wearing on the day I was apprehended ten years before. It had seemed to me that a ceremonial robing was required, that my outfit should somehow both proclaim my shriven state and mark me out as a pariah, and this was the best I could do. I must have looked as if I had dropped from Mars, an alien trying to pass for human, in my out-of-season suiting, which probably was risibly out of fashion too by now. Also, there was a cutting wind off the river and it was bloody cold.

I have always loved the river, the grand sweep of it, that noble prospect. The tide was high today, the water shouldering along swiftly with a dull, pewter shine. I leaned at gaze on the embankment, just breathing the dirty air, and sure enough my racing thoughts began to slow a little. There are certain harsh, knife-coloured mornings in springtime that are more plangently evocative than any leaf-blown autumn day. On the far bank the nine o'clock traffic flowed and stopped, flowed and stopped, the car-roofs darkly gleaming, humped like seals. By the river it is always the eighteenth century; I might have been Vaublin beside the Seine, I could see myself in a cloak and slouch hat, could almost smell the flowers and the excrement of Paris. The city, this dingy little city for which I have such a grim affection, seemed hardly changed. I scanned the skyline, looking for momentous gaps. A few landmarks had been taken away, a few incongruities added, but generally the view looked much as I remembered it. Strange to have been here all this time and yet not here at all. At dead of night I would lie awake in my cell, in that hour when the beast briefly ceased its bellowings, and try to hear the hum of life from beyond the walls; sometimes I would even get up, haggard with longing, and sit with my face pressed to the meshed window of my cell to catch the tiny vibrations in the glass, telling myself it was the noise of the great world I could feel beating there, its whoops and cries and crashes, that whole ragged, hilarious clamour, and not just the faint drumming of the prison generator.

I leaned out over the river wall and dropped my poor parcel of belongings into the oily water and watched it bob away. It was something I had planned to do, another ceremonial gesture; not very original, I suppose, but all the same a small sense of solemnity informed the occasion. The brown-paper wrapping came undone and rode the little waves like a sloughed skin, undulant and wrinkled. Here it is, I said to myself, here is where it really starts: my life. But I was not convinced.

By the window of a boarded-up shop two derelicts were having a confab. One was a tall, emaciated fellow with a woollen cap and matted beard and drooping, tragic eyes. It was he who caught my attention. I thought I remembered him, from former times; could that be, could he still be going about, haunting these streets the same as ever, after all these years? It seemed impossible, yet I felt sure I recognised him. A survivor, just like me! The idea of it was unwarrantedly cheering. His companion, in burst running-shoes and an outsize pair of maroon-coloured trousers, was short and rumpled-looking, with a babyish back to his head. He was doing most of the talking, jabbing a finger in the air and vigorously nodding agreement with himself, while the tall one just stood and stared bleakly into the middle distance, slowly champing his jaws, on the dim memory of his last square meal, probably, pausing now and then to drop in a considered word. Professional men, exchanging news of their world, its ups and downs. I wondered if I might become like them. I pictured myself falling through darker and darker air, tumbling slowly end over end, until the last, ragged net caught me. Down there in that shadowed, elemental state I would learn a new lingo, know all the dodges, be one of that band, one of the lost ones, the escapees. How restful it would be, traipsing the roads all day long, or skulking in rain-stained doorways as evening came on, with nothing to think about but hunger and lice and the state of my feet.

While I lingered there, idly watching these two, I became aware that I too in my turn was being watched. On the humpbacked bridge over the river a man was standing, with one hand on the metal rail, a thin, black-haired, shabbily dressed man. This one also I seemed to know, though I could not say how, or from where; he might have been someone I had dreamed about, in a dream long forgotten. His face was lifted at an awkward angle and although his eyes were not directly on me there was no doubt that it was me he was regarding, with peculiar and unwavering interest. He was very still. There was an air about him that was at once sinister and jaunty: I had an impression of hidden laughter. Standing above me there against the whitening sky, nimbed with soiled light and with people passing to and fro behind him, he looked flat and one-sided, like a figure cut out of cardboard. We remained thus for a moment, he scrutinising me with his covert, angled glance and I staring back boldly, ready to challenge him, why, or for what, I could not say. Then he turned away swiftly and slipped into the crowd and was gone.

After this encounter, if that is what it can be called, I found myself going along with a lighter step, almost gaily, despite the bitter wind and the ashen light. It was as if I had been sent a signal, a message of encouragement, from my own kind. All at once the world about me seemed more vivid, more dangerous, shot through with secret laughter: my world, and I in it. This was not what I had expected, this sudden, unlooked-for lightening, this chipper step and brisk straightening of the shoulders. Surely it was not right, surely in common decency the least I could do would be to put my head down and creep away abjectly into some dark hole where the world would not have to look at me. Yet I could not help feeling that somehow something like a blessing had been bestowed on me here, in this moment by the river. Oh, not a real blessing, of course; the paraclete will never extend forgiving wings above my bowed head. No, this was a benison from somewhere else. The angels sing in hell, too, remember, as the prophet K. tells us – and ah, how sweetly they sing!

Billy was waiting for me in the Boatman. It is not the kind of place I would have frequented in the old days. A handful of drinkers were at it already despite the early hour, rough-looking, indeterminate types hunched over their pints in the furry grey gloom. The sour stench from the quays outside was mingled with the smells of stale beer and cigarette smoke. At that hour the atmosphere of the place was watchful and faintly piratical; I would not have been surprised to glimpse a peg-leg under a chair, or the flash of a cutlass. Whenever the door opened a whitish cloud of light from the river came in like ectoplasm, hovered a moment and then sank down among the scarred tables and the plastic stools. Billy sat on a bench seat with a glass of beer untouched before him, tense as a pointer, gazing up in rapt attention from under a fallen lock of oiled black hair at the busy television set above the bar. He had been out for six months. He was dressed in a crisp white shirt, with the cuffs buttoned, and very clean jeans and very shiny black shoes with thick leather soles. A fag-end smouldered in one fist, and with the other hand he was kneading pensively the bunched muscles of his upper arm. When he saw me he stubbed out the cigarette hastily and scrambled up. He shook my hand with violent energy, rolling his shoulders and frantically smiling. Behind him on the television screen a cartoon bulldog was holding aloft by the neck a cartoon cat and slapping it back and forth rapidly across the snout with grim gusto.

This, I told myself, this is a mistake.

Billy was blushing. He blushes easily. He went on pumping my hand as though afraid that if he let it go he would have to do something even more awkward and embarrassing. His hand was as hard as stone. He has the body of a boxer, short and broad and packed with muscle. He seems made not of flesh but of some more solid stuff, a sort of magma, pliant and weighty and warm; beside him I feel bloated and cheesy, a big, soft, wallowing hulk. He exuded a faint, plumbeous smell, like the smell of machine oil; there used to be talk, I remembered, of an enthusiasm for motorbikes: perhaps this whiff of hot oil was their ghostly afterburn. He must be, my God, he must be nearly thirty by now, though he looks about eighteen. He still had a trace of that washed-out, tombal pallor that I suppose our kind never lose. His eyes, though, brown as sea-snails, were clear and clean as ever. Billy the butcher, we used to call him; very handy with a flensing knife, our Billy, in his younger days.

We sat down at the table and there was an awful silence, like something tightening and tightening in the air between us. I wondered if I still smelled of prison: something musty and mildewed, with a hint of wet wool and old smoke and cold cocoa. Billy kept shooting his white cuffs and plucking at the knees of his jeans. I pictured the nerves fizzing and popping under his skin like bundles of electric wires. He had a bag between his feet. It was a very small bag, black, solid, and peculiarly dangerous-looking; all Billy's things give off an air of casual menace. When I pointed to it and asked him if he was going somewhere he shook his head. 'Just gear,' he said, mysteriously. Billy always seems on the point of departure. Even in our early days inside, when I was still in shock, searching for the first hand-holds on the ziggurat of my sentence, he had the air of an innocent confidently awaiting imminent release. He would sit on his bunk, braced to leap up, his legs folded under him like a complicated pair of springs, or stand at the cell door beating out tense little rhythms with his fingertips on the bars, as if it had not sunk in even yet that this was real, that they were not going to come pounding down the corridor any minute now, red-faced and apologetic, to tell him it was all a preposterous mistake and slap him on the back and let him go. Ah, Billy. His trial was held on the same day as mine (a perfunctory and dispiriting affair, I'm afraid, much as I expected), which made us natural chums; he was by then already an experienced jailbird, having passed his adolescence in a variety of correctional institutions between riotous and increasingly brief bouts of freedom, and he was a great help to me in there in those first months, poor fledgling jailbird that I was.

The shirt-sleeved barman came over, wiping his reddened paws on a filthy rag. I asked for tea and got a sour look.

'Not drinking?' Billy said, with a sly, sideways grin. He has an unshakeable notion of me as a terrible fellow.

The barman slouched off. Why do barmen wear such awful trousers, I wonder? I hate to generalise, as I have probably remarked already, but they do, it is a thing I have noticed. On the screen before us the incorrigible cat, having suffered another whacking, sat slumped and skew-eyed under a spinning halo of multi-coloured stars.

'Well, Billy,' I said, 'tell me, how do I look? Honestly, now.'

'You look great.'

'No, really.'

He rolled his shoulders again and squinted at me, biting his lip.

'You look like shit,' he said, with a crooked little apologetic smile.

I took a breath.

'Do you know, Billy,' I said, 'the last time I was in a pub, a very long time ago, someone said the same thing to me. Exactly the same thing. Isn't that an amazing coincidence?'

All at once I thought I was going to weep; I felt that tickle in my sinuses and the tears squeezing up into my eyes. I stood up hurriedly, fumbling in my pockets for a hankie and muttering under my breath, terrified of making a spectacle of myself. I could not start blubbing now. I had thought I was finished with all that. Prison is supposed to harden but I'm afraid it softened me. I am like one of those afflicted sinners in a medieval altarpiece, skulking under my own little personalised cloud that rains on me a steady drizzle of grief.

There was a telephone at the far end of the bar. I hurried to it. I had difficulty getting it to work; I was out of practice with such things. The drinkers looked up from their pints and watched me with sardonic interest. 'Them are the wrong coins,' one of them said, and the barman, waiting for the kettle to boil, snickered. It is by such little signs – outmoded width of the trouser-leg, sideburns cut too long or too short, a constant expression of surprise at the price of things – that the old lag betrays his provenance.

My wife answered. She took her time. I was convinced, mistakenly, I'm sure, that she had known it was me and had deliberately waited to pick up the receiver until I was about to hang up. Why do I think such things of her?

'You,' she said.

It was a bad connection, hollow and crackly and overlaid with an oceanic surge and slush, as if great waves were breaking in the distance across the line.

'Yes, me,' I said.

She was silent for so long I thought we had been cut off. I leaned my back against the wall, hearing myself breathe into the clammy hollow of the mouthpiece, and watched Billy where he sat with his legs crossed, lighting another cigarette, self-conscious and ill at ease, glancing about him with studied casualness as if he thought there might be someone watching, waiting to laugh at him. He caught my eye and smiled uneasily and then let his gaze drift, dismantling his smile awkwardly in a series of small, covert readjustments of his facial muscles. He had seemed so natural when we were inside, so sure of himself, in his affably menacing way, padding along the catwalks with feline grace. I am convinced there are people who are born to go to jail. It is not a fashionable notion, I know, but I believe it. And I, am I one of those fated malefactors, I wonder? Was it all determined from the start? How eagerly, quaking like a rickety hound, my poor old conscience leaps for the well-gnawed bone of mitigation.

'You could have told me it was today,' my wife said.

'I would have,' I said, 'but . . .'

'But?'

'But.' Amazing how we had fallen straight away into the old routine, the deadpan patter that used to seem so sophisticated, so worldly, in the days when we had a world in which to perform it. 'I'm sorry,' I said.

I pictured her standing in the hall, a big, dark, serious woman waylaid for a moment in the midst of her day, a day in which until now there had been nothing of me. My wife. What shall I call her this time – Judy? Perhaps she will not need to have a name. I have dragged her deep enough into the mire; let her be decently anonymous.

'I'd like to see you,' I said.

Again she was silent. I listened to the harsh susurrus on the line and thought myself sunk in the deeps of the sea.

'I don't think,' she said slowly then, in a toneless voice, 'I don't think I want you to come here. I don't think I want that.' This time I said nothing. 'I'm sorry,' she said.

'You don't sound sorry.' In fact, she did. 'I need my things,' I said. 'My clothes. My books. I have nothing.' I was feeling aggrieved by now, in a happily sorrowful, self-pitying sort of way.

'I'll send them to you,' she said. 'It's all packed up. I'll post it.'

'You'll post it.'

Silence.

One of the drinkers at the bar tranquilly raised his backside off the stool and farted.

'Very well,' I said. 'I'll stay away.' I waited. 'How are you – ?'

'I'm fine,' she said, too quickly, and then paused; I could almost hear her biting her lip. 'I'm all right.'

'What do you mean, all right?'

'I mean I'm all right. How do you think I am?'

Was that a hint of tears in her voice? She does not weep easily, but when she does it is a terrible thing to see. I put a hand over my eyes. I felt weary all of a sudden. Come, I told myself, make an effort, this may be your last shot at what will be the nearest you will ever get to normal life. I still had hopes, you see, that the human world would take me back into its simple and forgiving embrace.

'Can't I see you?' I said plaintively.

She sighed; I imagined her tapping her foot impatiently. She is not unfeeling – far from it – but the spectacle of other people's sufferings always irritates her, she cannot help it.

'Someone was looking for you,' she said.

'What? Who?'

'On the phone. Foreign, by the sound of him. Or pretending to be. He seemed to think something was very funny – '

An angry bleating started up: my money was running out. I gave her the number and hung up and waited. She did not call back. The absence of that ringing still tolls faintly in my memory like a distant mourning bell.

My cup of tea was on the table, with one of those swollen brown bags submerged in it, its horribly limp string dangling suggestively over the rim. The tea was tepid by now. I put in four lumps of sugar and watched them slowly crumble. My sweet tooth: another vice I picked up in the clink.

'Everything all right?' Billy said.

'Oh, tip-top,' I said. 'Tip-top.'

He nodded seriously and took a sip of beer. How calm he is, how incurious! They expect so little from the world, these people. They just stand there quietly, looking at nothing and chewing the cud, until the bone-cart comes for them. Sometimes I think I must belong to a different species. Suddenly he brightened and reached down and unzipped his bag and brought out a bottle of gin and thrust it at me with another awkward dip of his shoulders and another embarrassed smile. A present! He had bought me a present! For a moment I could not speak, and sat, dumb with emotion, clutching the bottle in helpless hands and nodding gravely. I could feel him watching me.

'Is that kind all right?' he said anxiously. Billy does not touch spirits; he is quite the puritan, in his way. 'I got it from my brother-in-law.'

'It's splendid, Billy,' I said thickly. 'Really, splendid.' I was on the verge of tears again. Honestly, what a cry-baby I am.

Things improved after that. Billy became talkative and kept on laughing breathily in the enthusiasm of relief. He told me about his job. It seemed he delivered things, I cannot remember what they were supposed to be, for that brother-in-law, the gin merchant. It was all very vague. He had his own van. What he really wanted to do, though, was get into the army. He did not know if they would take him. He hesitated, sitting on his hands and gnawing the corner of his mouth, and then blurted it out: would I write a reference for him?

'You know,' he said excitedly, 'sort of a character reference.'

I laughed. That was a mistake. He looked away from me and brooded darkly, staring before him with narrowed eyes. There are moments, I confess, when I am a little afraid of him. Not that I think he might injure me – he would not dream of it, I know. I am just aware of a general uneasiness, a creeping sensation along the spine, the kind of thing I would feel walking past the cage of some crouched and simmering, green-eyed, big-shouldered animal. I wonder if others find me frightening in the same way? I can hardly credit it, yet it must be so, I suppose. Do they realise, I wonder, how afraid of them we are, on our side, for all our bruited ferocity, as we watch them sauntering abroad out there in the world, masters of the whip and chair?

A rain-shower clattered briefly against the window. Idly I watched the drinkers at the bar.

'Can they spot us, Billy, would you say?' I said.

He nodded. 'Oh, they can. They'd spot *us*, anyway.' He grinned and made a clockwork motion with his arm, wielding an invisible club. 'Two of a kind, you and me. Sort of a brotherhood, eh?'

A man with an orange face and desperate eyes and a mouth like a trap came on the television and began to tell jokes at breakneck speed, mugging and leering, mad as Mister Punch.

'Yes, Billy,' I said, 'that's right: sort of a brotherhood.'

WIND AND SMOKE and scudding clouds and wan sunlight flickering on the rain-splashed pavements. The river surged, steely and aswarm. Billy strode forward muscularly with his hands stuck in the pockets of his jeans and his bag under his arm, fairly springing along on his stout leather soles, careless of the cold wind. I remembered the two tramps at their colloquy; we must look an odd pair too, Billy all brawn and youthful tension and I scurrying at his heels huddled around myself as if I were running in a sack-race. We passed by junk shops and bargain stores and flyblown windows with the names of solicitors painted on them in tarnished gold lettering. A plastic bag flew high up into the sky, slewing and snapping. These are the things we remember.

Billy's van was a ramshackle contraption with fringes of rust around the mudguards and a deep dent in one wing. In the back seat a spring stuck up at a comical angle through a hole in the upholstery. I could see he was anxious to get away from me, making a great show of looking for his keys and frowning like a man awaited importantly elsewhere. I did not blame him: I find myself creepy company, sometimes. When he bent forward to open the door I looked down at the crown of his head and the little white twirled patch there and without thinking I said:

'Listen, Billy, will you give me a lift somewhere?'

He looked up at me in alarm. 'What? Where?'

'Down south. I have to get a boat in the morning.'

His frown deepened slowly.

'You mean, now?' he said. 'You mean just . . . go?'

'Yes,' I said. 'Just go.'

He turned his troubled eyes to the river. There was his Mam to think about, he said, she was expecting him home for his dinner, and he was supposed to see his girl tonight – and the day's deliveries, what about them? I said nothing, only waited. What was I thinking of, trying to hold on to him like that? Was it just that I did not want to travel alone, trapped with my haunted thoughts? Yes, that must have been it, I'm sure: I wanted company, I wanted to rattle along in Billy's banger with the wind whistling in the leaky doors and that spring waggling in the back seat like a broken jack-in-the-box. Loneliness: that, and no more. Sometimes it strikes me what a simple organism I must be, after all, without knowing it.

He gave in in the end. At first he drove hunched over the wheel, frowning worriedly out at the road, but as we got away from the city centre he cheered up. He has, like me, a fondness for the suburbs. What is it about these tidy estates, these little parks and shopping malls, that speaks so eloquently to us? What is still living there that in us is dead? The miniature trees were tenderly in leaf and the little clouds fleeted and the streets shimmered and swayed with pale swoops of sunlight. As we bowled along Billy talked, between long, thoughtful pauses, about his girl. She was, he confided, an apprentice hairdresser. She did not mind about his crimes, he said, even that rape business, regarding them it seemed as no more than the follies of youth. In fact, she rather fancied the idea of being a lifer's girl: Billy was a bit of a celebrity round their way, having cut out the tripes of a fellow on the street one night for making a remark about his sister. He was all for getting married right off, but she had said no, they should wait: when he got into the army they would have a place of their own at the camp and she would open a salon for the camp wives. I listened happily, slumped in my seat like a child at bedtime, as he filled in with loving strokes the colours – olive-drab, eiderdown-pink – of his dream of the future. This is how we used to while away the time inside, spinning each other stories of the life to come. In return now I told him my plans, how I was going to redeem myself through honest labour and all the rest of it; it must have sounded as much of a fairytale to him as his talk of a rosy future seemed to me. I even showed him my letter of introduction to Professor Kreutznaer, written for me by a kindly and forgiving woman. I was troubled to see that although I had kept it carefully it had already taken on that grubby, greyed, dog-eared look that prison somehow imparts to all important papers; how many such tired documents have I handled – my opinion was much sought after, inside – while young bloods such as Billy sat on the edge of their bunks twisting their hands and watching me with eyes in which anxiety and hopefulness struggled for command. Believe me, you do not know the tenderness of things in there, the strange mingling of violence and sorrow and unshakeable optimism.

'Anna who?' Billy said, squinting at the letter where I held it out for his inspection.

'Behrens,' I said. 'An old friend. Her late father was a very rich man who collected pictures. I borrowed one of them, once.' Billy quietly sniggered. 'They were very understanding about it, I must say. Anna has quite forgiven me. See what she says: *Please give him any help you can as he has lost everything and wants to make a new start*. Isn't that fine of her? I call that very fine, I must say.'

The van rattled and shook, lurching to the left every time Billy pressed the brakes, yet it felt as if we were flying swiftly through the soft, spring air. I love to travel like this, it is one of my secret joys. Any motorised mode of conveyance will do, car, bus, van – black maria, even. It is not the speed or the womby seclusion that works the magic, I think, but the fact of being enclosed on all sides by glass. The windscreen is for me one of the happiest inventions of humankind. Looked at through this moulded curve of light the travelling world outside seems itself made of crystal, a toylike place of scattering leaves and skimming shadows, where trees flash past and buildings rise up suddenly and as suddenly collapse, and staring people loom, standing at a tilt, impossibly tall, like the startled manikins in the shop windows of my childhood. If I were to believe in the possibility of anything other than endless and unremitting torment in store for me after I die – if, say, a power struggle on Mount Olympus were to result in a general amnesty for mortal sinners, including even me – then this is how I see myself travelling into eternity, reclining like this, with my arms folded, in a sort of happy fuddlement, at the warm centre of this whirling, glassy globe.

It must have been Billy's talk of his girl that got me thinking about my wife again. Idly I pictured her there in the hall after I had been cut off, listening to the hum of the dead line and then putting down the receiver and standing with a hand to her face in that sombre way she has when something unexpected happens. This time, however, as she stood there in my musings, I gave her, without really intending it, a companion. He was indistinct at first, just a man-shape hovering at the edge of fancy, but as my imagination – bloodshot, prehensile – took hold of him in fierce scrutiny the current crackled in the electrodes and a shudder ran through him and at once he began to walk and talk, with awful plausibility. Where do they come from, these sudden phantoms that stride unbidden into my unguarded thoughts, pushy and smug and scattering cigarette ash on the carpet, as if they owned the place? Invented in the idle play of the mind, they can suddenly turn treacherous, can rear up in a flash and give a nasty bite to the hand that fashioned them. This one was taking on attributes by the instant. He was tall and lean, with lank fair hair and a square jaw, togged out in tweeds and a checked shirt and scuffed, oxblood brogues. He would have a pipe about him somewhere, and strong, coarse tobacco in a fine, soft pouch. He cultivates an air of faint disdain, behind which lurks a crafty-eyed watchfulness. There is a touch of the rake about him. He drives a sports car and rides a large horse. He is probably a Protestant. And he is fucking my wife.

I had forgotten about the gin but now with trembling hands I fished the bottle out of my jacket pocket hurriedly and got it open. I love that little click when the metal cap gives; it is like the noise of the neck of some small, toothsome creature being snapped. I took a swig and gasped at the chill scald of the liquor on my tongue and an entire world came flooding back, silvery-blue and icily atinkle. I felt immediately drunk, as if that first mouthful had stirred up a sediment left over in me from the gallons of the stuff I used to drink in the old days. Billy glanced at me with a deep frown of disapproval; I know what he is thinking – that a gent like me should not be seen rattling along in a rusty jalopy and slugging from the neck of a gin bottle at ten-thirty in the morning. I would be in spats and a monocle if he had his way.

We were in the country now, lurching down a leafy road, with a preposterously lovely view before us of rolling fields and silver streams and vague, mauve mountains. Not once in all the years I endured inside had it occurred to me to be jealous. Oh, I knew that most likely I had lost my wife, yet I had thought of her all along as somehow safe, chained to the rock of my absence, like one of those mysteriously afflicted, big-eyed Pre-Raphaelite maidens. The idea of her cavorting with some hard-faced horseman of the kind who in the old days were always hanging around her struck me with the force of a blow to the heart. I sat aghast, hot all over, blushing in pain, and saw the whole thing. They are in a hotel on the market square of some small, nondescript midland town. The bedroom looks out on the square, where his roadster is discreetly parked under blossoming trees. Soft light of the deserted afternoon falls from the high window. She looks about her in faint surprise and a kind of amusement at the bed, the bureau, the worn rug on the floor: so, she thinks, what had seemed like accident was really something willed, after all, and here she is, on this blank Tuesday, in this anonymous room in a strange town miles away from her life. He stands awkwardly, not looking at her, a little nervous now despite all his easy talk on the way here, and takes things from his pockets and lines them up neatly on the bedside table: change, keys, that thing he uses to scrape the ash out of his pipe. The back of his neck is inflamed. The sight of that childish patch of pink makes something thicken in her throat. He turns to her, talking to cover his awkwardness, and stops and stares at her helplessly. She hears him swallow. They stand a moment, poised, listening to themselves, to that swelling inner buzz. Then a hand is lifted, a face touched, a breath indrawn. This is what shakes my heart, the thought of this wordless moment of surrender. All that will follow is terrible too – there is no stopping this imagination of mine – but it is here, when his fingers brush her cheek and her mouth softens and her eyes go vague, that my mind snags like a broken nail. Yet I know too there is something in me that wants it to have happened, wants to lean over them with face on fire and feed in sorrow on their embraces and drink deep their cries. What awful need is this? Am I the ghost at their banquet, sucking up a little of their life to warm myself? Her phantom lover is more real than I: when I look into that mirror I see no reflection. I am there and not there, flitting in panic this way and that in the torture chamber of my imaginings, poor, parched Nosferatu.

On a straight stretch Billy put his foot down and we fairly flew along. I sat watching the countryside rise up and rush to meet us and I drank more gin and felt faintly sick. She is a troubled sleeper, my wife, yet I always envied what seemed to me the rich drama of her nights, those fretful, laborious struggles through the dark from one shore of light to another. She would drop into sleep abruptly, often in the middle of a sentence, and lie prone on the knotted sheet with her face turned sideways and her mouth open and her limbs twitching, like a long-distance swimmer launching out flounderingly into icy black waters. She used to talk in her sleep too, in dim grumbles and sudden, sharp questionings. Sometimes she would cry out, staring sightlessly into the dark. And I would lie awake on my back beside her, stiff as a drifting spar, numb with that obscure anguish that wells up in me always when I am left alone with myself. Now I wondered if there was someone else who lay by her side at night with a dry throat and swollen heart, listening to her as she slept her restless sleep: not the prancing centaur of my inventing, but some poor solitary mortal just like me, staring sightlessly into the dark, still leaking a little, doing his gradual dying. I think I would have preferred the centaur.

'Stop here, Billy!' I cried. 'Stop here.'

I AM ALWAYS FASCINATED by the way the things that happen happen. I mean the ordinary things, the small occurrences that keep adding themselves on to all that went before in the running total of what I call my life. I do not think of events as discrete and discontinuous; mostly there is just what seems a sort of aimless floating. I am not afloat at all, of course, it only feels like that: really I am in free fall. And I come to earth repeatedly with a bump, though I am surprised every time, sitting in a daze on the hard ground of inevitability, like Tom the cat, leaning on my knuckles with my legs flung wide and stars circling my poor sore head. When Billy stopped the van we sat and listened for a while to the engine ticking and the water gurgling in the radiator, and I was like my wife in that hotel room that I had conjured up for her imaginary tryst, looking about her in subdued astonishment at the fact of being where she was. I had not intended that we should come this way, I had left it to Billy to choose whatever road he wished; yet here we were. Was it another sign, I asked myself, in this momentous day of signs? Billy looked out calmly at the stretch of country road before us and drummed his fingers on the steering wheel.

'Where's this?' he said.

'Home.' I laughed. The word boomed like a foghorn.

'Nice,' Billy said. 'The trees and all.' I marvelled anew at his lack of curiosity. Nothing, it seems, can surprise him. Or am I wrong, as I usually am about people and their ways? For all I know he may be in a ceaseless fever of amazement before the spectacle of this wholly improbable world. He twitches a lot, and sometimes he used to wake up screaming in his bunk at night; but then, we all woke up screaming in the night, sooner or later, so that proves nothing. All the same, I am probably underestimating him; underestimating people is one of my less serious besetting sins. 'Your family still here?' he said. 'Your mam and dad?'

He frowned. I could see him trying to imagine them, big, bossy folk with loud voices clattering down this road astride their horses, as outlandish to him as medieval knights in armour.

'No,' I said. 'All dead, thank God. My wife lives here now.'

I opened the door of the van and swung my legs out and sat for a moment with my head bowed and shoulders sagging and the gin bottle dangling between my knees. When I lifted my eyes I could see the roof of the house beyond the ragged tops of the hedge. I found myself toying with the notion that this was all there was, just a roof put up there to fool me, like something out of the *Arabian Nights*, and that if I stood up quickly enough I would glimpse under the eaves a telltale strip of silky sky and a shining scimitar of moon floating on its back.

'Did I ever tell you, Billy,' I said, still gazing up wearily at those familiar chimney-pots, 'about the many worlds theory?'

Of the few scraps of science I can still recall (talk about another life!), the many worlds theory is my favourite. The universe, it says, is everywhere and at every instant splitting into a myriad versions of itself. On Pluto, say, a particle of putty collides with a lump of lead and another, smaller particle is created in the process and goes shooting off in all directions. Every single one of those possible directions, says the many worlds theory, will produce its own universe, containing its own stars, its own solar system, its own Pluto, it own you and its own me: identical, that is, to all the other myriad universes except for this unique event, this particularly particle whizzing down this particular path. In this manifold version of reality chance is an iron law. Chance. Think of it. Oh, it's only numbers, I know, only a cunning wheeze got up to accommodate the infinities and make the equations come out, yet when I contemplate it something stirs in me, some indistinct, fallen thing that I had thought was dead lifts itself up on one smashed wing and gives a pathetic, hopeful cheep. For is it not possible that somewhere in this crystalline multiplicity of worlds, in this infinite, mirrored regression, there is a place where the dead have not died, and I am innocent?

'What do you think of that, Billy?' I said. 'That's the many worlds theory. Isn't that something, now?'

'Weird,' he answered, shaking his head slowly from side to side, humouring me.

Spring is strange. This day looked more like early winter, all metallic glitters and smooth, silver sky. The air was cool and bright and smelled of wet clay. An odd, unsteady sort of cheerfulness was gradually taking hold of me – the gin, I suppose.

'What's the first thing you noticed when you got out, Billy?' I said.

He hardly had to think at all.

'The quiet,' he said. 'People not shouting all the time.'

The quiet, yes. And the breadth of things, the far vistas on every side and the sense of farther and still farther spaces beyond. It made me giddy to think of it.

I got myself up at last, feet squelching in the boggy verge, and walked a little way along the road. I had nothing particular in mind. I had no intention as yet of going near the house – the gate was in the other direction – for in my heart I knew my wife was right, that I should stay away. All the same, now that I was here, by accident, I could not resist looking over the old place one more time, trying my feet in the old footprints, as it were, to see if they still fitted. Yet I could not feel the way one is supposed to feel amid the suddenly rediscovered surroundings of one's past, all swoony and tearful, in a transport of ecstatic remembrance, clasping it all to one's breast with a stifled cry and a sudden, sweet ache in the heart, that kind of thing. No; what I felt was a sort of glazed numbness, as if I were suspended in some thin, transparent stuff, like one of those eggs my mother used to preserve in waterglass when I was a child. This is what happens to you in prison, you lose your past, it is confiscated from you, along with your bootlaces and your belt, when you enter through that strait gate. It was all still here, of course, the ancient, enduring world, suave and detailed, standing years-deep in its own silence, only beyond my touching, as if shut away behind glass. There were even certain trees I seemed to recognise; I would not have been surprised if they had come alive and spoken to me, lifting their drooping limbs and sighing, as in a children's story-book. At that moment, as though indeed this were the enchanted forest, there materialised before me on the road, like a wood-sprite, a little old brown man in big hobnailed boots and a cap, carrying, of all things, a sickle. He had long arms and a bent back and bandy legs, and progressed with a rolling gait, as if he were bowling himself along like a hoop. As we approached each other he watched me keenly, with a crafty, sidewise, leering look. When we had drawn level he touched a finger to his cap and croaked an incomprehensible greeting, peering up at me out of clouded, half-blind eyes. I stopped. He took in my white suit with a mixture of misgiving and scornful amusement; he probably thought I was someone of consequence.

'Grand day,' I said, in a loud voice hollow with false heartiness.

'But hardy, though,' he answered smartly and looked pleased with himself, as if he had caught me out in some small, deceitful strategem.

'Yes,' I said, abashed, 'hardy indeed.'

He stood bowed before me, bobbing gently from the waist as if his spine were fitted with some sort of spring attachment at its base. The sickle dangled at the end of his long arm like a prosthesis. We were silent briefly. I considered the sky while he studied the roadway at my feet. I was never one for exchanging banter with the peasantry, yet I was loth to pass on, I do not know why. Perhaps I took him for another of this day's mysterious messengers.

'And are you from these parts yourself, sir?' he said, in that wheedling tone they reserve for tourists and well-heeled strangers in general.

For answer I made a broad, evasive gesture.

'Do you know that house?' I asked, pointing over the hedge.

He passed a hard brown hand over his jaw, making a sandpapery noise, and gave me a quick, sly look. His eyes were like shards from some large, broken, antique thing, a funerary jar, perhaps.

'I do,' he said. 'I know it well.'

Then he launched into a long rigmarole about my family and its history. I listened in awed astonishment as if to a tale of the old gods. It was all invention, of course; even the few facts he had were upside-down or twisted out of shape. 'I knew the young master, too,' he said. (*The young master*?) 'I seen him one day kill a rabbit. Broke its neck: like that. A pet thing, it was. Took it up in his hands and – ' he made a crunching noise out of the side of his mouth ' – kilt it. He was only a lad at the time, mind, a curly-headed little fellow you wouldn't think would say boo to a goose. Oh, a nice knave. I wasn't a bit surprised when I heard about what he done.'

What was this nonsense? I had never wrung the neck of any rabbit. I was the most innocuous of children, a poor, shivering mite afraid of its own shadow. Why had he invented this grotesque version of me? I felt confusion and a sort of angry shame, as if I had been jostled aside in the street by some ludicrously implausible imposter claiming to be me. The old man was squinting up at me with a slack-mouthed grin, a solitary, long yellow tooth dangling from his upper gums. 'I suppose you're looking for him too, are you?' he said.

A cold hand clutched my heart.

'Why?' I said. 'Who else was looking for him?'

His grin turned slyly knowing. 'Ah,' he said, 'there's always fellows like that going around, after people.'

He winked and touched a finger to his cap again, with the smug, self-satisfied air of a man who has properly settled someone's hash, and bowled himself off on his way. I looked after him but saw myself, a big, ragged, ravaged person, flabby as a porpoise, standing there in distress on the windy road, dangling from an invisible gibbet in my incongruous white suit, arms limp, with my mouth open and my bell-bottoms flapping and the neck of the gin bottle sticking out of my pocket. I do not know why I was so upset. There came over me then that sense of dislocation I experience with increasing frequency these days, and which frightens me. It is as if mind and body had pulled loose from each other, or as if the absolute, essential *I* had shrunk to the size of a dot, leaving the rest of me hanging in enormous suspension, massive and yet weightless, like a sawn tree before it topples. I wonder if it is incipient epilepsy, or some other insinuating cerebral malady? But I do not think the effect is physical.

Perhaps this is how I shall go mad in the end, perhaps I shall just fly apart like this finally and be lost to myself forever. The attack, if that is not too strong a word for it, the attack passed, as it always does, with a dropping sensation, a sort of general lurch, as if I had been struck a great, soft, padded punch and somehow had fallen out of myself even as I stood there, clenched in fright. I looked about warily, blinking; I might have just landed from somewhere entirely different. Everything was in its place, the roof beyond the hedge and the old man hobbling away and the back of Billy's seal-dark head motionless in the car, as though nothing had happened, as though that fissure had not opened up in the deceptively smooth surface of things. But I know that look of innocence the world puts on; I know it for what it is.

I found a gap in the hedge and pulled myself through it, my shoes sinking to the brim in startlingly cold mud. Twigs slapped my face and thorns clutched at my coat. I had forgotten what the countryside is like, the blank-faced, stolid malevolence of bush and briar. When I got to the other side I was panting. I had the feeling, as so often, that all this had happened before. The house was there in front of me now, quite solid and substantial after all and firmly tethered to its roof. Yet it seemed changed, seemed smaller and nearer to the road than it should be, and for a panicky moment I wondered if my memory had deceived me and this was not my house at all. (*My* house? Ah.) Mother's rose bushes were still flourishing under the big window at the gable end. They were in bud already. Poor ma, dead and gone and her roses still there, clinging on in their slow, tenacious, secret way. I started across the lawn, the soaked turf giving spongily under my tread. The past was gathering ever more thickly around me, I waded through it numbly like a greased swimmer, waiting to feel the chill and the treacherous undertow. I veered away from the front door – I do not naturally go in at front doors any more – and skirted round by the rose bushes, squinting up at the windows for a sign of life. How frowningly do empty windows look out at the world, full of blank sky and oddly arranged greenery. At the back of the house I skulked about for a while in the clayey dampness of the vegetable garden, feeling like poor Magwitch on the run. A few big stalks of last year's cabbages, knobbed like backbones, leaned this way and that, and there were hens that high-stepped worriedly away from me in slow motion, or stood canted over on one leg with their heads inclined, shaking their wattles and uttering mournful croaks of alarm. (What strange, baroque creatures they are, hens; there is something Persian about them, I always feel.) I was not thinking of anything. I was just feeling around blindly, like a doctor feeling for the place that pains. I would have welcomed pain. Dreamily I advanced, admiring the sea-green moss on the door of the disused privy, the lilac tumbling over its rusted tin roof. A breeze swooped down and a thrush whistled its brief, thick song. I paused, light-headed and blinking. At last the luminous air, the bird's song, that particular shade of green, all combined to succeed in transporting me back for a moment to the far, lost past, to some rain-washed, silver-grey morning like this one, forgotten but still somehow felt, and I stood for a moment in inexplicable rapture, my face lifted to the light, and felt a sort of breathlessness, an inward staggering, as if an enormous, airy weight had been dropped into my arms. But it did not last; that tender burden I had been given to hold, whatever it was, evaporated at once, and the rapture faded and I was numb again, as before.

I put my face to the kitchen window and peered inside. I could see little except shadows and my own eyes reflected in the glass, fixed and hungry, like the eyes of a desperate stranger. Crouched there with my breath steaming the pane and the bilious smell of drains in my nostrils, I felt intensely the pressure of things behind me, the garden and the fields and the far woods, like an inquisitive crowd gathering at my back, elbowing for a look. I am never really at ease in the open; I expect always some malignity of earth or air to strike me down or, worse, to whirl me up dizzyingly into the sky. I have always been a little afraid of the sky, so transparent and yet impenetrable, so deceptively harmless-looking in its bland blueness.

The back door was locked. I was turning to go, more relieved I think than anything else, when suddenly, in a sudden swoon of anger, or proprietorial resentment, or something, I don't know what, I turned with an elbow lifted and bashed it against one of the panes of frosted glass in the door. These things are not as easy as the cinema makes them seem: it took me three good goes before I managed it. The glass gave with a muffled whop, like a grunt of laughter, guttural and cruel, and the splinters falling to the floor inside made a sinister little musical sound, a sort of elfin music. I waited, listening. What a connoisseur of silences I have become over the years! This one had astonishment in it, and warm fright, and a naughty child's stifled glee. I took a breath. I was trembling, like a struck cymbal. How darkly thrilling it is to smash a pane of glass and reach through the jagged hole into the huge, cool emptiness of the other side. I pictured my hand pirouetting all alone in there, in that shocked space, doing its little back-to-front *pas de deux* with the key. The door swung open abruptly and I almost fell across the threshold; it was not so much the suddenness that made me totter but the vast surprise of being here. For an instant I say myself as if lit by lightning, a stark, crouched figure, vivid and yet not entirely real, an emanation of myself, a hologram image, pop-eyed and flickering. Shakily I stepped inside, and recalled, with eerie immediacy, the tweedy and damply warm underarm of a blind man I had helped across a street somewhere, in some forgotten city, years ago.

I shut the door behind me and stood and took another

deep breath, like a diver poised on the springboard's thrumming tip. The furniture hung about pretending not to look at me. Stillness lay like a dustsheet over everything. There was no one at home, I could sense it. I walked here and there, my footsteps falling without sound. I had a strange sensation in my ears, a sort of fullness, as if I were in a vessel fathoms deep with the weight of the ocean pressing all around me. The objects that I looked at seemed insulated, as if they had been painted with a protective coating of some invisible stuff, cool and thick and smooth as enamel, and when I touched them I could not seem to feel them. I thought of being here, a solemn little boy in a grubby jersey, crop-headed and frowning, with inky fingers and defenceless, translucent pink ears, sitting at this table hunched over my homework on a winter evening and dreaming of the future. Can I really ever have been thus? Can that child be me? Surely somewhere between that blameless past and this grim present something snapped, some break occurred without my noticing it in the line I was paying out behind me as I ran forward, reaching out an eager hand towards all the good things that I thought were waiting for me. Who was it, then, I wonder, that picked up the frayed end and fell nimbly into step behind me, chuckling softly to himself?

I went into the hall. There was the telephone she had delayed so long before answering. The machine squatted tensely on its little table like a shiny black toad, dying to speak, to tell all, to blurt out everything that had been confided to it down the years. Where had everyone gone to? Had they fled at the sound of my voice on the line, had she dropped everything and bundled the child in her arms and run out to the road and driven away with a shriek of tyres? I realised now why it was I could touch nothing, could not feel the texture of things: the house had been emptied of me; I had been exorcised from it. Would she know I had been here? Would she sense the contamination in the air? I closed my eyes and was assailed anew by that feeling of both being and not being, of having drifted loose from myself. I have always been convinced of the existence somewhere of another me, my more solid self, more weighty and far more serious than I, intent perhaps on great and unimaginable tasks, in another reality, where things are really real; I suppose for him, out there in his one of many worlds, I would be no more than the fancy of a summer's day, a shimmer at the edge of vision, something half-glimpsed, like the shadow of a cloud, or a gust of wind, or the hover and sudden flit of a dragonfly over reeded, sun-white shallows. And now as I stood in the midst of my own absence, in the birthplace that had rid itself of me utterly, I murmured a little prayer, and said, Oh, if you are really there, bright brother, in your more real reality, think of me, turn all your stern attentions on me, even for an instant, and make *me* real, too.

(Of course, at times I think of that other self not as my better half but my worse; if he is the bad one, the evil, lost twin, what does that make me? That is an avenue down which I do not care to venture.)

I climbed the stairs. I felt oddly, shakily buoyant, as if there were springs attached to the soles of my shoes and I must keep treading down heavily to prevent them from bouncing me over the banisters. On the first landing I stopped and turned from side to side, poor baffled minotaur, my head swinging ponderously on its thick tendons, a bullish weight, my humid, blood-dark glower groping stubbornly for something, for some smallest trace of my past selves lurking here, like the hidden faces in a comic-book puzzle. As a child I loved to be alone in the house; it was like being held loosely in the friendly clutches of a preoccupied, mute and melancholy giant. Something now had happened to the light, some sort of gloom had fallen. It was not raining. Perhaps it was fog; in these parts fog has a way of settling without warning and as quickly lifting again. At any rate I recall a clammy and crepuscular glow. I walked down the corridor. It was like walking in a dream, a sort of slow stumbling, weightless and yet encumbered. At the end of the corridor there was an arched window with a claret-coloured pane that had always made me think of cold churches and the word *litany*. The door to one of the bedrooms was ajar; I imagined someone standing behind it, breathless and listening, just like me. I hesitated, and then with one finger pushed the door open and stepped in sideways and stood listening in the softly thudding silence. The room was empty, a large, high, white chamber with a vaulted ceiling and one big window looking out into the umbrage of tall trees. There was no furniture, there were no pictures on the walls, there was nothing. The floorboards were bare. Whose room had this been? I did not remember it; that elaborate ceiling, for instance, domed and scooped like the inner crown of a priest's biretta: there must have been a false ceiling under it in my time that now had been removed. I looked up into the soft shadows and felt everything fall away from me like water. How cool and calm all was, how still the air. I thought how it would be to live here in this bone-white cell, in all this emptiness, watching the days ascend and fall again to darkness, hearing faintly the wind blow, seeing the light edge its way across the floor and die. And then to float away, to be gone, like dust, dispersed into the vast air. Not to be. Not to be at all. Deep down, deep beyond dreaming, have I ever desired anything other than that consummation? Sometimes I think that satyr, what's-his-name, was right: better not to have been born, and once born to have done with the whole business as quick as you can.

A bird like a black bolt came flying straight out of the trees and dashed itself with a bang against the window-pane.

Something jogged my memory then, the bird, perhaps, or

the look of those trees, or that strange, misty light in the glass: once, when I was sick, they had moved me here from my own room, I cannot think why – for the view, maybe, or the elevation, I don't know. I saw again the bed at the window, the tall, fluted half-columns of the curtains rising above me, the tops of the autumnal trees outside, and the child that I was then, lying quietly with bandaged throat, grey-browed and wan, my hands resting on the turned-down sheet, like a miniature warrior on his tomb. How strangely pleasurable were the illnesses of those days. Afloat there in febrile languor, with aching eyes and leaden limbs and the blood booming in my ears, I used to dream myself into sky-bound worlds where metallic birds soared aloft on shining loops of wire and great clouded glass shapes sailed ringingly through the cool, pellucid air. Perhaps this is how children die; perhaps still pining somehow for that oblivion out of which they have so lately come they just forget themselves and quietly float away.

A faint reflection moved on the glass before me and I turned to find my son standing in the doorway, watching me with a placid and enquiring smile. I thought, *I met Death upon the road.* I sat down on the window-sill. I felt feeble suddenly.

'Van!' I said and laughed breathlessly. 'How you've grown!'

Did he know me, I wonder? He must be seventeen now, or eighteen – in my confusion I could not remember his birthday, or even what month it falls in. I had not seen him for ten years. Would it upset him to come upon me suddenly here like this? Who knows what upsets him. Maybe nothing does, maybe he is perfectly at peace, locked away inside himself. I picture a far, white country, everything blurred and flat under a bleached sky, and, off on the horizon, a bird, perhaps, tiny as a toy in all that distance, flying steadily away. But how huge he was! – I could do nothing at first except sit leaning forward with my hands on my knees, gaping at him. He was a good half head taller than I, with a barrel chest and enormous shoulders and a great, broad brow, incongruously noble, like that of a prehistoric stone statue standing at an angle on a hillside above the shore of some remote, forgotten island. The blond curls that I remembered had grown thick and had turned a rusty shade of red; that is from me. He had his mother's dark colouring, though, and her dark, solemn eyes. His gaze, even at its steadiest, kept pulling away distractedly to one side, which created a curious, flickering effect, as if within that giant frame a smaller, frailer version of him, the one that I remembered, were minutely atremble. In my imagination I got up out of myself, like a swimmer clambering out of water, and took a staggering step towards him, my arms outstretched, and pressed him to my breast and sobbed. Poor boy, my poor boy. This is awful. In reality I am still sitting on the window-sill, with my hands with their whitened knuckles clamped on my knees, looking up at him and inanely, helplessly smiling; I never was one for embraces. He made a noise deep in his throat that might have been a chuckle and walked forward with a sort of teetering and unexpectedly light, almost dancing step, and peered at the stunned blackbird perched outside on the sill, glazed and motionless and all puffed up around its puzzlement and pain. It kept heaving shuddery little sighs and slowly blinking. There was blood on its beak. What a shock the poor thing must have had when what looked like shining air turned suddenly to solid glass and the world snapped shut. Is that how it is for my boy all the time, a sort of helpless blundering against darkly gleaming, impenetrable surfaces? He pointed to the bird and glanced at me almost shyly and did that chuckle again. He had a musty, faintly sweet smell that made me think of wheelchairs and those old-fashioned, cloth-padded wooden crutches. He was always fascinated by birds. I remembered, years ago, when he was a child, walking with him one blustery autumn day through the grounds of a great house we had paid a shilling to see. There was a peacock somewhere, we could hear its uncanny, desolate cry above the box hedges and the ornamental lawns. Van was beside himself and kept running agitatedly back and forth with his head lifted in that peculiar, angled way that he had when he was excited, looking to see what could be making such extravagant sounds. But we never did find the peacock, and now the day came back to me weighted with that little absence, that missed, marvellous bird, and I felt the pang of it, distant and piercing, like the bird's cry itself.

'Are you all right?' I said to him. That curious, dense light was in the trees and pressing like gauze against the window-panes. 'Are you happy?'

What else could I say? His only response was a puzzled, fleeting frown, as if what he had heard was not my voice but only a familiar and yet as always incomprehensible, distant noise, another of the squeaks and chirrups thronging the air of his white world. I have never been able to rid myself of the notion that his condition was my fault, that even before he was born I damaged him somehow with my expectations, that my high hopes made him hang back inside himself until it was too late for him to come out properly and be one with the rest of us. And no matter what I may tell myself, I did have hopes. Of what? Of being saved through him, as if the son by his mere existence might absorb and absolve the sins of the father? Even that grandiloquent name I insisted on hanging around his neck – Vanderveld! for God's sake, after my mother's people – even that was a weight that must have helped to drag him down. When he was still an infant I used to picture us someday in the far future strolling together down a dappled street in the south somewhere, he a grown man and I still miraculously youthful, both of us in white, my hand lightly on his shoulder and him smiling: father and son. But while I had my face turned away, dreaming of that or some other, equally fatuous idyll, the Erl King got him.

Suddenly, as if nothing at all had happened, the blackbird with a sort of clockwork jerk rose up and flexed its wings and flew off swiftly into the cottony white light. Van made a little disappointed mewling noise and pressed his face to the glass, craning to see the last of the bird, and for a second, as he stood with his face turned like that, I saw my mother in him. Dear Jesus, all my ghosts are gathering here.

Things are sort of smeared and splintery after that, as if seen through an iridescent haze of tears. I walked here and there about the house, with Van going along softly behind me with that dancer's dainty tread. I poked about in bedrooms and even looked through drawers and cupboards, but it was no good, I could make no impression. Everything gave before me like smoke. What was I looking for, anyway? Myself still, the dried spoor of my tracks? Not to be found here. I gathered a few bits of clothes together and took down from the top of a wardrobe an old cardboard suitcase to put them in. The clasps snapped up with a noise like pistol shots and I opened the lid and caught a faint smell of something that I almost recognised, some herb or fragrant wood, a pallid sigh out of the past. When I looked over my shoulder Van was gone, leaving no more than a fading shimmer on the air. I saw myself, kneeling on the floor with the case open before me, like a ravisher hunched over his splayed victim, and I stuffed in the last of my shirts and shut the lid and rose and hurried off down the stairs. In the kitchen the back door with its broken pane still stood open; it had a somehow insolent, insinuating look to it, like that of a tough lounging with his elbow against the wall and watching me with amusement and scorn. I went out skulkingly, clutching my suitcase and flushed with an inexplicable shame. I shall never, not ever again, go back there. It is lost to me; all lost. As I emerged from the gap in the hedge I felt myself stepping out of something, as if I had left a part of my life behind me, snagged on the briars like an old coat, and I experienced a spasm of blinding grief; it was so pure, so piercing, that for a moment I mistook it for pleasure; it flooded through me, a scalding serum, and left me feeling almost sanctified, holy sinner.

I was surprised to find Billy still waiting for me. After all I had been through I thought he would be gone, taken by the whirlwind like everything else I seemed to have lost today. Someone was leaning in the window of the van, talking to him, a thin, black-haired man who, seeing me approach, straightened up at once and legged it off around the bend in the road, stepping along hurriedly in a peculiarly comic and somehow ribald way, one arm swinging and the other hand inserted in his jacket pocket and the cuffs of his trousers flapping.

The air in the van was thick with cigarette smoke.

'Who was that?' I said.

Billy shrugged and did not look at me. 'Some fellow,' he said. He threw his fag-end out of the window and started up the engine and we lurched on our way. When we drove around the bend there was no sign of the black-haired man.

'See the family?' Billy asked.

'I told you,' I said, 'I have no family. I had a son once, but he died.'

I THINK OF THAT TRIP SOUTH as a sort of epic journey and I an Odysseus, homeless now, setting out once more, a last time, from Ithaca. The farther we travelled the lighter I felt, the more insubstantial, as if I were steadily throwing out bits of ballast as we went along. The van kept breaking down, and Billy, shaking his head in rueful amusement, would get out and hammer at something under the bonnet while I leaned across and pumped the pedals at his shouted command. It was strange, sitting there in the sudden quiet in the middle of nowhere. The countryside around wore a look of surprise and tight-lipped disapprobation, as if by these unexpected stops we were flouting some general rule of decorum; deep silence stood over the fields and the trees stirred restlessly, rustling their silks in the soft, varnished air. This lovely world, and we the only blot on the landscape. We, or just me? Sometimes I think I can feel the world recoiling from me, as if from the touch of some uncanny, cold and sticky thing. I recall one day when I was a child walking with my mother into a hotel in town, one of those shabby, grand places that are gone now, and halting on the threshold of the lounge as all the people there in the midst of their afternoon tea fell silent suddenly. It was only a coincidence, of course, it just happened that everyone had stopped talking at the same moment, but I was convinced it was because of me this dreadful hush had fallen, that somehow I had infected the air and struck the people dumb, and I stood there hot with shame and terror as stout matrons paused with teapots lifted and rheumy old men looked about them in startlement and blinked, until the next moment the whole thing calmly started up again, and my mother took my hand and gave me an impatient shake, and I trailed dully after her, stumbling in all that noise and light.

An early dusk was falling when we got to Coldharbour, a humped little town clinging to a rocky foreland facing the Atlantic. The houses shone whitely in the failing light and smoke swirled up from chimney-pots, mussel-blue against the paler blue of evening, and beyond the harbour wall the thick sea heaved like a jumble of big, empty iron boxes bobbing and jostling. I seemed to hear melodeon music and smell kippers being smoked. Billy parked outside a large pub that looked like a ranch and we went in for a drink. We sat before a turf fire in a low room with fake rafters and smoked yellow walls and listened to the wireless muttering to itself. Horse-brasses, plastic ivy, an astonished, stuffed fish in a glass case. We were the only customers. The publican was a big, slow man; he stood behind the bar ruminatively polishing a pint glass, frowning vacantly as if he were trying in vain to remember something very important. What did he make of us, I wonder? He seemed a decent sort. (Mind you, there are probably times when even I seem a decent sort.) His daughter, a skinny little thing with a pinched face and bitten fingernails and his eyes, came down from upstairs, still in her green school uniform, and said he was to help her with her sums, her mammy had said so. While he muttered over her jotter, a fat tongue-tip stuck in the corner of his mouth, she leaned against the bar and hummed a tune whiningly and made a great show of not looking in our direction. He showed her the solved sums and spoke to her softly, teasing her, and she kept saying: 'Oh, da!' and sighing, throwing up her eyes and making an El Greco face. We crouched over our grog, Billy and I, and watched them covertly, our noses pressed to the briefly lit window of all we had forfeited, and Billy, prompted I suppose by something in the example of this little familial scene, suddenly launched into a halting confession, keeping his head down and speaking in a stumbling monotone. He had no girl, he said. He had made it all up, the hairdressing salon, the wedding plans, everything. There was no job, either, no iffy brother-in-law in the delivery business; he had been on the dole since he got out. Even the stuff about his Mam was an invention: she had not been at home keeping his dinner hot for him, she was in the hospital, dying of a rotted liver. And now his parole officer would be after him for leaving the city without telling him.

We were silent for a long time, as if listening to the reverberations after an enormous crash, and then I heard myself in a flat voice say:

'Where did you get the gin?'

Hardly what you would call an adequate response, I know, but it was an awkward moment. Billy shrugged.

'Robbed,' he said.

'Ah. I see.'

I was not surprised by all this – I think in my heart I had known all along that the whole thing was a fantasy – and certainly I did not disapprove: after all, why shouldn't he make up a life for himself? I confess, though, that I was cross, not because he had lied to me but, on the contrary, precisely because he had changed his mind and owned up, damn it. Had I asked for honesty? I had not. In my opinion the truth, so-called, is a much overrated quantity. The trouble with it is that it is closed: when you tell the truth, that's the end of it; lies, on the other hand, ramify in all sorts of unexpected directions, complicating things, knotting them up in themselves, thickening the texture of life. Lying makes a dull world more interesting. To lie is to create. Besides, fibs are more fun, and liars, I am convinced, live longer. Yes, yes, I am an enthusiastic advocate of the whopper. But now bloody Billy had developed scruples and what on earth were we to do? From some things there is no going back. We sat and stared solemnly into the fireplace for a while, slumped in another horrible silence, and the publican's daughter went back upstairs and the publican returned to his glasses, and then – oh, my God, it was appalling! – Billy began to cry. In all the years we had spent together in the jug I had never once seen him shed a tear, even on his worst days. And this was not even proper crying, he did not blub or wail, as I would have made sure to do, but just sat there with his head bowed and the water squeezing out of his eyes and his shoulders shaking. The embarrassment of it! – I was thankful the place was deserted. I glanced at the publican but he was carefully looking the other way, his lips pursed, whistling without sound. I cannot imagine what he thought we were or what was happening. I had been sure it was I who would be the one to do the weeping today. I touched Billy's shoulder, less to console, I'm afraid, than as a signal to him that really I thought it was time for him to get a grip on himself, but I snatched away my hand at once, for the feel of that warmly quivering flesh brought back disturbing echoes of old intimacies: behind bars, Eros finds his comforts where he can. I finished my drink and stood up, clearing my throat, and said, still in that toneless voice that I hardly recognised as my own, that I had to go outside for a minute. Billy nodded but did not look up, and I walked away from him almost on tiptoe, a craven Captain Oates, and went through the lavatory and across a yard and came out in a lane at the back of the pub and stood for a little while in the marine darkness with my eyes closed, breathing deep the stink of another dirty little betrayal.

I got my suitcase out of the van and set off in the direction of the harbour. It was black night by now and I had nothing to guide me but the starshine on the cobbles and an occasional, dim streetlamp shivering in the wind. I seemed to be going somewhere. My steps took their own way, down a sloping street and along by the sea wall and on to the pier. A few dim boats reared at anchor out on the jostling water, their mast-ropes tinkling. Have I mentioned My Search For God? Every lifer sooner or later sets out on that quest; I have seen the hardest inmates, fellows who would slit your throat before you could say knife, kneeling meek as toddlers beside their bunks before lights-out, their fingers clasped and eyes shut tight and lips moving in silent communion with the Lord. I am glad to say I managed to hold out for what I consider was a creditably long time. I had never really thought about religion and all that; this world had always been enough of a mystery for me without my needing to invent implausible hereafters (the adjective is redundant, I know). True, I had, and have still, off and on, a hazy sort of half belief in some general force, a supreme malignancy in operation behind the apparent chaos and contingency of the world. There are times, indeed, when I even entertain the notion of a personal deity, a God out of the old books, He that laughs, the *deus ridens*. I remember, when I was a young man and tenderly impressionable, reading in some book of an event in the history of the Xhosa people of the eastern Cape Province. Do you know about the Xhosa? They were a proud and sophisticated race, and great warriors, too, yet unaccountably, for nigh on a hundred years, they had been losing battle after battle against the armies of the white settlers. Again and again they had stormed across the veldt and hurled themselves with perfect confidence against the bullets and the bayonets of these grub-coloured pygmies in their scarlet tunics and were repulsed every time, suffering terrible losses. Then one day in a vision a young girl whose name was Nongqawuse was instructed by the voices of her ancestors to inform her people that they must slaughter all their cattle and give up all forms of agriculture, after which sacrifices the tribe's ancestral dead would return to life, bringing with them great new herds and boundless supplies of corn, to form a ghostly, invincible army that would drive the white man into the sea. The tribal elders conferred and decided that the people must do as they were bidden; even the wise king Sandili (see, I have even remembered the names), who had been sceptical at first, in the end declared himself a believer in the New People. The livestock was slaughtered, the fields were laid waste, and the tribe settled down in confidence to await the day of days, which came and went, of course, without the appearance of a single phantom warrior. Nothing happened. The sun did not stand still in the sky, no great herds came thundering out of the dust, not a grain of corn appeared in the emptied bins. In that year of 1857 alone seventy thousand of the Xhosa died of starvation. Clearly I remember letting the book fall from my hand and staring before me with the mad light of the convert shining for a moment in my eyes and thinking yes, yes, there must be a God, if such things can happen! And I pictured Him, a rascally old boy with a tangled yellow beard and a drinker's nose, reclining on a woolly cloud with his chin on his fist and chuckling to himself as that proud people walked out in solemn ritual into the fields and butchered their cattle and burned their crops. Probably by the time the famine came He had lost interest, had turned his attention somewhere else entirely, leaving the Xhosa to die alone, huddled and speechless, on the parched savannah. In time, of course, I lapsed from my faith in this prankster God, preferring to believe in the Great Nothing instead, which when you think about it is itself a kind of force. However, the moment came one impossible night in prison when I felt so far from everything, so lost in fear and anguish, that I found myself reaching out, like an abandoned baby reaching out its arms beseechingly from the cold cot, for someone or something to comfort me, to save me from these horrors. There was no one there, of course, or not for me, anyway. It was like coming to in the dark on the battlefield amid the cries and the flying cannon-smoke and feeling around for a limb that had been shot off. I had never known a blackness so vast and deep as that which my groping soul encountered that night. Almost as bad as the emptiness, though, was the fact of the need itself, that bleeding stump I could not bring myself to touch. And now as I stood on the pier, whirled about by the night wind, I felt pressing down on me the weight of another vast darkness and another unassuageable need, for what, I could not say precisely. I looked back at the town; how far off it seemed, how distant its little lights, as if I had already embarked and my voyage were under way. It came to me that I had reached the end of something, that this long day drawing to a close was the last of its kind I would know. What next, then? The voices spoke to me out of the wind, the dead voices. I stood above the black, heaving water and imagined how it would be, the blundering leap and then the plunge and the sudden, bulging silence as I sank. And in the morning they would find my suitcase standing on the pier, unique and incongruous, a comic prefigurement of my tombstone. Strange: I never seriously considered doing away with myself, even in prison, where regularly fellows were found strung up by ropes of knotted bedsheets from the waterpipes in their cells. But what did I have to lose now, that I had not lost already, except life itself, and what was that worth, to me? Cowardice, of course, plain funk, that was a stalwart that could be counted on to keep me dragging along, but there are times when even cowardice must and does give way to stronger, irresistible forces. Yet I knew I would not do it; not even for a moment did I think I might. Was it that in a way I was already dead, or was I waiting for some new access of life and hope? Life! Hope! And yet it must have been something like that that kept me going. Unfinished business, a debt not paid – yes, that too, of course, of course, we know all about that. But beyond even that there was something more, I did not know what. I felt that whatever it was – is! – it must be simple but so immense I cannot see it, as immense as air: that secret everyone is in on, except me. When I look back all seems inevitable, as if under everything there really were a secret structure, held immovably in place by an unknown and unknowable force. Every tiniest action I ever took was a grain of sand in the flow of things tapering towards that moment when I let go of myself, when with a great *Tarraa*! I flung open the door of the cage and let the beast come bounding out. Now I am condemned to sit here in my filthy straw and sift through the bones of it all over again. Eternal recurrence! That is what I realised that night, standing in the blackness at the end of the pier above the roiling, seductive sea: there was to be no end of it, for me; my term was just beginning. But what I was sentenced to this time was freedom. Freedom! What a thought! The very word gave me the shivers. Freedom, formless and ungraspable, yes, that was the true nature of my sentence. For ten terrible years I had yearned to be free, I had eaten, slept, drunk the thought of it, lay in my bunk at night, heart racing and eyes popping, panting like a decrepit masturbator towards that fantastic moment when the gates would swing open and I would be released, and now it had arrived and I was appalled at the prospect. I am free, I told myself, but what does it signify? This objectless liberty is a burden to me. Forget the past, then, give up all hope of retrieving my lost selves, just let it go, just let it all fall away? And then be something new, a sticky, staggering thing with myriad-faceted eyes and wet wings, an astonishment standing up in the world, straining drunkenly for flight. Was that it, that I must imagine myself into existence before tackling the harder task of conjuring another? I closed my eyes. My poor brain throbbed. I did not know what to do, whether to go on or go back or just stay here, somehow, forever. Presently I turned and retraced my steps to the town, ploddingly, confused as always, lost, and alone.

Statues. I am thinking of statues. I have always found something uncanny about these sudden, frozen figures, the way they stand so still among moving leaves, or off at the end of an avenue, watching something that is not us, that is beyond us, some endless, transfixing spectacle only they can see. Time for them moves as slow as mountains. I am remembering, for instance, that great photographer old Père Atget's matutinal studies at Versailles and St Cloud of rain-stained Venuses and laughing fauns, Vertumnus removing his winter mask, that rapt Diana with her bow starting out of the shrubbery into the sunlight beside the motionless pond; how vivid and rounded his lens makes them seem, how immanent with intent, these bleached, impetuous creatures poised as if to leap down from their plinths and stride away, trailing storms of dust behind them. Diderot developed a theory of ethics based on the idea of the statue: if we would be good, he said, we must become sculptors of the self. Virtue is not natural to us; we achieve it, if at all, through a kind of artistic striving, cutting and shaping the material of which we are made, the intransigent stone of selfhood, and erecting an idealised effigy of ourselves in our own minds and in the minds of those around us and living as best we can according to its sublime example. I like this notion. There is something grand and tragic in it, and something of essential gaiety, too. Diderot himself had great reverence for statues; he thought of them as living, somehow: strange, solitary beings, exemplary, aloof, closed on themselves and at the same time yearning in their mute and helpless way to step down into our world, to laugh or weep, know happiness and pain, to be mortal, like us. *Such beautiful statues*, he wrote in a letter to his mistress Sophie Volland, *hidden in the remotest spots and distant from one another, statues which call to me, that I seek out or that I encounter, that arrest me and with which I have long conversations* . . . I like to picture him, that cheerful *philosophe*, at St Cloud or Marly or the great park at Sceaux, talking to the cherubs on a carved vase or lecturing a stone Pygmalion on the hegemony of the senses.

What statue of myself did I erect long ago, I wonder? Must have been a gargoyle.

Here's a story. Chap I knew in Spain once, in a previous life, painter, not very good, got a commission to do a portrait of a local bigwig in the village where we were both scraping a living at the time. My pal would go to the old boy's house in the mornings and work on the canvas for an hour or so while it was still cool; he had not much Spanish and anyway in those parts they spoke an incomprehensible dialect, so conversation was at a minimum. For a long time the work did not go well. It was very hard to fix a likeness. The mayor, I think he was the mayor, an ugly old peasant with enormous hands and a simian brow, would sit very stiffly in his best blue suit in a white room staring fixedly before him with a hunted look, as if, said my friend, he were at the oncologist's waiting to hear the worst. Some subjects, my friend explained, simply do not look like themselves; shyness, embarrassment, self-consciousness, something compels them to put on a mask and hide behind it; they will look like their mothers, their siblings, complete strangers, even, but not themselves. With such sitters the painter must coast along, biding his time, waiting for them to relax and forget themselves for long enough to be themselves. The mayor was such a one. He just sat there like a stuffed barbary ape, blank, featureless, folded up in himself. Until one morning my friend arrived and found him transformed; he was no more animated than at other times, but suddenly at last his face was open, the mask cast aside, his character – violent, rapacious, fearful, melancholy – legible in every wrinkle and mole and ill-shaved whisker. Well, the portrait was finished within the hour – and damned good it was, too, according to my friend – yet still the mayor sat there, gazing before him with a pensive and faintly puzzled look. You know of course what had happened, you saw it coming, didn't you: the old man was dead, had died calmly of a stroke a few minutes before the painter arrived. You see, you see what I mean? To thine own self be true, they tell you; well, I allowed myself that luxury just once and look what happened. No, no, give me the mask any day, I'll settle for inauthenticity and bad faith, those things that only corrode the self and leave the world at large unmolested.

I am reading Diderot on actors and acting, too. He knew how much of life is a part that we play. He conceived of living as a form of necessary hypocrisy, each man acting out his part, posing as himself. It is true. What have I ever been but an actor, even if a bad one, too much involved in my role, not detached enough, not sufficiently cold. Yes, yes, it's so. You think me cold? I am not. Harsh, perhaps, uncaring of the proprieties, too apt to make poor jokes, but not cold, no. Quite the opposite, in fact, hot and sweating in my doublet and hose, trying not to see the upturned faces beyond the footlights, the eyes greedy for disaster fixed on me as I stumble among my fellow players, stammering out my implausible lines and corpsing at all the big moments. This is why I have never learned to live properly among others. People find me strange. Well, I find myself strange. I am not convincing, somehow, even to myself. *The man who wishes to move the crowd must be an actor who impersonates himself*. Is that it, is that really it? Have I cracked it? And there I was all that time thinking it was *others* I must imagine into life. Well well. (To act is to be, to rehearse is to become: Felix *dixit*, or someone like him.) This has the feel of a great discovery. I'm sure it must be a delusion.

Do you notice how the gull's cry echoes through these pages, sounding its note of hunger and harsh beseeching? It is my emblem; my watermark. Next morning it was everywhere around me, a disembodied keening in the calm, white air. The wind had died and there was a kind of luminous, faint fog. I walked along the pier again, carrying my suitcase, but in daylight now, the scene a developed print of last night's heartsick negative. The boat was a blunt vessel with a rusted chimney and a limp flag dangling in the cordage. When I arrived it was already loaded up with a cargo of tomatoes and potato crisps and bales of toilet paper and mysterious, complicated machine parts, all gleamingly, implausibly new. The skipper, a big-bellied man with a red face, stood in the wheelhouse and yawned. (If I were a visitor from another planet – but then, am I not a visitor from another planet? – I think that of all the earthlings' quirks it is the act of pandiculation that would surprise and fascinate me most, that slow stretch and then the soundless ape-howl, in which they indulge themselves with such languorous relish.) There was a boy also, a nimble, bow-legged fellow with red hair and buck-teeth; he did all the work, scurrying about the deck and cursing violently to himself while Bulkington in the wheelhouse watched him with amusement and a kind of fond contempt, taking a quick nip now and then from a secret bottle stowed under a shelf behind the wheel. I seemed to be the only passenger. As soon as the cargo was loaded we got under way. I always feel a childish surge of excitement when the last mooring rope is cast off and the boat backs away shudderingly from the dock. We swerved into the middle of the harbour and swung about smartly and headed out past the lighthouse into the open sea. I stood in the bow and watched Coldharbour turn into a miniature of itself, complete with smoking chimneys and bristling masts and tiny figures moving on the quayside. I spotted Billy's van, still parked outside the pub. Probably he had slept in it last night, huddled on the back seat with that wobbly spring sticking up and his knees in his chest. I, of course, had passed the hours of darkness in my accustomed fashion, hanging upside down under the tavern eaves wrapped in my leathern wings.

The morning was extraordinarily still under a sky of pure pearl. The coast dwindled behind us; when I looked out from the prow we might have been a thousand leagues from land. The sea stretched away empty save for a white ship far off on the high horizon, unmoving, it seemed, impossibly tall and lit somehow from below, a glimmering, ghostly vessel. I like the sea; I am afraid of it, but all the same I like it, its strangeness, its indifferent thereness; in all that space I can forget for a while who and what I am. A pair of dolphins broke the surface and swam with us, criss-crossing our bows and gambolling in the wash, seeming emblematic of something, and now and then long-necked brown birds appeared out of nowhere, singly, flying low and straight at great speed above the water. The skipper kept to the wheelhouse and the boy sat on the deck with a transistor radio pressed to his ear, dead-eyed and rhythmically twitching. Soon the sky cleared and a delicate wind sprang up and the water turned to splintered sapphire. I lay and drowsed on a pile of tarpaulins, lapped about by sea-sounds and cool zephyrs. I slept briefly and dreamed that I was back in prison and could not understand why the floor of my cell was swaying; then a warder wearing a seaman's cap at a jaunty angle came and told me not to worry, that I would soon be let out, and laughed extravagantly, pointing a finger at me through the bars.

I woke with a start and struggled groggily to my feet, rubbing my eyes. It was as though I had fallen asleep in one world and woken up in another. The air seemed brisker, the sky bluer. The boat fairly skimmed along, tensed in every timber, eager and light, as if at any moment it might take to the air in a great, groaning leap. I felt light-headed; when I looked out to the horizon it seemed it was not the boat but rather the sea itself that was swaying. Despite the early hour I brought out the gin bottle and took a steely swallow straight from the neck and walked to the bow-rail and stood and watched our wake unfurling behind us. Cloud-shadows, whale-blue and swift, skimmed the glittering surface of the sea. Have I said all this already? Suddenly there came to me the memory of a day when I was a boy and I cycled across country to the coast with my friend Horse. My friend; I had not many such, and those that I had did not last long, and nor did Horse. But that day our friendship was still at the tremulous, solemn stage that I sometimes think is all I have ever known of what they seem to mean when they chatter about love. We left our bikes hidden in a ditch and made our way through a little, dense dark wood and came out on the river estuary and found moored in the shallows among the reeds the punt that Horse's father kept there for duck shooting. A keen hunter, Horse's father, I remember him, a big, slow-moving, smooth-faced man, which Horse in his turn must be by now, I imagine. Horse undid the mooring rope and pushed us out of the reeds with a negligent deftness that filled me with envy and made me feel proud to be his pal. How lightly, with hardly a sound, the white punt glided over the water, seeming barely to touch the swiftly running surface. Horse stood above me in the bow and plied the scull, his eye fixed on a far horizon. We saw not a soul; we might have been alone in the world. For a mile or two we went along close to the river bank and then all at once sky and sea opened before us and we crossed a broad reach and came in sight of a long, low, khaki-coloured shore. I can see it, I can see it all, as clear as day, the white punt and that sunlit shoreline and the two of us there, Horse and me. It must have been a place where the river waters met the open sea, or perhaps it was something to do with the currents, or the tide was turning – I do not understand these things – but for a minute we were halted and held motionless on the unmoving water in the midst of a golden calm. The burnished surface of the sea was high and heavy and smooth as metal, and a small, repeated wave gambolled like an otter along the margin of the shore. The sun was hot. Nothing happened. We just stayed there for that minute, poised between sea and sky, suspended somehow as if in air, no, not air, but some other, unearthly element, and it seemed to me I had never known such happiness, and never would again, though happiness is not the word, not the word at all. That is where I would like to live, on some forgotten strip of sandy shore, with my back to the land, facing out into the limitless ocean. That would be freedom, watching in solitude the days pass, marking the seasons, observing the spring tides and the autumn auroras, weathering the summer sun and the storms of winter. Pure existence, pure existence and nothing else.

Now, a grown-up, so-called, I stood there in the bows, for how long I do not know, watching the white waters purling behind us and the little clouds flying overhead, and then all at once I heard that soft, roaring noise coming to us across the water and I turned, startled, and there it was, the island, looming up in front of us, with sheep-strewn hill and tiny trees and the narrow road winding away, as if it had been conjured up that moment out of sea and clouds. We chugged into the deserted harbour past jagged, chocolate-coloured rocks such as the Italian masters liked to set at the backs of their madonnas. Red-headed Pip had put aside his radio and was furiously at work again with ropes and winches while the skipper in the wheelhouse, his bottle empty, plied the wheel with ample and unsteady grapplings. I took another drink of gin and looked about me brightly at the harbour and the hill as they disposed themselves glidingly like well-oiled stage machinery around our smooth advance.

We docked. Everything went quiet suddenly. The skipper came out of the wheelhouse and spat over the side. The boy was already on the pier, winding a rope around a bollard. When I stepped up after him on to dry land the world went on moving under my feet. Hyperborean Apollo, I prayed, make haste to help me! Mr Tighe's van came bumping along the pier and drew to a shuddering halt at the dockside where the boy was unloading the cargo from the deck. How vivid and gay everything seemed to my gin-tinted gaze, the acid-green hill and the opalescent water shimmering under a lemon light. I set off up the hill and presently Mr Tighe in his laden van drew level with me and offered me a lift which I declined, making large gestures of thanks. He nodded in friendly fashion and drove on, the van farting petrol-blue billows of exhaust smoke. Shall we describe him now? I think not. Mr Tighe, and that old dog that comes and goes, and the horse I am supposed to have heard but never saw: holes in the backdrop, through which the bare sky twinkles. When I looked back from the last bend of the road the boat was already under way again, veering out past the jetty like an offer of reprieve being unceremoniously withdrawn. What had I done, coming to this far-flung place? Yet how light I felt, how fleet, as if I were aloft on wings! I went on and soon spotted the house, perched in its solitude under the oak ridge. The hawthorn was in blossom. Here is the little bridge. Wind, shine, clouds, the unwarranted yet irrepressible expectancies of the heart. I am arrived.

I MUST HAVE LOOKED like something out of a Bible story, toiling up that stony track in my soiled suit with my cardboard suitcase in my hand and my collar turned up against the wind. I should have been on my knees, of course, or, better still, barefoot, with staff and falcon, like the penitent pilgrim I was pretending to be. I could still feel the sway of the sea, and of that other sea of gin sloshing around inside me, and the ground kept rearing up under my feet in the most alarming way, like a carpet with the wind under it; I stumbled more than once, making the stones fly and getting grit in my shoes. I could hear myself breathing. I always know I am drunk when I can hear myself breathing; it sounded as if I were carrying a large, fat, winded man on my back. At the gate I paused to gather my wits but that only made my head spin; I set off again sternly, marching up the path to the front door like a wooden man, snorting and muttering, with my head thrown back and swinging my free arm. I rapped the knocker smartly and turned and surveyed the scene before me, chest out and nostrils flared, snuffing up the air.

I had to knock a second and then a third time before Licht came at last. He opened the door a crack and stuck out his little face and peered crossly past my shoulder, the tip of his sharp little nose twitching. I told him my name and he pursed his lips and sniffed.

'Oh, it's you, is it,' he said. I thought he might shut the door on me, but after a moment of sullen indecision he stood aside grudgingly and motioned me in. 'I'm Licht. The Professor said you were coming.'

He sniffed again.

The hallway was high and hung with shadows. I experienced a mysterious shock of recognition: it was as if I had stepped inside myself, into the shadowed vault of my own skull.

'He's working,' Licht said truculently. 'There's a room ready for you.' That seemed to amuse him.

He shut the door, fussing with the lock. I stood breathing; I could feel a horrible, tipsy leer slipping and sliding uncontrollably about my face. I seemed to be floating in some heavy, sluggish substance, a Dead Sea of the mind. I had a sense of vague, violent hilarity, and there was an inner roll and lurch as if something inside me had come loose and was yawing wildly from side to side. Licht still would not look directly at me but eyed vexedly a patch of the floor between us with his mouth pursed and a hand twitching in his pocket and one leg jigging. Never still, never still. I did not know what to say to him. At bottom I am a shy soul – yes, yes, I am, really. My kind always are. When I hear on the wireless a report of some grimy little atrocity – the bloodstained body discovered in the wood, the pensioner beaten to death in his bed, the mother-in-law dismembered and packed in a trunk and sent off on the night mail to Dundee – I think at once not of the victim, as I know I should, but of the other one, the poor, shivering, dandruffy, whey-faced fellow in his sleeveless pullover and cheap shoes, with his shaking hands and haunted eyes, caught there, frozen in the spotlight, realising with a falling sensation in the pit of his stomach that he will never again have a moment's privacy, never a second he can call his own, that they will poke at him and probe him and ask endless questions and then put him in the dock to be gawped at and then send him for life – life! – to that panopticon where he will not even be able to void his bowels without an audience looking on. This is how you lose yourself, this is how they wrench you out of what you thought you were and hang you up by the hair and invite the world to gather round and point and laugh and take a shy at you for free. And all the time of course you know you deserve it, deserve it all, and more.

'You look awful,' Licht said with satisfaction and grinned uncontrollably and bit his lip. 'Were you seasick?'

'No, no,' I said. 'Just a little, just a little . . . tired.'

I tramped behind him up the stairs. The upper flights grew progressively narrower and our footsteps thudded ringingly on the uncarpeted boards. My room was cramped and low, with peeling wallpaper and a tilted floor. I could see why Licht had been amused. There was a rush-bottomed chair – a relic of St Vincent – and a pine dressing-table and a coffin-sized wardrobe. On the floor beside the bed there was a worn, blue and grey rug. (How many more such cells must I invent?) One of the panes in the little window was broken and someone had mended it by wedging a bit of cardboard in the hole. Pigeons had got in, there were droppings on the sill and down the wall, hardened to a whitish stuff, like coral. The window framed a three-quarters view of indistinct greenery and the corner of a sloped field. I put my suitcase on the bed and looked about me. There was a steady, pulsing hum in my head as if a delicately balanced pinion spinning in there had developed a wobble.

Licht hovered on the threshold with a hand on the doorknob, frowning hard at the wardrobe.

'So,' he said, 'you're another expert, are you?'

'An expert?' I said blearily.

'On art.' His lip curled on the word.

'Oh no,' I said, 'no, not at all.'

'Good,' he said. 'One is enough.'

We stood a moment saying nothing, each thinking his own thoughts. I felt a weight in my jacket pocket and brought out the half-empty gin bottle. We both looked at it dully.

'How is the Professor?' I said.

He glanced at me sharply.

'He's all right,' he said. 'Why?' I had no answer to that. He looked away from me again and nibbled the nail of his little finger. 'So you were in jail,' he said and tittered, and then quickly recomposed his sullen glare. 'What was it like?'

'Like hell,' I said. 'Very warm and crowded.'

He nodded, thinking, still chewing his fingernail. We might have been talking about the weather.

'I wouldn't like that,' he said, 'jail.'

'No,' I said.

He slid a rapid glance across the floor and let it settle somewhere near my feet.

'Bad, was it, yes?'

I said nothing. Still he waited, eyes aglitter with eager malice, hoping for the worst, I suppose, for some tearful cry or terrible, blurted confession. The wind in the chimneys, the gulls, all that: the strangeness of things. The strangeness of being here – of being anywhere.

'When did you get out?' he asked.

'Yesterday,' I said, and thought: Yesterday!

Licht nodded.

'I'll tell Professor Kreutznaer you're here,' he said. 'We have our tea at five o'clock.'

He tarried a moment more, then muttered something under his breath and abruptly withdrew, shutting the door behind him with a soft bang.

I sat down on the side of the bed with my hands on my knees, gazing at the floor between my feet and sighing the while, in a kind of weary and not wholly unpleasant dejection. Thus the prodigal son must have felt – shaky, dazed, a little hollow – as the haunch of veal was wheeled in and the infuriate brother slunk away gnawing his knuckles.

Professor Kreutznaer did not fall upon my neck. The first thing that struck me about him was how plausible he appeared, how authentic, at least when looked at from a decent distance; compared to him I seemed to myself a thing of rags and smoke, flapping helplessly this way and that at the mercy of every passing breeze. I had met him once before, many years ago, in a golden world now gone. He had hardly changed at all; I do not imagine he has ever been much different from what he is now. I see receding versions of him – young man, boy, babe in arms – all nestling inside each other, each one smaller than the next and yet all the same, with the same big bloodless head and filmy stare and that same air of standing somehow sideways to the world. He is calm, remote, taciturn, possessed of a faintly shabby imperium; he is, or was, at least, a legend in the world of art, foremost authority on Vaublin, frequent guest at I Tatti in the great days, co-author with the late Keeper of the Queen's Pictures of that controversial monograph on Poussin, consultant for the great galleries of the world and valued adviser to private collectors on however many continents there are. It used to be said that a Thyssen or a Helmut Behrens would not lift a finger in the auction room without first consulting Kreutznaer. Yet when Licht ushered me at last into his presence and left me there, the thing I felt most strongly was the urge to laugh. Yes, laugh, as I want to laugh for instance in the concert hall when the orchestra trundles to a stop and the virtuoso at his piano, hunched like a demented vet before the bared teeth of this enormous black beast of sound, lifts up deliquescent hands and prepares to plunge into the cadenza. I was immediately ashamed of myself, of course, convinced this tickle of raucous glee must be the self-protective reflex of the second-rater before the spectacle of excellence, the guffaw of the half-educated in the presence of the scholar. I thought of a monkey leaping among the palms, pointing and shrieking and hilariously hurling excrement as the famous naturalist in his baggy shorts comes tramping down the jungle track on the heels of his burdened bearers, his nose buried in his field-notes. It has always been thus with me. Even in what I like to think of now as the renaissance period of my life, when my interests were catholic and everything was a matter of perspective, I always worried that I would burst into shrieks of laughter in the face of this or that grand savant and so show myself up for the hopelessly shallow creature that I am. But then sometimes too I comfort myself with the thought that, as someone or other has rightly pointed out, shallowness has no bottom. Is it any wonder I went to the bad?

So there we are in the turret room, with the transparent sky of morning all around us, he seated in his sea-captain's chair and I standing meekly before him, exchanging solemnities with him and trying to keep a straight face while with protruding lower lip he read over yet again my letter of introduction from the administrator of the Behrens Collection. I was still three-quarters drunk, but the hot, brassy taste of gathering sobriety was in my mouth and I could hear in the distance the dull tom-tom beat of an approaching headache. It was like being up before the beak – and I should know, after all. Presently, however, and most unexpectedly, another sensation came over me, a sort of burning flush, which it took me a moment to identify. It was shame. I mean the real thing, the sear, the scald, the pure, fat, fiery stuff itself: shame. Do you know what it is to feel like that, to cringe and writhe inside yourself as if your flesh were on fire? It is not given to every man to know without the shadow of a doubt that he is a scoundrel. (It takes more courage than you think to name yourself as you should be named. You do not know what it costs to bring yourself to that pass, I can tell you.) I wanted to abase myself before him, to cast myself down at his feet with cries and imprecations, drumming my fists and weeping, or wrap my arms around his knees and cry my sins aloud and beg forgiveness. Oh, I was in a transport. In the end, however, I only put my head back and snuffled up a deep breath, like a diver surfacing, and brought out with a certain ceremonial air the fact of our previous meeting, as if it were the broken half of the precious amulet that would identify me as the long-lost son of the palace, despite my rags and sores. He stiffened, I thought, and rolled his soft-boiled eyes at me suspiciously.

'We met?' he said. 'Where was that?'

'At Whitewater,' I said. 'Oh, twenty years ago. We were house-guests there one weekend. We walked together in the gallery, I remember; you spoke of Vaublin.'

Talk about another life! The windows of the great house filled with greenish summer light and the pictures on the walls like high doorways opening on to other, luminously peopled worlds. The Professor wore black that day, too; for all I know it may have been the same outfit as the one he was wearing now, the same rusty velvet jacket and tubular trousers and boots so old the uppers looked as if they were made of crêpe paper. He had reminded me, I remember, with his big body and little legs and great, round, suet-coloured head, of one of the mighty Germans, Hegel, perhaps, someone like that, someone solemn and ponderous and faintly, unconsciously ridiculous. It struck me how he managed to be both abstracted and sharply watchful. What did we talk about as we paced the polished timbers of that long, high gallery, stepping through blocks of sunlight streaming in the immense windows? I can't remember, though I can see us there, clear as anything. The Professor, however, was firmly sceptical.

'No no,' he said brusquely, 'you have mistaken me for someone else.'

I persisted gently, determined to establish my connection, however tenuous, with the great days of Whitewater when Helmut Behrens was still alive and I had not yet forfeited my place in the realm of light. I should have married his daughter, I would be master there now, would even have a Vaublin of my very own. Whitewater! I think of permed girls in old-fashioned tennis shoes and pleated skirts and slacks – remember slacks? – and the grass green as it only can be in memory, and gin-and-tonics on the terrace and everyone smoking, and all day long that general air of idleness shot through with languid lusts. When I conjure up those days I feel like old Adam pausing in anguish in the midst of the stony fields, mattock in hand, pierced by paradisal visions of a past now hardly to be believed in. The more I insisted, the more firmly the Professor denied we had ever met; a sort of tussle resulted, elaborately polite, of course, I pushing and he pulling, our teeth gritted. It was all very awkward and in the end embarrassing. We fell into a rueful silence and looked out of the windows for a while, he fiddling with things on his desk and I standing behind him with my hands plunged in the pockets of my jacket; we must have looked like something out of one of Munch's more melancholic studies. A sea-fret had blurred the far dunes and clouds the colour of wood-smoke were piling up from the horizon, and as we watched, two thick, butter-coloured pillars of sunlight stepped slowly over the far, unmoving waves; sometimes even Dame Nature overdoes her effects. The Professor cleared his throat, huffing and frowning. He dropped Anna Behrens's letter on the desk and sat brooding, palping his lower lip with a thumb and forefinger.

'A very great collection,' he said.

'Yes, wonderful, wonderful,' I said, with what I suppose

must have seemed a horribly suggestive, pushy coyness. 'There is that Vaublin, for instance.'

He shot me a rapid, sideways glance and cleared his throat. What had I said? His chair gave a stifled cry of protest under him as he rose. He walked heavily to the window and stood looking out, hunched and motionless, his fat, bloodless little hands clasped tight behind his back, the two stubby thumbs busily circling each other. Whenever I think of him this is how I see him, in the act of turning away from me like this, in the furtive way that he has, with one fat shoulder lifted and that great, round head bowed, like a man anticipating a hail of brickbats. Outside, rain fell glittering through sunlight.

'Miss Behrens speaks highly of you,' he said, and directed at me over his shoulder a sort of fishy rictus.

'She's very kind,' I said. 'We have known each other a long time.'

'Ah.' He sniffed.

'I would like to have seen *Le monde d'or*,' I said. 'It is the centrepiece of the collection, as you know.' A definite plumminess was creeping into my tone; I was beginning to sound like the suave cat-burglar in the old movies – where was my silver cigarette case, my patent-leather pumps, my cummerbund? The Professor sniffed again, louder than before. 'Of course,' I said, 'I would not go to Whitewater now. It would hardly be . . .' I could not think of the word; the language is not commodious enough to encompass the notion of a return by me to – well, yes, to the scene of the crime. 'I can't go home either,' I said and essayed a light, melancholy laugh. 'I have burnt my boats, I'm afraid.'

He did not seem to be listening, standing motionless at the window with his back firmly set against me. At length he turned, frowning abstractedly at the floor between us.

'There is a lot to be done,' he said. 'Papers, notes . . .' He waved a hand over the disorder on his desk. 'Secretarial work, really. Licht does what he can, but of course . . .' He shrugged.

'Then I can stay?' I said.

It came out like a whoop. He flinched, as if he had been pounced upon by something large and heavy.

'Yes,' he said, shrugging his shoulders again, trying to extricate himself from the woolly embrace of my enthusiasm, 'yes, I suppose you . . . I suppose . . .'

I thanked him. There was a catch in my voice, thick as it was with the pent of unshed tears; had I let them flow they would have come out forty per cent proof. Feeling the unabating waft of my gratitude he blinked and gave me one of his consternated, slow stares and turned away from me again uneasily. You must understand, this was a fraught moment for me, the commencement of my return from the wilderness into the place of humankind. I had come prepared to throw myself at his feet and here I was, still standing. Conceive of my joy, spiced though it was, I confess, with the actor's secret triumph at having moved the house to tears (I have said it before, I shall say it again, the stage has lost a star in me). I went down the stairs and locked myself in the lavatory on the landing and sat on the bowl and gazed at the space between my knees, swaying a little and humming to myself, lost in a euphoric, unfocused introspection. I brought out my broad-shouldered comforter and took another good stiff nip of gin. My nose was running. Here I was, hardly a day out of prison and already a hand had come down from the clouds to haul me up to celestial heights. Why then, behind the euphoria, did I have the impression that something was being palmed off on me? Was there, I asked myself, a trace of dirt under the fingernails of that helping hand? Oh, not the greasy black stuff flecked with blood and hair that is lodged immovably under my splintered nails, but just the ordinary grime, the stuff that humans naturally accumulate as they claw their way through this filthy world. Would the Professor draw me up out of myself, or was I to help him to descend?

*

Thus I had alighted at last in what I suppose I may as well call my destination. I had a feeling of weightlessness, a floating sensation, which I recognised; I always feel like this when I first come to a new place, as if something of me were lagging behind the physical arrival, some part of myself hanging back, out on the ocean, or in the air, dazed by speed and change. Thus the angel when he came to Mary must have felt, trembling on one knee with his wings still spread in this other, denser azure, stammering out his amazing message. But what annunciation did I bring, what grotesque incarnation did I herald? What word? What flesh?

We ate our tea in the kitchen, the Professor frowning at his plate and Licht eyeing me narrowly and saying things under his breath. I felt like the interloper that I was. Interloper: what an apt word: as if I had run up quietly and pressed myself between them. I had an awkward sense of myself caught up in a sort of antique dance, smiling and wincing and mouthing excuse-me's as together they trod out the measures of their ancient minuet, their eyes fixed on something elsewhere and their feet dragging leadenly.

Licht could not contain himself.

'Why don't we open a hostel?' he said at last, loudly, his voice shaking.

The room cringed. The Professor put on a bland expression and did not lift his eyes, and Licht, white-faced and furious, glared across the table at his inclined, broad bald pate. 'Why not turn the place into a doss-house?' he cried. 'We could take in every tinker and drunkard that happens to be passing by.'

A long and weighty silence followed. Licht sat and stared before him with livid fixity, his knife and fork clutched in his fists and his knuckles white and one leg going like a sewing-machine under the table, making the cruets rattle.

'How was the crossing?' the Professor enquired of me at last, in a resonantly courteous tone.

The effects of the gin were wearing off and the faint buzzing of a hangover had started up. My eyes felt as if they had been toasted and my breath came out in furnace blasts.

'There's the extra work,' Licht shouted. 'There's the cooking, for instance. Am I expected to do all that? – because I won't.' He beat a fist softly on the table; there were tears in his eyes, big, shining drops brimming on the lids. 'You never tell me anything!' he cried. 'You never consult me!'

Professor Kreutznaer fixed his eye on a patch of the tablecloth beside his plate and sighed.

I fell to quiet contemplation, as is my wont at times of social awkwardness such as this. How shyly chance portions of the world dispose themselves – a bit of yard spied through a doorway at evening, clouds crowding in the corner of a window – as if to say, Look at us! we mean something!

The dog came waddling in from the yard (yes, yes! – Mr Tighe will make a full appearance yet, arm in arm with Miss Broaders the postmistress, and a winged horse will put its head over the half-door, and there will be no mysteries left). Licht took our plates and set them on the floor for the beast to finish off the scraps. Its name was Patch; all dogs are Patch, to me. It had a bad case of pink-eye. As it gulped and gasped Licht talked to it loudly in angry good humour that was meant to sound a general rebuke, tousling its rank fur and slapping it on the rump, raising a cloud of brownish dust.

Another prison, I was thinking, its walls made of air, and the old self inside me still in its white cell snarling for release.

'Good dog,' Licht said heartily. 'Good old dog!'

That's me.

*

In time of course we got used to each other. Even Licht in the end reconciled himself, not without a lingering and occasionally eruptive resentment, to my invasion of his little world. What an oddly assorted trio we would have seemed anywhere else; the island, however, with its long tradition of inbreeding and recurring bouts of internecine strife, was well used to peculiar and contingent arrangements such as ours. We were like a family of orphaned, elderly siblings, the resentments and rivalries of childhood calcified inside us, like gallstones. When I think of it I am surprised at myself for the brazen way in which I insinuated myself here – it is not like me, really it's not – but the truth is I had nowhere else to go. The house, the Professor, the work on Vaublin, all this represented for me the last outpost at the border; beyond were the fiery, waterless wastes where no man or even monster could survive.

Eventually the house too in its haughty way accommodated itself to my coming, though there were still times when the whole place seemed to twang like a spider's web under the weight of my unaccustomed tread. I suspect it was not any noise that I made but on the contrary the uncanny quiet of my presence that was most unsettling. I have always moved gingerly, excessively so, perhaps, among the furniture of other people's lives, not for fear of disturbing things but out of an obscure terror of being myself somehow caught out, of being surprised among surprised surroundings, red-handed. At times I fancied I could hear everything going silent suddenly for no particular reason, listening for me, and then of course I too would stop and stand with held breath, straining to catch I knew not what, and so the silence would stretch and stretch until it could bear the strain no longer and snapped of its own accord when a floorboard groaned or a door banged in the wind. At moments such as that I sympathised with the aboriginal tenants as they too stood stock-still, Licht in the kitchen and the Professor in his tower, straining despite themselves to catch the faint, discordant note of my presence. It must have been as if some large and softly padding animal had got into the house and was hiding somewhere, in the dark under a bed, or behind a not quite closed door, breathing and waiting, half fierce and half afraid. Licht in particular seems unable to prevent himself from listening for me, from the moment I wake in the morning until I drag myself up to my room again at dead of night. He wants to ask me things, I know, but cannot formulate the questions. He is like a child longing to learn all the thrilling, dirty secrets of the big world. He listens to the beast stirring, and smells blood.

Poor Licht. I seem unable to utter his name without that adjective attached to it. He keeps himself busy; that is his aim, to keep busy, as if he fears dissolution, a general and immediate falling apart, should he stop even for a moment in his headlong stumble. He cleaves to the principle of the perfectability of man, and gives himself over enthusiastically to self-improvement programmes. He sends off for things advertised in the newspapers, kitchen utensils, hiking boots, patented remedies for this or that deficiency of the blood or brain; he possesses books and manuals on all sorts of matters – how to set up a windmill or grow mushrooms commercially, how to draw and paint, or do wickerwork; he has piles of pamphlets on bee-keeping, wine-making, home accountancy, all of them eagerly thumb-marked for the first few pages and in pristine condition thereafter. He writes letters to the newspapers, does football competitions, labours for days over prize crossword puzzles. Always busy, always in motion, frantically treading the rungs of his cage-wheel. Nor does he neglect the outer man: at morning and evening, unfailingly, he strips down to his vest and drawers and spends a quarter of an hour ponderously bending knees and flexing arms and touching fingertips to toes; on occasion, looking up from the garden, I catch a glimpse of him in his room engaged in these shaky callisthenics, his strained little face yo-yoing slowly behind the shadowed glass like a lugubrious moon. He aims to get in shape, he says – but what shape, I wonder, is that? I suspect that, like me, he is convinced that large adjustments need to be made before he can consider himself to have reached the stage of being fully human.

We each of us have our ceremonies. There is the Professor's nightly bath, for instance, which has all the solemn trappings of a royal balneation. I hear him in the cavernous bathroom on the second-floor return, vigorously sluicing and sloshing; then for a long time all goes quiet except for an occasional aquatic heave or the sudden, echoing plop of a big drop falling from chin or lifted elbow. I picture him sitting up in the tub like a big, mottled frog, just sitting there with the steam rising around him, quite still, water-wrinkled, hardly breathing, the lids dropping abruptly now and then over those little bulging black eyes and as abruptly lifting again. Afterwards I discover his damp trail on the stairs, dumbbell-shaped footprints dark in the moonlight, at once comic and sinister, winding their splayed way upwards to the mysterious fastness of his bedroom.

Strange, now that I think of it, how many of the rituals of the house involve water; we are a little Venice here, all to ourselves. There are the plants to be watered, the kettle to be kept simmering on the stove for the endless pots of tea the house requires, the washings-up, the launderings. I do our clothes, the girl's and mine, in an old tin bath in the scullery; there is an antiquated washing-machine I could use, but like all lifers I am set in my ways. I used to hang the laundry in bits and pieces out of the window of my room to dry, until Licht complained ('We're not living in a tenement here, you know'), and then I rigged up a line in a corner of the garden. Still Licht was not pleased – he is pained I suppose by the sight of my flapping shirts excitedly embracing the girl's slip. I confess I derive a certain wan pleasure from annoying him; it is wrong of me, I know, but somehow he invites cruelty. He patronises me, seeing in my ruin an encouragement to lord it over me. I do not mind, motheaten old lion that I am, and obligingly open wide my toothless jaws and let him put in his head as far and for as long as he likes. He confides in me, despite himself, under cover of a blustering anger that does not convince either of us, telling me how he loathes the life here, the harshness of it, the isolation. The villagers laugh at him, Mr Tighe cheats him on the grocery bill, Miss Broaders listens in when he goes to the post office to use the telephone. He professes to hate the house, too, speaking of it with deep disgust, in a furious, spitting undertone, as if he thinks the walls might be eavesdropping; it bears him along like a big old broken-down ship, its ancient timbers shuddering; he looks forward to the day when it will founder at last. He is convinced it plays tricks on him. Inanimate things rear up at him, trip him up, give way under his feet, fall on his head. He will put down something and return an hour later and find it gone. Door handles come away in his hand, curtains when he tries to draw them will collapse suddenly in a muffled cascade of dust and jangling brass rings. He retaliates, letting the rain come in through open windows, allowing filth to gather in hidden corners of the kitchen, neglecting things until they break, or get scorched, or overflow. He dreams of escape, of getting up one morning before dawn and sneaking off like a hotel guest doing a flit. He has no idea where he would go to, yet flight, just flight itself, is a constant theme, a kind of hazy, blue and gold background to everything he does. I could tell him about freedom, but I have not the heart; let him dream, let him dream.

How at a word things shift suddenly, the whole pattern falling apart and reassembling itself in a new way out of the old pieces. I had been here some time before I discovered that it is not Professor Kreutznaer who owns the house, but Licht. This was a great surprise. I had, naturally, I believe, taken it for granted that the Professor was the man of property and Licht his vassal, but not so; in fact, the Professor is as much the parvenu as I am. Licht has lived here since he was a child – he may even have been born here. I would not have thought of him as a native, mind you, he is not exactly the craggy, weatherbeaten type one would expect an islandman to be. His mother it seems was a widow of many years; I pictured her as a scattered, birdlike creature with wild white hair and demented eyes, a sort of anile, genderless version of her son, but then Licht showed me a picture of her and she was nothing like my imagining, but a big strapping termagant with an implacable stare and a boxer's biceps. It is not clear when she died, or even that she did die; an inexplicably imperative sense of delicacy prevents me from enquiring too closely. He may have her in the cellar, or boarded up in the attic, for all I know. He speaks of her, on the rare occasions when he does speak of her, with the startled, heart-in-mouth air of a man stepping over a gaping crevice that has suddenly opened up before him in the pavement, frowning, his eyes cast down in alarmed despondency. I understand, however, that she had been long gone, by whatever means of departure she had chosen, by the time the Professor turned up, like me, looking for shelter. It seems he came over on the boat and climbed up here to enquire after lodgings and has been here ever since. In retirement from life, just like me.

Thus the days passed, the weeks. I walked the island, taking consolation from stray things, a red geranium in a blue window, a white sail in the bay, the suspense and then the sudden plummet of a hawk. In the evenings I lay on the frowsty bed in my room with my back against the wall and my hands behind my head and watched the dusk deepen in the window and the world out there fade from green to grey and turn at last to glossy black. I felt nothing, almost nothing. All my life I had been on my way elsewhere, despising the present, pressing always into the future, wanting the next thing, always the next thing; now at last I had come to rest, if that is what it can be called, as sometimes in my dreams I land with unexpected lightness after a long, tumbling, heart-stopping plunge through emptiness and dark air. I had sailed the sea and come to Cythera. That much I could say. Now I was waiting. The days would whiten and then flutter to the floor like so many leaves torn from a calendar; I would write my notes, do my chores, eat, sleep, be. And then one day, a day much like any other in that turning season between spring's breathless imminences and the first, gold flourishings of summer, I would look out the window and see that little band of castaways toiling up the road to the house and a door would open into another world. Oh, a little door, hardly high enough for me to squeeze through, but a door, all the same. And out there in that new place I would lose myself, would fade and become one of them, would be another person, not what I had been – or even, perhaps, would cease altogether. Not to be, not to be: the old cry. Or to be as they, rather: real and yet mere fancy, the necessary dreams of one lying on a narrow bed watching barred light move on a grey wall and imagining fields, oaks, gulls, moving figures, a peopled world. I think of a picture at the end of a long gallery, a sudden presence come upon unexpectedly, at first sight a soft confusion of greens and gilts in the calm, speechless air. Look at this foliage, these clouds, the texture of this gown. A stricken figure stares out at something that is being lost. There is an impression of music, tiny, exact and gay. This is the end of a world. Birds unseen are fluting in the trees, the sun shines somewhere, the distances of the sea are vague and palely blue, the galliot awaits. The figures move, if they move, as in a moving scene, one that they define, by being there, its arbiters. Without them only the wilderness, green riot, tumult of wind and the crazy sun. They formulate the tale and people it and give it substance. They are the human moment.

3

HE STANDS BEFORE US like our own reflection distorted in a mirror, known yet strange. What is he doing here, on this raised ground, in this gilded, inexplicable light? He is isolated from the rest of the figures ranged behind him, suspended between their world and ours, a man alone. Has he dropped from the sky or risen from the underworld? We have the sense of a mournful apotheosis. His arms hang loosely forward from his sides, his splayed feet are arranged in a parody of the mannered stance of prince or soldier posing for an heroic portrait. He seems trapped, held fast by invisible constraints. He might be in the stocks, or worse. We notice the pipe-clayed slippers tied with crimson ribbons in enormous, floppy bows, the broad satin trousers that are too short for him, the outsize coat of white twill, with its sixteen buttons, the rucked sleeves of which seem ample enough to accommodate the arms of an ape. Who has dressed him up in this clown's attire? For he has the look of having been bundled into his costume and thrust unceremoniously out of the wings to stand up here all alone, dumbfounded, mortified, afraid to move lest an unseen audience break into a storm of laughter; yet although for now he is lost for words, we have the feeling that at any moment he may burst out and talk and talk, unstoppably. He wears a limp ruff of white lace, a skullcap, or perhaps it is a headband, and a hat with a wide, circular brim pushed far back on his head. The head is oval, with a broad brow and receding chin. His gaze is at once remote and penetrating, his eyes are a greenish brown. His hair, what we can see of it, is black, or perhaps red. He seems weary. The eyelids, lips and nostrils are tinged with pink and appear to be inflamed; has he been weeping? Yet the corners of his fleshy mouth are dimpled in a sort of smile, distant, pained perhaps, without warmth. We have the impression of past suffering and a present numbness. Perhaps behind that pensive gaze he is laughing at us.

The X-rays show beneath his face another face which may be that of a woman. Pentimenti will out. (See fig. 1. Behrens Collection, recent acquisition.)

The figure of Pierrot derives from the Italian stock characters Pedrolino and the Neapolitan Pulcinella. These characters were introduced to the Paris Fairs by the King's Company of Italian Comedians towards the close of the 17th century and were transformed into the more familiar French form not long before Vaublin's arrival in Paris from his native Holland in the early 1700s; he would have seen the part played at the Comédie-Française by the great Biancolelli among others. Pierrot, disguised in outfit and in personality, is the childish man, the mannish child. Traditionally, as here, he wears a headband or skullcap and pleated ruff, broad silk trousers, a buttoned coat of silk or white twill with loose sleeves and white or black pumps. He appears in whiteface, though not always. Not always. In certain manifestations he is endowed with a humped back and a protruding chest, reminding us of his roots also in the character of Punch, that malign figure which itself dates from the time of the Roman circuses. He does not usually carry a club; in this instance, he does.

*

It is a large work, more than two metres high. Pierrot is slightly greater than lifesize. This disproportion, and the elevated placing – he seems somehow to hover in mid-air – lend a sense of lowering massiveness to an otherwise unremarkable, even absurd figure. Note too that Pierrot, for all his centrality in the design, is not centrally placed in the composition, but set a little way to the left; the small displacement creates an unsettling subliminal effect, which it is hard to believe is not intentional. Yes: a subtle harmonics is at work here, which plays upon our expectations of symmetry and balance; in the overall arrangement is there perhaps a sly parody of the rules of golden section? It is difficult to say which effects are intentional and which accidental.

The design of the work, the strange yet strangely pleasing asymmetry in the placing of the figures within the enveloping frame of trees and clouds and hazy, far-off sea, which strikes the viewer as at once arbitrary and inevitable, generates an air of mystery over and above the question of what it is that is happening and who or what the figures may be meant to represent – beyond, that is, their *commedia dell'arte* roles. Similar treatments of such subjects, by the same artist and others (Pater, Lancret, Watteau in particular), are equally baffling as to *plot*, if the term may be so employed, yet these works have not become the objects of unremitting, often ingenious yet for the most part futile speculation, as is the case with this work. Evidently there is an allegory here, and symbols seem to abound, yet the scene carries a weight of unaccountable significance that is disproportionate to any possible programme or hidden discourse. It is first of all a masterpiece of pure composition, of the architectonic arrangement of light and shade, of earth and sky, of presence and absence, and yet we cannot prevent ourselves asking what it is that gives the scene its air of mystery and profound and at the same time playful significance. Who are these people? we ask, for it seems to matter not what they may be doing, but what they are. Above all, who is this Pierrot? He is presented to us upright in darkening air, like a figure from the tarot pack, lost inside his too-large costume, mute and solitary, sorrowful, laughable perhaps, and yet unavoidable, hardly present at all and at the same time profoundly, palpably *there*, possessed it seems of a secret knowledge, our victim and our ineluctable judge.

Who is he? – we shall not know. What we seek are those evidences of origin, will and action that make up what we think of as identity. We shall not find them. This Pierrot, our Pierrot, comes from nowhere, from a place where no one else lives; nor is he on his way to anywhere. His sole purpose, it would appear, is to be painted; he is wholly pose; we feel ourselves to be the spectators at a melancholy comedy. See how strangely he fits into his costume; he seems not so much to be wearing it as standing behind it, like a cut-out paper doll. Notice the small size of the head in relation to the trunk, the unnatural length of the arms, the very broad hips, the oversized feet. He is almost deformed – almost, when we look long enough, a freak. He seems someone to whom something terrible has happened, or who has done some terrible thing, the effects of which upon his personality are suggested by these marked and at the same time subtle physical exaggerations. What is it he has done, what crime is he guilty of? And from whom is he hiding, if he is hiding? That smirking Harlequin mounted on the donkey seems to know the answers. Is it he who has lent Pierrot his club?

How deeply do we look into these depths? There is no end to what we may see. Consider this sky. Supposedly it is blue; we say, *Pierrot stands outlined against a blue sky*. In fact, what blue there is is more a faded, bluish green, and the effect is further softened by a scumbling of ochreous pinks;

lower down, the shades range from turquoise through a watered mauve to deep indigo towards the barely discernible horizon of the sea; as is frequently the case in this master's work, evening is coming on, seeping up like a violet mist out of the earth. The cloud-mass on the right, behind the trees, is particulary well executed, a tarnished, whitish gold bundle, corpulent and dense. We might think that this is one of those high, smoky gold skies of early October, were it not for the tender foliage of the trees and the general sense of movement and expectancy. It is spring, surely, a cool, restless evening late in spring. We note the crepuscular, fulvous light, the softly thickening shadows; we feel the wind in the trees, in the clouds, and sense the stirring of the earth, the green shoots rising and the tight buds preparing to unfold. This is the springtime not of fêtes and fairs and gambolling milkmaids, but a more savage season, quick with a sense of the struggle in pain and darkness of things being born.

The crowded assortment of trees – oaks, poplars, umbrella pine – suggests a park or pleasure garden by the sea. Is this a calculated irony, a mocking gesture towards our feeble notions of pastoral? We have only to look more closely and the wildness of the scene becomes apparent. The wind blows, the clouds tumble, the trees shiver before the encroaching dark, while that statue of the scowling satyr – Pan, is it, or Silenus? – looks down stonily upon the action, his fleshy lips curled. Perhaps this tawny light is not the light of evening but of storm; if so, has the tempest passed, or is it only gathering? And whence comes this fierce luminescence falling full on Pierrot's breast, transforming his white tunic into a shining cuirass? It is as if some radiant being were alighting behind us from out of the sky and shedding upon him the glare of its shining wings.

*

The question has frequently been asked if the figures ranged behind Pierrot are the products of the artist's imagination or portraits of real people, actors from the Comédie-Française, perhaps, or the painter's friends and acquaintances, got up in the costumes of clowns and carnival types. They have a presence that is at once fugitive and fixed. They seem to be at ease, languorous almost, yet when we look close we see how tense they are with self-awareness. We have the feeling they are conscious of being watched, as they set off down the slope towards that magically insubstantial ship wreathed round with cherubs that awaits them on the amber shore with sails unfurled. The boy at the rear of the little procession is puzzled and frowning, while his slighter, somewhat wizened companion seems prey to a sort of angry longing. The woman dressed in black casts a backward glance that is at once wistful and resigned. The mood she suggests is a complex one; it is as if she were on her way to a sublimer elsewhere yet filled with regret for the creaturely world that she is leaving. There is about her a suggestion of the divine. If this is the Golden World, or the last of it, is she perhaps Astraea, regretfully withdrawing into the innocent sky? And is it Pierrot upon whom her last, lingering glance is fixed, or something or someone beyond him, which it is not our privilege to see?

The little girl with braided hair who leads the woman by the hand is eager to be away; what is Aphrodite's island to her, what does she know yet of the pains of love? At the other extreme of this little human chain of youth and age is the old man in the straw hat who looks away from us, over his shoulder, as if he has just now heard someone call to him from the shadows under the trees.

The presence of the donkey has puzzled many commentators. This creature is simultaneously one of the most mysterious and most immediate of the group, despite the fact that we see no more of it than a part of the head and one, pricked-up ear, and, of course, that single, soft, auburn, unavoidable eye. What is it that looks at us here? There is curiosity in its look, and apprehensiveness, and a kind of startled awe. We see in this unwavering gaze the windy stable and the stony road, the dawn-light in the icy yard and the rain-lashed corner of the field at evening; we feel the hunger and the beatings, the moment of brutish warmth in the byre, we taste the harsh straw of winter and the lush grass in the summer meadow. It is the eye of Nature itself, gazing out at us in a kind of stoic wonderment – at us, the laughing animal, the mad animal, the inexplicable animal.

Of that smirking Harlequin mounted on the donkey's back we shall not speak. No, we shall not speak of him.

At the window of that distant tower – we shall need a magnifying glass for this – a young woman is watching, waiting perhaps for some figure out of romance to come by and rescue her.

What happens does not matter; the moment is all. This is the golden world. The painter has gathered his little group and set them down in this wind-tossed glade, in this delicate, artificial light, and painted them as angels and as clowns. It is a world where nothing is lost, where all is accounted for while yet the mystery of things is preserved; a world where they may live, however briefly, however tenuously, in the failing evening of the self, solitary and at the same time together somehow here in this place, dying as they may be and yet fixed forever in a luminous, unending instant.

4

I CONFESS I had avoided them all day. Oh, I know I pretended that I recognised in them what I had been waiting for since I first came here, the motley troupe who would take me into their midst and make a man of me, but the truth is I was afraid of them. I am not tough, not worldly-wise at all. It takes courage to expose yourself to the possibilities of the world and I am not a courageous man. I want only comfort, what little of it can be squeezed out of this life on a planet to which I have always felt ill-adapted. Their coming was a threat to the delicate equilibrium I had painstakingly established for myself. I was like a hungry old spider suddenly beset by a terrifying swarm of giant flying things. The web shook and I scuttled off into the foliage for shelter, legs flailing and eyes out on stalks. I saw old Croke walk up the hill and saw him too when he returned, staggering, from the beach where he had fallen, with the boy at his heels. I watched from hiding as Sophie set off into the hills to find the ruins she had come to photograph. I witnessed Felix pacing the lawn in the sun with a hand in his side pocket, smoking a cheroot. Oh yes, I skulked. And when late in the afternoon I screwed up my nerve and ventured back into the house it was I who seemed the intruder.

The kitchen was deserted. The debris of their lunch was still on the table, looking disturbingly like the remains of a debauch. I poured out the tepid dregs of Licht's chicken soup and ate it standing at the stove. I wanted one of them to come in and find me there. I would nod in friendly fashion and perhaps say something about the weather, claiming by this show of ease that I was the true inhabitant of the house while they were merely transients. No one came, however, and anyway, if someone had, probably I would have dropped my soup bowl and taken to my heels in a blue funk. I have always suffered from a tendency to generate panic out of my own fears and imaginings; I think it is a common weakness of the self-obsessed. There are moments of quiet and isolation when I can feel within me clearly the tiny, ceaseless tremor of impending hysteria that someday may break out and overwhelm me entirely. What is its source? It is the old emptiness, I suppose, the black vacuum the self keeps rushing into yet can never fill. I'm sure there is a formula for it, some elegant and simple equation balancing the void on one side and the endless inward spin of essence on the other. It is how I think of myself, eating myself alive, consuming myself always and yet never consumed.

Some incarnation this is. I have achieved nothing, nothing. I am what I always was, alone as always, locked in the same old glass prison of myself.

Why is it, I wonder, that silent, sunlit afternoons always remind me of childhood? Was there some marvellous moment of happiness that I have forgotten, some interval of stillness and radiance in which the enchanted child lingered on the forest path while his other self stepped out of him and blundered on oblivious into the dark entanglements of the future? I stood in the ancient light of the hallway for a long time, gazing up into the shadows thronging on the stairs, listening for them, for the sounds of their voices, for life going on. I do not know what I expected: cries, perhaps, arguments, sobs, wild laughter. I had got out of the way of ordinary things, you see; life, being what others did, must be all alarms and confrontations and matters coming to a head. I could hear nothing, or not nothing, exactly, only that faint, pervasive pressure in the air, that soundless hum that betrays the presence of humankind. How thoroughly the house had absorbed them, as if they really were the ones who belonged here; as if they had come home.

Flora was waiting on the landing, hanging back in the shadowed corner between the window and the bedroom door. She had thrown a blanket over her shoulders, she clutched it about her like a shroud. The dark mass of her hair was tangled and damp and her eyes were swollen. Through the window beside her I could see far off in the fields a toy dog chivvying a toy flock of sheep. She had to clear her throat to speak.

'I thought you were Felix,' she said.

And almost smiled.

Licht had put her in my room; his idea of a joke, I suppose. Startling what a transformation her presence had wrought already; nothing was changed yet I would hardly have recognised the place as mine. The air was warm and thick with her smell, the musky smell of her hair and her hot skin. I shut the door behind me. She walked to the window and stood looking out at the dwindling afternoon, thick with slanted sunlight. Although she was on the far side of the room from me I had an extraordinarily vivid sense of her as she stood there with her arms folded around herself and her shoulder-blades unfurled, barefoot, in all her wan, popliteal frailty. I tend not to take much notice of other people – I have mentioned this before, it is one of my more serious failings – and on the rare occasions when I do put my head outside the shell and take a good gander at someone what strikes me as astonishing is not how different they are from me, but how similar, despite everything. I go along imagining myself to be unique, a sport of nature, a sort of tumour growing on the world, and suddenly I am brought up short: there it is, not I but another and yet made of skin, hair, clothed bone, just like me. This is a great mystery. Sex is supposed to solve it, but it doesn't, not in my experience, anyway (not that nowadays I have anything more than the haziest recollection of that universal palliative). Perhaps that is all I ever wanted to do, to break open the shell of the other and climb inside and slam it shut on myself, terrible spikes and all. What a way that would be to end it all.

'Have you lived here long?' Flora said.

I felt nauseous suddenly. My palms were clammy and my innards did a slow heave, as if there were something alive in there. I had a teetering sensation, as if I had grown immensely tall, looming over the room, a great, fat, wallowing thing, a moving puffball stuffed with spores. I was frightened of myself. Not many people know the things they are capable of; I do. I wanted now to take this girl in my arms, to lift her up and hold her hotly to my heart, to feel the frail bones of her ankles and her wrists, to cup the delicate egg of her skull in my palm, to smell her blood and taste the silvery ichor of her sweat. How brittle she seemed, how easily breakable. This is what the poor giant in the old tales never gets to tell, that what is most precious to him in his victims is their fragility, the way they crack so tenderly between his teeth, giving up their little cries like lovers in the extremity of passion. He will never know what he yearns to know, how it feels to be little like them, gay and gaily vicious and full of fears and impossible plans. The human world is what he eats. It does not nourish him.

What she wanted, she was saying, was to stay here, on the island, just for a little while. She was sick, she was sure she was getting the flu. She stood for a moment frowning and biting her lip. The thing was, she said, she had made a mistake and now Felix had the wrong idea and she was afraid of him.

'He said he's going to stay on here,' she said. 'In this house. He knows something about that old man. He told me.'

Although her face was turned towards the window she was watching me. I still had that sensation of nausea. I felt shaky and almost tearful in what I imagined must be a womanly sort of way.

'Would he let *me* stay, do you think?' she said.

She meant the Professor.

'Yes,' I said, 'if I ask him.'

I meant Licht.

'If Felix was gone,' she said.

'Yes,' I said, so stoutly I surprised myself, 'yes, Felix will go.'

She nodded, still gnawing at her lip.

'I don't want to go back to that hotel,' she said, narrowing her eyes. 'They're not nice to me there. They boss me around. The parents expect me to do everything and the manageress is a bitch.'

Stop! I wanted to say, stop! you're ruining everything. I am told I should treasure life, but give me the realm of art anytime.

She went and sat down on the bed and hugged the blanket around her and stared at her bare feet. A girl, just a girl, greedy and dissatisfied, somewhat scheming, resentful of the world and all it would not give her. But that is not what I saw, that is not what I would let myself see.

Mélisande, Mélisande!

I still had, still have, much to learn. I am, I realise, only at the beginning of this birthing business.

I went downstairs, manoeuvring the way with difficulty in my newly swollen state, the gasping ogre, seeming to flop from step to step like an enormous bladder now, filled to the brim with slow, fat liquid. I was still queasy, still on the verge of tears, no, not tears, but a vast overflowing, an unstanchable flood of gall and gleet, my whole life oozing out of me in a final, foul regurgitation. I stopped at the window on the landing and rested a moment, leaning on the sill. How quickly the dusk was gathering, an oyster-grey stain spreading inland from the reaches of the sea, a darkness slowly, irresistibly descending.

Something had happened in that little room up there that before had been mine and now was hers, a solemn warrant had been issued on me, and I felt more than ever like the hero in a tale of chivalry commanded to perform a task of rescue and reconciliation. There they were, the old man in the tower with his books, the damsel under lock and key, and the dark one, my dark brother, waiting for me, the knight of the rosy cross, to throw down my challenge to him.

I laughed a soundless laugh and went on, down the stairs.

They were in the hall, ready to depart. They turned to look at me. What must I have seemed?

This toy dog, that toy flock.

We walked down the hill road in the blued evening under the vast, light dome of sky where Venus had risen. The fields were darkening on either side, the bay below us glistered. Everyone had acquired something. Croke his invisible companion that had risen with him from the sand at the sea's edge and walked at his shoulder now step for step, Sophie her photographs that tomorrow would swim into her red room like water sprites, the boys that sly phantom that had run up swiftly and insinuated itself between them while they fought and would not go away, Alice her image of a girl reclining in a sunny bed.

A moth reeled out of the gloaming and there was a sense of something falling and failing and I seemed to feel the faint dust of wings sifting down. The god takes many forms.

We rounded a bend in the road where there was a little copse and a stream running by and found Felix sitting perched on a dry-stone wall in the dark with his arms around his knees and his face turned to the sky. The others walked on in calm procession, Sophie arm in arm with Croke and holding Alice by the hand and the boys trudging behind them, kicking stones. You see? They have their party favours and now they are going home, after the long day's doings, Sophie to her developments, Croke to die, the children to grow up and become other people. This is what happens. What seems an end is not an end at all.

'What a start you gave me,' Felix said to me amiably, 'rearing up out of the dark like that. I thought you were Old Nick.'

It was as if all along we had been walking side by side, with something between us, some barrier, thin and smooth and deceptive as a mirror, that now was broken, and I had stepped into his world, or he into mine, or we had both entered some third place that belonged to neither of us. He lit one of his cheroots, bending his narrow face to the flare of the match in his cupped hands. A flaw of smoke shaped like Africa assumed itself into the leaves above him. Behind the tobacco smell I caught a faint whiff of his own unsavoury, stale stink. I found it hard to keep a hold of him, somehow. He kept going in and out of focus, one minute flat and transparent, a two-dimensional figure cut out of grimed glass, the next an overpowering presence pressing itself against me in awful intimacy, insistently physical, all flesh and breath and that stale whiff of something gone rank. He began to sing to himself softly, in a jaunty voice, crowingly.

Allo, allo, who's yer laidy friend,
Who's 'at little girl I sawre yer wiv larst night?

He mused a while, gazing into the thickening shadows.

'I cannot set my foot on board a ship,' he said, 'without the memory coming back of sailing to the frozen northern pole. I wonder, have you ever been up there? The tundra and the towering bergs, the sun that never sets: such solitude! such cold! And yet how beautiful, this land of ice! We sailed out of Archangel and due north we ploughed our way, all day, and all the night, for weeks. And then one morning when I looked out from the deck I saw the strangest sight: a figure, in the distance, on a sled, a giant man, it seemed, with whip and dogs, at great speed travelling on the floes, due north, like us. And then another – ' There he paused, and said: 'I think you know this story, though?'

A drowsy bird in the branches above us stirred a wing. The stream muttered to itself. Felix considered me with his head on one side.

'Tell me,' he said, 'don't I know you? I mean from somewhere else. Your face looks familiar.'

The last light was ascending in the zenith. Stars swarmed. A big white gloating moon had hoisted itself clear of the velvet heights behind us.

'Time to go, I think,' he said. 'I had thought of staying for a bit, but now you're here there is no need. Definitely *de trop*, what?' He lowered his lashes almost shyly and smiled a thin-lipped smile that made it seem as if he were nibbling a tiny seed between his teeth. 'Anyway, you're inviting me to leave, aren't you. *Luxe, calme et volupté*, eh?'

In the gathering dark the trees kept lisping the same slurred phrase over and over. Felix sighed and unwound his legs and nimbly scrambled down from the wall. 'Time to go, yes,' he said, brushing himself off, and linked his arm in mine and together we set off down the hill towards the bay.

On the brow of the hill he paused and looked back and laughed and waved a hand and softly cried:

'Farewell, happy fields!'

None of it was as I had thought it would be. I do not know what I had expected – some sort of tussle, I suppose, a contest on the road, maybe even fisticuffs, and then me pushing him protesting down to the boat, his nose bleeding and his collar sticking up and his heels furrowing the dust. What did I think I was, the avenging angel of the Lord? No, Felix would not fight, he would go quietly, or pretend to. I know his type, I know it only too well.

'And you are going to stay here, are you?' he said. 'You have it all worked out?' He laughed in the dark. We could see below us now the lights of the harbour and the dark bulk of the waiting boat crouched at the jetty. We heard the noise that the island makes, that deep, dark note rising through the gloom. We paused to listen, and Felix struck a dramatic pose and inclined an ear and shouted out softly in a stage-actor's voice, making it seem uncannily as if it were someone calling to us from an immense distance:

'*Thamous! Thamous! The great god Pan is dead!*'

And laughed.

We walked on.

'You know I too knew the Professor, long ago?' he said. 'Oh, yes. As you are now so I was once, his friend, his confidant.' He squeezed my arm against his side and I felt the meagre armature of his ribs. 'Tell me,' he said in a confidential tone, 'do you respect him? I mean, is he a great man, do you think? I thought so, at first. Alas, we all have our weaknesses. You realise that painting is a fake? Yes, more of gilt in it than gold, I fear. Poor Miss Behrens was taken in. Do you know her too? What a coincidence! She does not know she bought a fake. I may tell her, or I may not. What do you think? Which is better, ignorance or enlightenment? The Professor was the one who verified it.

And made a killing on it, of course. Not for the first time either.' He chuckled. 'Curious phrase, that, don't you think – a killing?'

We had reached the harbour, and walked out now along the pier still arm in arm. The boat reared gently at its moorings, sending up a soft puttering of smoke from the rusted stack. The skipper was in his lighted wheelhouse, the others stood about the deck, dim shadows of themselves, like the Pequod's swarth phantoms, fading already. A storm lantern hanging in the bow shed a frail, apricot glow around which the night seemed to gather itself and find a brief definition. Felix stopped on the dockside and released my arm only to take my hand in both of his.

'I say, old chap,' he said in his actor's voice with a fake sob in it, 'look after the girl for me, will you? She likes a bit of rough stuff, but these things can go too far, as you well know.'

I should have seen him go. I should have waited until he was safely on board and the boat under way. When I had walked back along the pier and turned he was still standing where I had left him on the dock, waving one hand slowly, like a mechanical man. Was he smiling?

No riddance of him.

Flora has decided she is recovered. She is getting ready to leave, I can feel it, the change in her, like the season changing. She is ruffling her feathers, testing the buoyant air. I shall be glad to see her go – glad, that is, as the hand is glad when the arrow flies from the bow. If she were to remain I should only engrey her life. Better that, you will say, than if I had incarnadined it, but that is not the issue. There was never any question but that I would lift her up and let her go; what else have I been doing here but trying to beget a girl? Licht of course will be heartbroken. We shall stand on the windy headland, he and I, bereft together, and watch her skim away over the waves. The Professor will hardly notice she is gone. I think he is the one whose heart is really breaking. I make no mention to him of the Golden World and its clouded provenance; we have both made killings, he in his way, I in mine; there is no comparison. I am still puzzling over the problem: if this is a fake, what then would be the genuine thing? And if Vaublin did not paint it, who did? Who was *his* dark double? Perhaps the Professor will tell me, in his own time; I think I detect a speculative something in his filmy glance these days; I fear a deathbed confession. Maybe he painted it himself? He does have a touch of the old master to him; I can just picture him in velvet cap and ruff, peering from under the murk of centuries, one bleared, pachydermous eye following the viewer round the room and out the gilded door: *Self-portrait in the Guise of a Dutchman*. Well. He does not mention Felix, any of that. Matters go on as before, as if nothing had happened. My writing is almost done: Vaublin shall live! If you call this life. He too was no more than a copy, of his own self. As I am, of mine.

No: no riddance.

Also available in Minerva

JOHN BANVILLE

The Book of Evidence

'Freddie Montgomery is a gentleman first and a murderer second . . . He has committed two crimes. He stole a small Dutch master from a wealthy family friend, and he murdered a chambermaid who caught him in the act. He has little to say about the dead girl. He killed her, he says, because he was physically capable of doing so. She annoyed him. It made perfect sense to smash her head in with a hammer. What he cannot understand, and would desperately like to know, is why he was so moved by an unattributed portrait of a plain middle-aged woman that he felt compelled to steal it . . .

'I have read books that are as cleverly constructed as this one and I can think of a few – not many – writers who can match Banville's technical brilliance, but I have read no other novel that illustrates so perfectly a single epiphany. It is, in its cold, terrifying way, a masterpiece'

Maureen Freely, *Literary Review*

'Compelling and brutally funny reading from a master of his craft'

Patrick Gale, *Daily Telegraph*

'Banville must be fed up being told how beautifully he writes, but on this occasion he has excelled himself in a flawlessly flowing prose whose lyricism, patrician irony and aching sense of loss are reminiscent of *Lolita*'

Observer

'Completely compelling reading . . . not only entertains but informs, startles and disturbs'

Irish Independent

JOHN BANVILLE

Mefisto

'Fable, intellectual thriller, Gothic extravaganza and symbolist conundrum . . . a sign in this book is never just a sign . . . like a literary Rubik cube for which there is no solution . . . The novel accordingly embodies its own theme, the impulse to discern a definitive symbolic order constantly defeated by the changing conditions of a literary text attentive to chance as well as to possible structure . . . a true work of art'

Sunday Independent

'*Mefisto* renders all superlatives woefully inadequate . . . Undisputed master of language, the laconic pause and the blackly comic, Banville is a supreme stylist . . . He is a magician . . . another expectedly astonishing and very daring display from this richly, almost wickedly, gifted artist'

Time Out

'Beautifully written . . . wonderful stuff . . . the sort of thing you have to read more than once . . . this excellent novel'

Punch

'Few writers in Ireland today can arouse such expectation by the advent of a new novel . . . a profound beauty of words displayed by their lover . . . Banville's great enterprise does not falter . . . read *Mefisto* straight through; it deserves it'

Irish Times